Praise for Sarah Jamila Stevenson's
The Latte Rebellion

"Asha is engaging and the depiction of her journey—a realistic mess of vague hopes, serendipitous events, serious missteps and gutsy choices—[is] compellingly original."

—*Kirkus Reviews*

"This coming-of-age story is craftily written, fast paced and delivers a message of doing the right thing under difficult circumstances. *The Latte Rebellion* is a wonderful, conceptual story from a new author with strong promise of becoming established in the YA genre."

—*VOYA*

"The portrayal of Asha's initially misguided but relatable social awakening is so honest that readers will find themselves first cringing at her efforts, then cheering her on."

—*Booklist*

"Stevenson's debut novel expertly handles complex issues around race and ethnic identity without seeming pedantic. A welcome addition to a rapidly evolving genre of multiethnic young adult literature."

—*School Library Journal*

"Young readers facing real life racism are sure to be inspired by the story."

l Magazine

"*[The Latte Reb*   igh school story. [It] will s   .ts who are trying to find their place in society."

—*Library Media Connection*

The Truth
Against
The World

The Truth

Against

The World

SARAH JAMILA STEVENSON

flux®

Woodbury, Minnesota

First Edition
First Printing, 2014

Book design by Bob Gaul
Cover design by Lisa Novak
Cover art: iStockphoto.com/6718553/Giorgio Magini
iStockphoto.com/6010440/bkindler
iStockphoto.com/18913555/Stacey Newman
iStockphoto.com/3414358/Appleguy

Flux, an imprint of Llewellyn Worldwide Ltd.

Library of Congress Cataloging-in-Publication Data
Stevenson, Sarah Jamila.
  The truth against the world/Sarah Jamila Stevenson.—First edition.
    pages cm
  Summary: Fifteen-year-olds Wyn, an American, and Gareth, an Englishman, share dreams of a young girl who shares Wyn's name and, when Wyn's great-grandmother asks to go to Wales to die, they join forces to solve the mystery that brought them together.
  ISBN 978-0-7387-4058-4
  [1. Ghosts—Fiction. 2. Supernatural—Fiction. 3. Great-grandmothers—Fiction. 4. Death—Fiction. 5. World War, 1939-1945—Wales—Fiction. 6. Wales—Fiction. 7. Wales—History—20th century—Fiction. 8. Mystery and detective stories.] I. Title.
  PZ7.S84826Tru 2014
  [Fic]—dc23
                                                                    2014004535

Flux
Llewellyn Worldwide Ltd.
2143 Wooddale Drive
Woodbury, MN 55125-2989
www.fluxnow.com

Printed in the United States of America

To Gramp

1

Truth shines in the dark.

....

Welsh proverb

"Right over there, behind the old church." Gareth's mother pointed. "You used to love rolling down that hill. Over and over until you got dizzy." She laughed, the wind blowing her pale hair out of its ponytail and whipping it around.

Gareth glanced up from his phone. The hill looked a lot smaller than it had seemed in his memory. It soared gently upward, its grassy flanks covered in purple and yellow wildflowers. The trail they were on meandered past it, looping around picturesque ruins and mysterious heaps of stones before ending in a rocky cliff overlooking the sea.

"Good thing we left Tommy back at the house with

Great-Granddad," he said. "He'd start rolling around and we'd never get him to leave."

"Bit chilly out here for a little tyke," his dad said, zipping his nylon jacket closed.

That was true. The gusts blowing in from the Bristol Channel carried the tang of salt, and misty gray clouds formed a cottony ceiling that stretched to the horizon. Gareth could feel the clammy moisture condensing on his face as he walked. Still, it wasn't so bad out here. Quiet.

Maybe too quiet. He should have brought his earphones.

He looked back down, his thumbs flying over the keypad of his mobile.

Wales: land of sheep, rain, and boredom. He found Amit's name in his contacts list and hit Send. A reply came a moment later.

Told u. Should've stayed in London this week.

He remembered coming to this spot with his dad, about a year before their family moved to London. The two of them had spent the afternoon making grave rubbings, and then they'd gone back down to the beach for a picnic. In those days they'd spent a lot of weekends in the village, driving out from Swansea to visit Great-Granddad.

Nice scenery, tho. Rolling hills. Bit of a workout.

Just like yr mum last night.

Gareth huffed a laugh.

"Gareth! Look where you're going," his mother called, somewhere behind him. He stopped short, just in time to avoid tripping over a half-fallen rock wall, and almost dropped his phone. "Keep hold of that thing!" she added. "I'm not paying for a new one."

"It's truly amazing." His dad came up the path, a little breathless. "You spend the entire week whinging about being bored, so we take you somewhere, and then you spend the entire time texting your friends." He exchanged a look with Gareth's mum. "We could have left you at the house and had a lovely quiet afternoon."

"Sorry," Gareth said.

"A romantic afternoon," his mother added.

Gareth groaned. "Go ahead then. I'll catch you in a sec."

The truth was, it wouldn't be such a bad place if somebody actually bothered to care for it. The building that used to be a church was nothing but a ruin. Piles of rocks and rubble; a tumble of headstones. A few dried remains of flower bouquets. Presumably that meant someone made the occasional visit, but nobody was around today except for Gareth and his parents. The place was silent except for the ocean's murmur.

He walked behind one of the fallen walls and was about to kick at a knee-high pile of stones, encrusted with lime-green lichen, when he realized it was a cairn—some villager's memorial to a lost loved one. A plaque of dark gray slate was embedded in the ground in front of it, weeds and shrubs encroaching on its edges.

He was about to walk on when the inscription caught his eye. Hunching in his jacket against the chilly breeze, he stooped to look closer.

Er Cof Cariadus ~ In Loving Remembrance
"Our Little Girl"
Olwen Nia Evans
1944–1950

That was depressing.

A corner of metal was sticking up out of the dirt, half-buried in the ground next to the plaque. He nudged it with his toe, but it didn't move. An urn, probably. Disgusting *and* depressing. He took a photo with his phone, in case anybody asked him how he spent his spring holidays. Then he took a photo of himself making a pathetic face, the grayish-blue sea in the background, and sent it to Amit with a note that said *nary an Internet in sight. pity me.*

Shuffling along through the gathering mist, Gareth scrolled through the photos he'd taken at dinner the previous night in his great-granddad's kitchen. He particularly liked the one where his little brother was standing on his chair and his great-granddad had his eyes raised to the heavens as if wondering how he'd been cursed with this family.

Seemingly out of nowhere, a crooked headstone loomed up at him, the inscription long ago weathered to nothing. He tried to veer around it but tripped, landing on his hands and knees with a grunt, his phone flying off into the gloom. When he looked up after it, his heart sank.

In front of him was a cromlech, a Neolithic stone monument. It had a huge, slablike capstone several feet thick, gray and weathered, that was supported by squat, smaller boulders. Though the top of the structure was higher than his head, the gatelike opening between the stones only came up to his shoulders; beneath it, a dark hollow yawned into the ground. A white shroud of water vapor rose from the grass around it, as if it wasn't already creepy enough.

Gareth shivered involuntarily. "Mum is going to kill me," he muttered. He'd better at least try to retrieve his phone, even if it was broken. He approached the hole and peered in.

It was dark inside, but he thought he could see the dirt floor a few feet down. Cromlechs were supposed to be ancient burial chambers, but he really did not want to think about that. He needed his phone.

Gareth lowered himself to a sitting position and scooted forward until his legs dangled inside the opening. He still couldn't quite feel the floor, so he pushed off and dropped down, landing in a crouch. A cloud of dirt and dust swirled up from where his feet had landed, obscuring the weak sunlight. He squinted into the shadows of the cave. The chamber inside was about five feet high and just a bit wider, but he couldn't tell how long it extended. His phone couldn't have gone far, though.

He started feeling around, scooting ahead inch by inch until he was completely underneath the earthen ceiling, the opening a wide square of light behind and above him. He patted the dirt floor around him and hoped he didn't find something *other* than the phone. Of course, if he did, it would officially become the most exciting trip to Wales he'd ever had.

"Who are you?"

Gareth jumped, knocking his head hard on the packed, rocky soil above him. The voice was high and soft, and he took darting glances all around, searching for its source, his heart racing.

Off to one side, half-hidden by the shadows, was a little girl, small and thin. She had wispy dark hair and was wearing a white dress. He blinked, sure it must be a trick of the light, but she was still there.

"You gave me a heart attack," he said.

"What are you doing here?" the girl asked sternly, with a strong Welsh cadence.

"What are *you* doing here?" Gareth said. Little urchin. No doubt her parents were somewhere up on the path looking for her.

"I asked first!" she said, shuffling her feet soundlessly.

"Oh. I dropped my mobile." Gareth rubbed gingerly at the sore spot on his temple and looked around again. There wasn't much down here that he could see. He moved toward the girl. Maybe she had the phone. "Do you need me to help you out of here?"

She backed away. "You're not supposed to be down here," she shrilled. Her face showed a slight frown in the dim light. She peered closer at him, and then her face relaxed, as if she'd recognized him. "But it's all right. You came to visit then, didn't you! My name is Olwen." Even as she smiled, her gaze shifted away, restless.

"Olwen?" Gareth thought back to the plaque at the other end of the churchyard, the one that said "Olwen Nia Evans." Interesting coincidence. She was probably playing a game. He crouched down in the dirt, trying to seem nonthreatening. "Who are you? Where's your mum and dad?"

"I don't know," she said, seeming momentarily confused. Then she giggled. "You can be my friend if you want. I think you're funny!"

Funny. Something was definitely funny about this girl. Gareth's head pounded. He needed to find his phone, and then he needed to get out of here and find his parents. They were much better at coaxing small children. He straightened up as much as he could, and finally caught sight of his phone glinting in the girl's hand.

"You found it! My mobile." He reached his hand out, slowly, as if she were a shy cat. "Please?"

She looked down. "This?" The phone's screen momentarily flashed on. She met his gaze again, her eyes questioning. But she never moved from the shadows.

"We're—we're friends, right?" Gareth said, a bit desperately. He decided to try to play along. "I came to visit you, yeah? So, er, if you give me back my phone, I'll be able to ring you up, because we're friends."

Her eyes widened, and a tiny hint of a smile brightened her wan face. "We *are* friends," she said.

She held the phone out to him, but the moment he reached for it, she snatched it back. "Wait." She peered more closely at it, tilting her head, curious and intent. Her fingers hovered over the keys for a moment, not touching them, and he could have sworn he saw a spark flare in the dark. He gritted his teeth.

"Don't play with it," he said, trying not to sound impatient. The girl was as bad as Tommy.

"Only promise me that you'll come back to visit me?

I'm so lonely." Her voice faded, as soft as an echo. "I won't let you go unless you promise."

"Of course, I promise," Gareth said, resisting the urge to roll his eyes.

She smiled and held out the phone. When he leaned forward to grab it, a static charge jolted his fingers and he almost dropped it again. Pocketing the phone, he rubbed his hand on his pants to ease the tingling. His head had started to throb again, too, and he sank to his knees for a moment, the shadows spinning around him until the dizziness passed.

Straightening, he turned just in time to see his dad's head peering in from the opening above.

"For God's sake, Gareth. What are you doing in there? On second thought," his dad said, "don't tell me." He reached a hand down. "Here; I'll pull you up. Quick, before Mum notices."

"Thanks." Gareth got to his feet carefully, brushing the dirt off his jeans. He stretched for his dad's hand and then hesitated. "Wait, Dad. What about the little girl? She's lost her parents or something…" He looked back into the shadows.

Olwen was gone.

2

Four white trefoils sprang up behind her
wherever she went; and for that reason she
was called Olwen, of the white track...

....

"Kilhwch and Olwen," from *The Mabinogion,*
in The Red Book of Hergest

I still felt like I was caught in a dream; my mind, all cobwebs. Seven a.m.

By seven p.m., we'd be back home again and everything would be different.

I pulled on a block-printed skirt and sat on the edge
of the bed, lacing up my calf-high boots, then paused
for a moment, listening to the prerecorded voice coming
through my computer speakers.

"*Mae'r tywydd yn braf,*" I repeated haltingly, trying to concentrate. The weather is fine. "*Sut dych chi?*" How are you?

"*Olwen ydw i.*" My name is Olwen.

With every repetition, I tried to remember how Gee Gee, my great-grandmother, added that special lilt at the end of every word. When she spoke Welsh, it almost sounded like singing, more magical than ordinary speech.

I'd learned the words, but I wanted to get it *right*.

I swallowed past a sudden lump in my throat and closed my eyes for a moment.

"*Wyn!* Five minutes! And bring those empty boxes down with you."

I winced, my mother's voice piercing even through the closed bedroom door. "Coming!" I called.

With one hand, I grabbed my black sweater off the back of the chair; with the other, I hit *Publish* on my latest blog post, letting the past few weeks of my life fly off into the ether. Disappearing into unread oblivion, probably, like everything else I'd posted. In a way, it freed me up to write whatever I felt like writing, no matter how weird.

Language is like music, and each language is a different instrument, one of my posts began. *Welsh is like gently plucked harp strings.*

Another one: *Finished up book on Norse mythology. Back to the Mabinogion—Ceridwen and Gwion Bach, the original story. So much better than the Black Cauldron movie. Mind blown.*

Or: *Sometimes I feel like I'm too strange to relate to anyone. Even my strangeness is strange.*

Ruminations, obsessions, fascinations. Things I couldn't

even talk about with Rae, let alone any of my other friends. But this morning's post was different.

It was harder than I'd anticipated: putting into words all the constantly shifting feelings that well up inside you when you find out someone you love is going to die.

I closed my laptop and grabbed the stack of empty file boxes from under my desk. The drive to Gee Gee's house in Mendocino would take three hours, and then we'd bring her back here to San Francisco and move her into Mom's cramped office. There was already a hospital bed, delivered yesterday and wedged into the corner under the window.

"*Gwely*," I mumbled, maneuvering the stack of boxes through the hallway and dropping them near the front door. Bed.

I'd been learning a lot of new words.

Metastasized. Carcinoma.

I closed my eyes for a moment and leaned against the wall next to the door.

My mom walked in, footsteps clacking on the hardwood. "Where's your father?"

I shook my head.

"I need him to hang up his bike so we can put Gee Gee's boxes on that side of the garage," she said, dropping a roll of packing tape into my hands as she breezed past into the back of the house.

I slipped the roll of tape onto my wrist. Everything around me was changing so quickly. But I had to keep up. I had to learn; I had to feel like I was accomplishing something.

If I didn't, then I'd have to admit that I really didn't

know anything about *anything*. That this situation—Gee Gee's illness—was something I couldn't control or fix, no matter how many words I repeated to myself, no matter what I wrote or who might read it.

———————

That night, after hours of driving, of carrying boxes and unpacking the car and moving Gee Gee's life into our small Victorian-style flat, I was exhausted, and so was Gee Gee. But she called me into her room in Mom's office anyway.

She was already holding the musty old book open on her lap, carefully turning its thin, foxed pages until she reached the right spot. This had been our bedtime ritual for years, whenever she visited, but this time it felt different. It felt like there was a catch in my heart.

Not quite able to look at her, I settled in on the adjustable bed, snuggling in the way I used to when I was little. As a child, I'd had no trouble fitting under the covers beside her, but today, at age fifteen, I felt tall and ungainly next to her fragile frame.

"'Kilhwch and Olwen, or the Twrch Trwyth.'" It was a myth from the *Mabinogion*, a collection of medieval Arthurian legends. A book I'd loved almost to tatters. A story I'd heard a thousand times.

I wished I could hear it a thousand times more.

It wasn't just because of the name "Olwen"—the name Gee Gee herself suggested for me on the day I was born. It was *all* the names, the sounds of Welsh rolling off my great-grandmother's tongue like the strange liquid language of some unearthly being, undulating like the hills of the seaside town in Wales where she grew up, whispering, beckoning. The language of heaven, Gee Gee always said.

She cleared her throat, adjusted her reading glasses, and began to speak.

"Kilydd, the son of Prince Kelyddon, desired a wife as a helpmate, and the wife that he chose was Goleuddydd, the Daylight One."

Her voice always comforted me, like a warm blanket of sound. While she read, I reached onto the end table for the lovespoon that had hung on her kitchen wall for as long as I could remember. My fingers traced the carvings in the rich reddish-brown wood: an intricate tracery of knotwork and heart shapes, twining together and apart like vines until they joined at the bottom in the smooth bowl of a spoon.

"They had a son through the prayers of the people. From the time of her pregnancy, Goleuddydd became wild, and wandered about…"

The knots and twists of the spoon symbolized togetherness, two becoming one; the hearts symbolized love. I could almost hear the echo of Gee Gee's voice explaining it to me. That morning, I had carefully swaddled it in bubble wrap and put it into a box of other keepsakes, scrawling the word "fragile" across the lid with a blue marker.

The wood was soft under my hands, surprisingly unworn despite year after year—decade after decade—of being nestled in the palms of my great-grandmother, and then in the hands of Grandpa William, who'd died in Vietnam long before I was born; and, much later, my father's. And mine. The only thing interrupting the smooth surface was a tiny incised shape on the back of the spoon's bowl, the carver's mark—two tiny squared-off hillocks like a blocky M, or an E. I knew every millimeter of that spoon and it felt familiar, reassuring.

" ... And Kilhwch's father inquired of him, 'What has come over thee, my son, and what aileth thee?' 'My stepmother has declared to me that I shall never have a wife until I obtain Olwen ... '"

I closed my eyes and let Gee Gee's voice wash over me, rich and low. It wasn't the voice of someone with less than a year left to live. I tried to picture her as a girl in love; tried to picture a handsome young man presenting her with the lovespoon as a token of affection, like in a fairy tale or an Arthurian legend. An old friend, maybe, or a former love. Not my great-grandfather; I knew that much. All she would ever say about the spoon was that it was from someone in her past, someone who was gone now.

If only I could have known her then. If only we had more time.

3

Ni ddaw doe byth yn ôl.

Yesterday will never return.

Welsh proverb

Gareth sat up in bed and rubbed grit out of his eyes. His legs were tangled in the sheets, half-exposed to the chilly air, and the rest of him was drenched in sweat. He'd been dreaming about—what was it? Some kind of headstones and whatnot. Next he'd be dreaming about zombies drooling their way out of the graveyard and eating his brains. Playing *Resident Evil* late into the night had perhaps not been his cleverest idea.

After shaking off the cobwebs, he had a shower. His dream had been vivid and sharp, like a memory, though it was dissipating rapidly now. Was it possible to have a dream that was a memory at the same time? Pondering, Gareth rinsed the shampoo out of his hair and shut off the water. The problem was, you'd never really be able to tell whether it was more than just a dream. The brain was good at making things up. He suspected you couldn't really even trust your memories, could you? It was all subjective. Shaking his head, he wrapped a towel around his waist and jogged barefoot down the drafty hallway back to his room.

He pulled on his school uniform—dark blue pants and jacket, white shirt, dreadful striped tie—and wandered down the narrow staircase looking for breakfast. His mum was just running out the door with Tommy, and his dad was already gone.

He glanced at the clock; how did it get so late? After rapidly inhaling two bowls of muesli, he stuffed various books and papers into his school bag and dashed to the bus stop just as the bus was pulling up, wiping the sweat from the back of his neck.

His first day back at school after the holidays, and he already felt tired.

After a history test, double maths, a horrifying lunch of gray mystery stew, and a new project in Information Technology on web animations, Gareth was eager to get outside and be somewhere that didn't require higher brain functions. He joined the crush jostling through the hallway toward the doors.

On the way out, Amit fell into step next to him, grinning. "Brought a souvenir back from the countryside, I see."

"What?"

"Your head. You look like you're wearing a miniature tan sheep." Amit snickered.

"Don't take the piss. I *will* kill you. Very slowly and painfully." Gareth tried to pat down his hair, but without a comb it was useless.

"Oh, speaking of death and destruction," Amit said, "I started animating a zombie for the IT project. Decaying bits falling off and everything."

Gareth frowned. "I wanted to do a mythology thing," he said, "but so far I can't get Medusa's hair to writhe properly." They stepped onto the bus behind a crowd of other uniformed students.

"It seems like I should have something obscene to say about that. But I can't think of anything," Amit replied a bit mournfully, sliding into a seat near the back of the bus. "I'm off my game."

"Your brain must still be on holiday." Gareth slid in next to his friend and jabbed an elbow into his ribs.

After a brief scuffle, Amit said, "Speaking of the holidays, how were the wild Welsh hinterlands? That sad photo was the last thing I got from you."

"Yeah, sorry. The charge ran out on my mobile. I dropped it down a hole and it must have dislodged the battery or something." Gareth pulled out his phone and scrolled through the pictures from the past week. "Look at Tommy," he said, pointing to a photo of his brother wearing Great-Granddad's old mining helmet. It covered the entire top half of his head. Great-Granddad was in the midst of reaching out to snatch the helmet back, looking furious.

"What's the old guy's problem, then?" Amit asked.

"Dunno. He always looks like that." Gareth scrolled through a few more photos. "He's all right, though."

"For a Taff."

"No need to be racist."

"Sorry, Mum." Amit grinned. "Seriously, I was afraid you'd come back spouting all that Welshy unpronounceable gibberish."

Gareth gave him a look. "You're one to talk."

"Gujarati is a noble language."

"The only words you know are insults," Gareth pointed out. "Anyway, what'd you do here all week? Play *Halo* until your eyeballs started bleeding?"

Amit launched into a lengthy story about his cousins visiting from Blackpool. Meanwhile, Gareth continued flipping through pictures. He rather liked the one he'd taken of the ruined church, the sea in the background a pale blue blur blending into the cloudy sky. There was a faint figure just disappearing around the back of the collapsing building; probably one of his parents. He scrolled to the next photo: a view of the dismal churchyard with its lichen-covered headstones, the ancient cromlech looming behind them, and his parents holding hands and looking out to sea. It had been a peaceful day, just the three of them. No Tommy to give him a headache.

Just the three of them, and the girl. Gareth suppressed a shiver. He hoped she'd found her parents. He really hadn't seen anyone anywhere else around; he was sure of it. She seemed a bit young to run away from home, but what did he know? And then she'd just vanished. Maybe her family lived somewhere nearby.

Had to be.

Amit finished his story and turned to talk to a girl across the aisle, so Gareth scrolled to the next picture: a shot of the sad little cairn with the grave plaque of the girl who'd died in 1950. The greenery grew close, partially obscuring the inscription, but he could still read it.

As he stared at the photo, something else began to take shape. It was a faint, fuzzy outline, a small figure, transparent white against the background of dark gray stone and slate. He blinked his eyes rapidly, took off his glasses and cleaned them, and then held the phone close to his face.

The shape was even clearer than before. Gareth knew it hadn't been there when he'd taken the photo.

He knew *she* hadn't been there.

It was a little girl in a white dress, her feet bare. The same girl he'd seen under the cromlech. The one who'd called herself Olwen.

Just a moment ago, the photo had been normal—just a picture of old rocks and a grave. He'd swear to it. He remembered the moment he'd taken the shot, too, and he'd been completely alone. But now there was something else there—some*one* else.

The skin prickled on the back of Gareth's neck. He scrolled back to the photo of the ruined church and zoomed in on the figure he'd thought was one of his parents.

A flash of white dress. Slender, almost skinny limbs. A bare foot. Long, dark hair.

He frantically scrolled ahead again, to the picture of the cairn. He could see the girl's face relatively clearly now, though her whole image looked like someone had gone into Photoshop and smudged it with a Gaussian blur. He grasped onto that thought—maybe this was someone's idea of a joke? Had Amit gotten hold of his phone? Altered his photos somehow?

But Gareth's entire body had gone cold, because he knew for a fact that there was only one person who'd handled his phone in days, besides himself.

And he wasn't even sure that person was real.

4

Hir yw pob ymaros.

All waiting is long.

Welsh proverb

I picked up my spoon and slurped up a mouthful of min-estrone soup, organic store brand. My parents were argu-ing without trying to sound like they were arguing. I stared blankly across the dinner table, thinking about verb conju-gations and wondering how I'd ever learn to pronounce the letter "ll" and trying not to worry about Gee Gee, alone in the hospital overnight.

"*Ll*," I muttered, but I couldn't seem to do it without spitting. "Llangollen. Llanelli. Llyn y Bala." I could just see myself visiting Wales someday, riding the bus somewhere, asking where Llangollen was and everybody laughing at me. "*Llwy.*" Spoon.

"Everyone speaks English there, Wyn," my mom burst out, sounding annoyed.

"Don't take this out on Wyn," Dad said mildly.

I was sick of this. "Don't take what out on me?"

There was a long silence, then Dad put his spoon down inside his empty soup bowl. I got a strange feeling, suddenly scared of what he might say, and I stopped eating.

"What?" I asked.

Mom sighed. "There's no sense in keeping it from her, Rhys."

"I know." Dad looked right at me, shut his eyes tightly for a moment as if in pain, and then opened them again. "It's Gee Gee. She wants to—" He broke off.

I twisted my hands in my lap, looking from one to the other.

"She doesn't want her life to end without having seen her home one last time," Mom said bluntly. "She wants to go back to Wales."

Dad pressed his lips tightly together. "We can do this. As a family."

"Wait—what?" I stared at him. "Right now?"

"Summer," Mom said shortly.

There was a long, painful pause. "It's going to be expensive." She was talking to Dad again, and I could sense the argument threatening to boil over. "A month, maybe two, abroad? With only a few weeks to plan?"

I couldn't believe it. I'd always wanted to go to Wales.

And yet now I wanted to cry, because I knew what it meant. I knew what they weren't quite saying.

Gee Gee wanted to die there.

Dad put a hand on my shoulder. "Your Welsh will come in handy," he said, his voice strained. "You'll be able to pronounce all the place names."

He was trying so hard. Too hard. I forced a smile.

"Just don't let it interfere with your sleep," my mother added. "You've been awake a lot lately. I hear you muttering in there." My smile disappeared. I hadn't been sleeping well and the whole family knew it. It was impossible to hide anything in our house; all four of us were crammed into our second-level flat. It had only been a few months since Gee Gee first moved in, and I started having the dream soon after that.

Stress, my mom said. I wasn't so sure.

I'd always had vivid dreams, but this was... different somehow. Maybe because it just didn't *feel* like a dream. Or maybe because I would wake up with my heart pounding, covered in sweat. Sometimes more than once a night.

"My sleep is fine," I said flatly, not meeting my mother's eyes. Lately, whenever I woke up in the wee hours, I'd turn on my laptop and start listening to things in Welsh—podcasts, Internet radio, anything at all—losing myself in the rhythms, the music of the words. It was better than lying in bed and staring at the ceiling, one word repeating itself over and over in my head: *cancer*. One word my parents never seemed to say.

"When is Gee Gee getting home again?" I asked, trying to change the subject.

"The day after tomorrow," my mom said. "She's finished with that clinical trial, but they want to run a few more tests." Tests. Once liver cancer metastasizes, the prognosis isn't good; I didn't need more tests to tell me that. That was why Gee Gee had refused further treatment. That was why there was a hospital bed in our office.

That was, clearly, why we were going to Wales.

I'd be surrounded by Welsh people, speaking Welsh for an entire summer. It felt unreal. I'd tried out other popular Celtic stuff: Irish folk dancing, Scottish Highland Games, Elizabethan dress-up at the Renaissance Faire, even steampunk outfits at the Edwardian Ball. You can do anything you want in San Francisco, and I had cardboard boxes full of costumes to prove it. But Wales was better. The minute I heard the language, I knew.

And in a few short weeks, we'd be there for real. I looked down at my hands, turning my Celtic knot ring from the Ren Faire around and around on my finger. It would be my first time overseas, my first vacation out of the country.

It might be Gee Gee's last.

Born to Wyn, May 15, 12:32 p.m.

I've learned enough Welsh to say "Hello, my name is Olwen Nia Evans and I come from California." I can also say "Please," "Thank you," and "Where are the toilets?" If I can manage to hold a conversation by the time we get there—even a boring one—I'll be happy.

Other than visiting Grandma Hazel in Orlando (and her new husband Angus, who served with Grandpa William in Vietnam—a long sad story that actually had a sort-of happy ending!), this will be the farthest I've ever traveled. I've even started dreaming about the trip.

It's a nice change from the other dream, the recurring nightmare.

I deleted the last line and typed instead, *Maybe if I keep listening to Welsh music while I sleep, I'll learn by osmosis.*

I didn't talk much about the dream, even though my blog wasn't really all that public. Judging from the lack of comments, I was pretty sure nobody was reading it. Not even Rae. I tried to tell myself that a minimum of unsolicited advice is a sign of a good listener. If so, my blog was definitely a good listener. A bit less satisfying than talking to a real person, but better than nothing.

The after-lunch bell rang. I logged out and pushed my chair back from the computer in the library. Rae just kept having more and more student government meetings, leaving me in lunchtime limbo. There were too many days like today, spending my lunch period doing homework or blogging in the library.

I tried to make it romantic somehow; tried to see myself as a solitary writer, not needing anyone. In the long vintage sundress I was wearing today, at least I looked the part. But it still felt like an act.

I hitched up my backpack and pushed open the library doors, squinting into the late spring sunlight—pretty, but I preferred our usual gray weather, the sky pearly with soft clouds and the air cool and smelling like the sea. Clearly everyone else disagreed with me. The masses of Geary High School students were a rowdy, happy, shouting mob in jeans and T-shirts, ready for the weekend to start.

I stood off to one side, feeling very alone.

Maybe it was a good thing I was going to be gone this summer.

———

Just a couple of hours later, I paced back and forth across the living room, all the lights blazing. Being home alone in a converted Victorian that creaked and cracked during a rainstorm was too creepy. Mom and Dad had called to say they were stuck in traffic and wouldn't be home with Gee Gee until later. Plus, water was pouring out of the sky, complete with thunder *and* lightning, which would make their drive even slower.

I really didn't want to be alone right now. But I didn't want to brave the storm, either. My steps led me into the kitchen. Silent and empty. Then back to the living room.

This was crazy. I had to talk to *someone*. I grabbed my phone, sat in the tiny window seat at the corner of our living room, and called Rae. She would know the right thing to say;

she always knew how to distract me, how to make me laugh. The first day we met, in third grade, she made vampire fangs out of French fries and made me snort milk out of my nose in the middle of the cafeteria. We *still* laughed about that.

The phone rang seven times, long enough for me to wonder what she was doing and whether she'd been avoiding me all day, and then she finally picked up.

"What's up?" She sounded distracted.

"Are you busy?" I asked.

"Um … kind of," she said. "I'm helping my mom make wontons for the student government meeting tomorrow."

"I could help," I said, frowning. I'd made wontons with Rae and her mom a million times. "I feel like we haven't talked in ages."

"Eh, they don't deserve your magic touch," she said. "Anyway, what's up?"

I ticked off each point on my fingers, even though she couldn't see me. "My house is empty and creepy. My Gee Gee is sick. Mom and Dad keep arguing. Nobody reads my blog. Oh, and I haven't been sleeping well because I keep having weird dreams."

"Have you been snacking late? It might be an indigestion problem," Rae asked innocently.

"Har har." I looked out the window, down at the street: the rain had stopped. People were shaking off and closing up their umbrellas, either hurrying home with briefcases held close or dressed up and heading out for sushi in Japantown. It was like looking at an aquarium of strange, colorful fish, only I was the one trapped inside the tank.

The figures blurred behind the wet glass, and I wondered if I should tell Rae the truth: that there was something weird about this dream. Something scary, uncanny. I shuddered, not wanting to think about it.

Rae spoke again, sounding serious now. "If it's a real problem, maybe you should tell your parents?"

I shook my head. "They'll probably just make me see a therapist. I don't want to talk to a stranger."

"Better a therapist than Chinese herbs," Rae said. "Trust me, you do not want to drink my mom's stinky tea. It works, but—" She stopped abruptly and let out an *eep*. "I'm so sorry, Wyn. I have to go. Listen, though, I think you *should* talk to someone." She paused. "Maybe your great-grandma?"

I thought for a moment. "Maybe," I allowed.

"Okay, good," Rae said. "I promise I'll call you on Sunday, 'kay?"

"Okay," I said forlornly, and ended the call.

I leaned my forehead against the cold glass of the window. How could I ever explain something that was so completely off the wall? I hadn't even known where to start with Rae. I hadn't even had a chance to tell her how lonely I was feeling.

Tears welled up in my eyes. I wondered if this was just another thing that was changing, ending, like everything else in my life right now.

Born to Wyn, May 15, 6:37 p.m.

It's raining outside, and everything is slipping through my fingers like water.

I'm alone. Maybe that's why it feels like the right time to say this. If any of you are faithful readers of this blog, you should probably know this about me: I have recurring dreams. I always have. But the one I've been having lately—it's different. Scarier.

In this one, I'm standing in front of a mirror, the huge one with the wooden frame that takes up half my dresser, the one Gee Gee gave us when Great-Grandpa John died and she had to move into a smaller place. We've had it since I was a kid. I reach out to run my fingers over the carved frame, the wood seeming warm and alive under my hand.

There is a girl reflected in the mirror. Is it me? She looks familiar. I reach up to touch my hair; the girl in the mirror reaches up to touch her long, dark hair. She's wearing a dress, a white, billowing dress. And then her hair is turning white and she's going blurry like an unfocused camera lens, but she's still smiling although she's old now, wrinkled. As I touch my own face, my skin crawls with nameless dread, but my face feels normal.

A small black fuzzy patch appears on the old woman's dress, like mold, then grows in snaking tendrils that spread over the white figure, faster and faster, until she's completely obliterated and the mirror shows only darkness.

I moved my mouse to the *Save as Draft* button. I wasn't sure I was ready to let this one out into the world, nonexistent audience or not. I let the cursor hover over *Publish*, then moved back to the draft button. I closed my eyes, listened to the rain pouring down. Washing everything clean. Almost everything.

My hand trembled, sliding the mouse a millimeter. Darkness behind my eyes.

I had to let go.

I clicked the button and turned away.

5

It is no secret unless it is between two.

Welsh proverb

Gareth shoved the front door open with his shoulder, his hair flopping into his eyes as he juggled keys, school bag, and a plastic bottle of water.

"Coming in or not?" he shouted.

"Keep your pants on." From the sidewalk, Amit gave the soccer ball one last kick; it arced high and landed in Gareth's mum's neatly weeded flower bed. "Oops." He retrieved the ball and set it next to the gate, then jogged up the front walk. "What's wrong with you these days? You're all grumpy and weird. Is it a girl thing?"

"What? No. I'm just tired," Gareth said. He switched on the light in the narrow front hallway, and Amit followed him inside.

"Are you sure? I heard Anita saying that the Year Nine with the red hair fancies you." Amit paused. "Or maybe she said 'Aaron,' not 'Gareth.' But still. My point is, you're being a tosser."

"You're the tosser," Gareth retorted automatically.

"Knobhead. Arseface." Amit dumped an armload of books on the living-room floor. "Did you start your history project? It's due next Monday."

"Yeah, I was just thinking about that. I still have loads to do on it," Gareth said. "Family history. It's such a primary-school assignment."

"I don't even want to think about it." Amit sat on the floor and started rummaging through his bag, pulling out a notebook and pen.

Gareth sat at the desk under the side window and switched on the computer. Next to it was a handwritten list his dad had left for him, for the family tree part of the project, with names and birthdates of all his aunts, uncles, and cousins. He scanned the list briefly: Uncle David. Aunt Liz. Uncle Nick, Aunt Rhian. Cousins Bronwen and Nia...

Something about that name "Nia" rang a bell. But he was sure he didn't know any other girls by that name. Except...

"Olwen Nia Evans." The words slipped from Gareth's mouth involuntarily, almost a whisper. He hardly noticed he'd said anything, just stared into space until a crumpled-up wad of paper hit the side of his head.

"Oi," Amit said. "What're you muttering about over there?"

"Eh? Nothing. Talking to myself." Gareth shook his head. What had he been doing? Oh, right; the history project.

"Better not be programming mumbo-jumbo. IT exam's not until next year." Amit poked Gareth in the foot with his pencil. "Even *you* don't need to study that long."

"Ha ha." Gareth threw the wad of crumpled paper back at his friend.

Amit caught it easily, then flopped onto his back on the paisley carpet, tossing the wad of paper and catching it again. On his second toss, it hit the ceiling and ricocheted back down onto his forehead. "Bloody Christmas!" Amit rolled around theatrically.

Gareth laughed, and swiveled back around to face the computer. "Yep. Tosser."

"I," Amit declared, "am amazing. Even your mum loves me. She wishes she had a daughter so I could marry right into your family." He sat up and opened his math book.

"The horror," Gareth said. He clicked into the browser so he could start researching public records. The browser window was open, the cursor poised over the blank URL field waiting for him to type, but there was something....

His head felt fuzzy all of a sudden. Something was nagging at him, like he was trying to remember an important date or name. But he didn't know what he was trying to remember. If he'd been sleeping better lately, maybe he could actually remember—

Olwen Nia Evans. The name drifted into his mind like a

thread of music into a silent room. This time he was acutely aware of it, heard each syllable as if someone were speaking right into his ear. His entire body shuddered like someone had run their finger down his spine. But nobody was there. Just Amit, studying trigonometry formulas across the room as if nothing had happened.

Then it hit him.

Weeks ago, during the spring holidays. A deserted hillside trail through green meadows, a cliff overlooking the waves. And the grave. The plaque had said "Olwen Nia Evans." Just to make sure, he pulled out his phone with the snapshots of his trip and scrolled to the one with the cairn.

There it was: *"Our Little Girl," Olwen Nia Evans, 1944–1950.*

This time, there was nobody in the photo.

Gareth felt cold sweat on his forehead and wiped it away impatiently. He didn't have time for this. He'd probably imagined the girl appearing in the picture, anyway. Or dreamed it or something. He turned his attention back to the screen, trying to focus. Family history project. All he really had left to do was research the public records and fill in the missing dates on his family tree. Then he'd type up his interview with his dad and be done with it.

"Hey, which of the essays did you pick?" he asked Amit. "The interview or the one about the history of your surname?"

Amit groaned. "Oh, no. Don't remind me."

"I know," Gareth said. "I picked the interview. I didn't

think my dad could *be* that boring. But my great-granddad didn't want to do it, so…"

"The frowny one who lives in Coom-Whatsit?"

"Cwm Tawel, yeah. 'Quiet Valley' in Welsh. Really quiet, I guess, since he didn't have anything he wanted to say about it." Gareth shook his head and tried to get back to work. But something was still rattling around in his mind. Great-Granddad… Cwm Tawel… It was as if his brain was trying to make some connection but wasn't there yet.

He accessed the Office of Public Records website and typed in a few names, copying down dates of marriage for his great-grandparents. "Married, Ellen Angharad Hughes, Swansea, 1952," he mumbled under his breath. He stopped and put down his pen. Cwm Tawel. The cromlech.

Olwen Nia Evans.

He was struck with a sudden urge to type "Olwen Nia Evans" into the Public Records search box. He took off his glasses and wiped the sweat off his forehead again.

"You look positively green," Amit said. "You didn't eat in the canteen again, did you?"

"Ugh… no." Gareth leaned back in the chair and closed his eyes. What was wrong with him? "Sorry. Maybe it's the flu."

"Maybe it's that time of the month," Amit said, and then ducked the flying pen Gareth aimed at him.

"Very funny."

Amit grinned, checking the time on his phone. "I should go, anyway." He gathered his books and notes into an untidy stack and pulled on his Arsenal Football Club stocking cap. After a moment, Gareth heard the front door shut with a bang, and the room was blessedly silent.

He let out a lungful of air. A strange feeling had been building up inside him, and his shoulders were tense and aching.

Olwen Nia Evans. It wasn't a whisper this time; it was just a thought drifting past. But he'd had enough. The photos. The name. The weirdness. "Fine!" he said loudly, and typed the name into the search box before he could change his mind.

Despite all logic, a shiver of anticipation ran through him and he crossed his fingers. Maybe if he found something out on Public Records, he could stop fixating.

The search results came back as he watched. For a moment, all Gareth could see on the screen was the reflection of blue eyes peering intently from his worried-looking face. He swallowed and stared at the results page. Odd. There was no entry. More precisely, there was an entry, but a blank one. Just a name with birth and death dates. No other information.

They were the right dates, though. At least now he knew for sure she existed. *Had* existed. That had to be enough to satisfy his subconscious curiosity, didn't it? The girl in the cromlech couldn't have been the same Olwen. It was impossible. End of story.

All this bloody research into his family tree. It was making him obsessive.

Gareth scrolled down the screen to find the *Search Again* button and realized he'd missed something, just below an inconspicuous heading labeled *External Search Results*. It was a single line of hypertext: *Olwen Nia Evans (Blogsite)*. No further information.

 He clicked on the link. He didn't know what he'd find— maybe historical records or old pictures scanned in. If he could find something on Cwm Tawel, it might be useful for his project.

The page loaded. Gareth stared for a moment. It wasn't what he'd expected at all.

Born to Wyn.

That was what it said at the top of the page, in a fake typewriter font. It was someone's blog. A prefab template—he could tell by the simple layout.

On the right he could see the top part of a photo, still loading. Below was the blogger's bio. It said: *Call me Wyn. Short for Olwen Nia Evans. San Francisco native. Mythology buff. Language nerd. Compulsive writer. Self-confessed geek girl.*

Interesting. His eyes kept returning to her name: Olwen Nia Evans.

Before he could read more, before he could check out any of the actual posts, the rest of the picture appeared. Gareth froze, his pulse beating in his ears. Long dark hair; thin oval face; dreamy smile. It could almost have been her. The girl from the cromlech, from the photo. The ghost girl.

Or whatever. He told himself to be logical. This Olwen was years older than the little girl he'd seen in the cromlech, and obviously existed now, somewhere in San Francisco. He looked more closely. This girl—Wyn—had brown hair, not black. She really wasn't quite the spitting image of the other girl, like he'd thought at first. Still, there was a resemblance, wasn't there? It was eerie.

And her name...

He had satisfied his curiosity, all right. But now he had a new nagging question: Who was this other Olwen, the living Olwen Evans? Was there some sort of a connection, or was he reading too much into it?

Before he could talk himself out of it, he started typing.

Hello Wyn,

My name is Gareth Lewis. I live in London. I don't know quite how to put this without sounding cheesy, but in a way I feel like I already know you.

It sounded like a chat-up line, a bad one. But it was the simple truth.

6

Henaint ni ddaw ei hunan.

Old age does not come by itself.

....

Welsh proverb

Born to Wyn, May 17th, 10:15 a.m.

*I had the dream again last night. The very same one.
I am officially weirded out.*

I shivered and set my laptop on the coffee table, wiping my
sweaty palms on my skirt. Why did I wait until I was alone in
the house to think about these things? Right—Mom worried
the blog was a waste of my time, so I saved it for when she
wasn't watching.

I didn't mean to be secretive. But I didn't want to get that raised-eyebrow look every time I wrote a blog post, either. My mom was a talker, in the courtroom *and* at home, so she didn't understand why I'd rather work it out in writing than spill my guts out loud. It seemed like every ten minutes she was asking if I wanted to talk about what was happening with Gee Gee.

More things I didn't want to think about. Too many things. Clenching my jaw, I got up and started pacing restlessly, wandering into the kitchen and then the living room again, and then back into the kitchen. But it didn't help. Desperately, I recited words into the empty room.

"*Mam-gu.*" Grandmother.

"*Cymru.*" Wales.

"*Breuddwyd.*" Dream. My voice trembled slightly, echoing off the walls of the spotless kitchen.

I caught a glimpse of myself in the glass of the microwave door. My face was drawn, my eyes tired. It was the waiting that drove me crazy every time they took Gee Gee to an appointment. I went back to the living room and sat on the couch, determined not to cave in and call Rae again. I pulled my computer back onto my lap.

As I typed, I felt my muscles tense again.

I don't know if I'm having the dream more because of my great-grandmother Rhiannon. Because of the cancer. I wake up at night and I turn on my computer. I learn words like "cyfrifiadur" and "merlyn" and "gwyntog."

But it doesn't help, because the only words in my head
are "sick" and "sad" and "not enough time."

A horrible image formed in my mind: Gee Gee looking sicker, thinner, like the gaunt, sparse-haired cancer patients on TV. For a moment I squeezed my eyes shut.

My email account, open in another window, dinged quietly. New message. Probably nothing, but I checked anyway.

"Your blog," said the subject line, from someone named Gareth Lewis. Could be spam. I didn't recognize the name, and anyway, who was reading my blog? Curious, I opened it. As I scanned it, something in the message caught my eye.

A single word—possibly the only one that would get me to read some random stranger's email—and that word was "Wales."

Hello Wyn,

My name is Gareth Lewis. I live in London. I don't know quite how to put this without sounding cheesy, but in a way I feel like I already know you. See, I sort of used to know an Olwen Nia Evans, back in Wales. It's a long story, but I was researching family history online for a school project and I found your website. We're not related, are we? Haha! Anyway, I thought you sounded interesting so I decided to write you. I enjoy writing, too, but just in a journal. Nothing exciting. What else? I'm 15 too. I spend a lot of time

on the computer; I'm doing an IT course at school.
Well, write me back if you feel like it.

—Regards, Gareth.

Related? Was this for real?

I knew it had to be a joke, but I couldn't help thinking about it. Wales. It couldn't really be possible, could it? I did still have some distant family there, but ... I sat frozen for several minutes. Had I missed something, during my conversations with Gee Gee over the years? What if I'd missed some random tidbit about long-lost cousin Gareth?

Guilt came rushing in a moment later, because it was kind of late for what-ifs. What if I'd been home more? What if we had more time? There was no more time.

I closed the browser window and put my head down on my knees.

After a moment, I heard the front door open. Dad boomed out "Wyn, we're home!" in the fake cheerful voice I was growing to dread. I looked up. Mom walked in briskly with a large overnight bag, and Gee Gee followed.

I rushed to Gee Gee and hugged her, cautiously, like I couldn't help doing now. Afraid I'd be too exuberant and hurt her; afraid to be too tentative and seem like I was pulling away. I tried to hide my indecision by going back over to the couch and patting the cushion next to me.

"*Croeso!*" I said, managing a smile. *Welcome.*

Gee Gee's eyes crinkled as she smiled broadly in reply. "*Diolch yn fawr!* Don't mind if I do." Tiredly, she navigated around the coffee table and sat down next to me. My dad put her bag in the office and returned with a huge throw pillow for her back, strangely awkward in his movements as he settled her against it.

She'd lost a lot of the plumpness that I recalled from childhood, and even since she'd moved in. A blurry memory drifted through my mind of being very small, sitting on Gee Gee's lap. I'd reached up toward the dimples in her smiling face, which was framed with soft, wavy gray hair that tickled my hands. Her face had gotten so much thinner now that the dimples were all but gone, but her warm smile was the same, her strong features, and her bright, sharp eyes. Eyes that made me feel a bit awed under their powerful gaze.

"Gran, can I get you anything else? Do you need a blanket?" Dad rested his hands on the back of the couch for a moment, looking more exhausted than I'd seen him in ages.

"No, thank you, Rhys dear." She smiled up at him. "We're both fine."

Dad left to join Mom in the kitchen. In a moment I heard clinking noises, and the sound of water filling the electric teakettle.

"How was the hospital?" I asked, and then felt like cringing. What a stupid question.

"Oh, I detest those places." Gee Gee waved off the question, then reached over and tucked a lock of my hair back behind my ear.

Another image flashed through my mind, an old picture from Dad's family photo album: Gee Gee with long, straight dark hair similar to mine, standing proudly next to my great-grandpa. *Rhiannon and John* said the handwritten note on the back. Great-Grandpa John had died suddenly of a stroke eight years ago, but Gee Gee might suffer for weeks, even months.

I clenched my hands in my lap, bunching up my skirt into a crinkly wad. "Me too. I'm glad you're back," I said, my voice almost a whisper.

"I'm glad to be back, too," she answered, her mouth curving up into a gentle smile.

I tried to smile in response, but I couldn't think of anything else to say. My breath hitched in my chest for a moment. I looked at my hands in my lap, the vase of slightly wilted lilies on the end table, the prints on the walls; everywhere except at Gee Gee. Why was talking so hard all of a sudden?

I glanced at my laptop. "Gee Gee, can I ask you something?"

"Of course, *cariad.*" Her face was serene, and I wished I had even an ounce of that serenity.

"Are we … are we related to anyone whose last name is Lewis?"

Gee Gee raised her eyebrows and I rushed to explain.

"The thing is, I got a random email from this guy named Gareth Lewis who was reading my blog. And he's from the UK and recognized my name and thought, wouldn't that be funny if we were related somehow." I trailed off, realizing how ridiculous it all sounded. I wished I'd thought of something else, anything else, to talk about.

I could have tried practicing my Welsh. Too late.

Gee Gee was looking back at me, keenly. "Well, as you

know, Rhiannon Davies is my maiden name. There were plenty of us Davies in our village. All of us related somehow, it seemed at the time." The ghost of a smile passed across her face, then disappeared. "The war killed one of my brothers, the Second World War. The ones left, my younger brothers—we weren't close. And on your great-granddad's side, they were all named Evans, you know."

"Nobody named Lewis married in later? Maybe Gareth is related to some random cousin." I realized that deep down, I was hoping for a connection. Another small part of Gee Gee that would still be alive even after she was gone.

"Heavens, love, I can't speak for everyone in the extended family." Gee Gee leaned back onto the overstuffed pillows and yawned. "But that's about the sum of it. Davies and Evans," she said, the conversation obviously closed.

It felt kind of strange, because normally Gee Gee was happy to tell me about Wales. I didn't even have to press her. We'd had a ton of conversations about what it would be like this summer, how it would be different from here: Accents. Driving. Village life. How it would be the same: Gray skies. Ocean. Rolling hills.

"I wonder what happened to that tea?" Gee Gee mused. It almost sounded like she was trying to distract me.

I frowned, but I let it go. She was probably just tired. "I'm on it." I got up, wanting to ask more but not knowing exactly what I wanted to ask about.

As I walked toward the kitchen, she said, "Oh, Olwen *fach*. My lovey." Her voice was like a sigh, apologetic. "We could read the Olwen story again tonight if you like. Or do you remember how much you loved *Peter Pan* when you were a little one? Maybe you don't recall, but you always wanted to be Wendy, soaring through the starry sky. Too old for that, now, I expect," she finished. My heart constricted.

"I do remember," I said, my voice breaking. "I never want to forget those moments."

"No, we mustn't forget," Gee Gee said softly, but her eyes weren't meeting mine now. They looked elsewhere, somewhere above my left shoulder, or inward, to something still unsaid.

———

It seemed to take a monumental effort to pick up the phone, even though I had Rae on speed dial. I felt awkward. It was Sunday night, and she still hadn't called even though she'd said she would.

She picked up after one ring and started talking. "Wyn, ohmigod, did you finish the Chem homework?"

"The molar equations? Yeah, I finished it yesterday. Are you still not done?"

"No! Crap. I'm so screwed." I could tell she was flitting around, doing stuff; I heard papers rustling in the background. "I've been so busy. There was a tennis tournament last night, and we had to hold the ASL meeting at my house today so I spent all week trying to get everything cleaned up and my brother's crap out of the way. You know."

I didn't know. "You should have called me," I said pointedly. "I would have helped."

"But I didn't want to bother you! I figured you'd want to spend time with, you know, your family and all." I could picture her flapping her hands, all flustered, but the mental image didn't make me giggle like it normally did. She still should have called me. What if I *wanted* her to bother me?

"Or you were 'too busy' to call," I muttered. "Or text."

"Look, I'm sorry. I—things are just crazy. Is everything going okay? Did you have a chance to talk to your Gee Gee? Or someone?" Rae's voice was solicitous, but I felt cranky now. Like things weren't crazy for me, too? I decided that if she wasn't going to keep me posted, I wasn't going to talk, even if that was petty.

"Everything's fine," I said, trying to sound blasé. "I'm fine. We're dealing with it."

"Oh. Uh. Okay." Rae sounded disconcerted, and I was perversely glad, even though it really wasn't *her* I was upset at. Not entirely.

I hung up the phone, flopped back on the bed, and turned out the light. The three weeks left until the end of the school year felt like an eternity—slogging through final projects and essays I couldn't bring myself to care about, waiting in the wings for Rae. Watching Gee Gee get sicker.

At least someone was reading my blog now. I'd have to decide whether to answer his email or not.

I'd only been lying on the bed for a minute when raised voices started filtering through my open door. I lifted my head. Mom and Dad were having what they called a "reasoned debate" in the kitchen. Dad sounded annoyed. I got up and crept to the door. Their voices got quieter, rising and falling, until I heard Dad say something like, "If that's where she wants to stay, we'll find a way! We have to. It's what Dad and Granddad would have wanted."

"I know it's no question for *you*," Mom said, "but you've got *us* to think about. And your mother, too. She always had a good relationship with Rhiannon before your father passed." There was a tense silence. "Anyway, she's going on that Alaskan cruise and the timing couldn't be worse. I just wish we were . . ." Their voices dwindled to a murmur again.

I sighed. Even the littlest things were a big deal now—what we ate for breakfast, the type of pillows on Gee Gee's bed. The amount of time I was spending on the computer, which my mother blamed for my lack of sleep.

I returned to bed and twisted onto my right side, then my left, trying to get comfortable. I was *not* going to give in and turn on the light tonight. Instead, I composed sentences in my head using my limited vocabulary. Maybe this Gareth character spoke Welsh. I could try to email him in Welsh tomorrow and see what happened. For instance, I could say:

Mae Cymru yn hyfryd. Wales is lovely.

Mae'r tywydd yn braf heddiw. The weather is fine today.

Dw i'n hoffi te. I like tea.

I must have been dozing. My mind went fuzzy for a while, free-associating, and then I heard a voice, singing:

Ar lan y môr mae rhosus cochion.

I sat bolt upright and looked around. Of course, nobody was there. My room was dark and empty; the house was silent. It had sounded like . . . well, it had sounded like Gee

Gee, singing me to sleep the way she had when I was little. I touched my face and felt tears on my cheeks.

When I lay down to go back to sleep, I couldn't help hearing the haunting, soft melody as I slipped into dreams, a woman's soft voice singing low and sweet.

Ar lan y môr mae rhosus cochion
Ar lan y môr mae lilis gwynion
Ar lan y môr mae 'nghariad inne
Yn cysgu'r nos a chodi'r bore.

Beside the sea there are red roses
Beside the sea there are white lilies
Beside the sea my sweetheart lives
Asleep at night, awake at morning.

This dream was different; new. I was walking by the sea. A field of white flowers. My footsteps made no sound, but waves crashed and wind whistled.

The smell of salt air; the faint tang of nearby farm-lands. Real enough to touch.

On a clifftop stood a man and a woman. The man, tall and rangy with short brown hair riffled by the breeze. The woman with long black hair and a homespun dress.

Nearer now. The man and woman were Gee Gee and Great-Grandpa John, but younger, like in old photos. The woman held a baby in her arms, and both their heads were bent toward him.

Then somehow there was a little girl standing there, too, but the couple still did not look up. The little girl was thin, frail, and her face was contorted with anguish. She opened her mouth but I couldn't hear what she said. The girl reached out to the couple, but suddenly they receded into the distance. Farther and farther. She turned and looked directly at me, pleadingly. Her eyes were dark little caves of sorrow.

I jerked away in fear. Suddenly the little girl, the couple, the seashore were all gone. The woman with white hair stood before me, but not blurry this time. No, her features were clear, and it was Gee Gee, white hair hanging down long and brittle. The skin-crawling sensation of dread returned, all too familiar, and a black cancerous patch of mold spread over her dress, her limbs, her face, until she was no longer recognizable.

I kicked away the covers, opening my eyes to bright morning light. It was Monday morning, and the sun was streaming through my flimsy curtains onto my bed, making me sweaty. The clock read 7:05 a.m., but I felt as though I'd hardly slept.

I hurried out of bed and into the shower, letting the hot spray rinse the sweat off my body. Drying off afterward, I noticed Gee Gee's lily-scented powder in a small cylindrical container on the edge of the sink. I pulled off the lid and a small cloud of powder drifted into the air. The flowery fragrance was sweet, almost cloying. That had been the smell of her house. Sweet and strong.

Gee Gee was alone in the kitchen, and I slipped quietly into one of the blocky wooden chairs at the kitchen table.

"Good morning, my dear." She smiled, moving with

slow and measured steps across the kitchen with a plate of hot muffins.

"*Bore da*," I answered, yawning.

Gee Gee set down the muffins and sat down across the table from me, her eyes lingering on my face. "Didn't you sleep well, *cariad*?"

Was it that obvious, again? "It was just a nightmare. A really vivid one," I said. I couldn't meet her gaze. "There was a little girl, and you and Great-Grandpa John were there with a baby, by the sea, and..." I realized I didn't want to tell her about the image in the mirror, the spreading darkness. I didn't want her to think I couldn't handle her illness. I didn't want her worrying about me on top of everything. "I guess I still feel weird. I know it's stupid."

Gee Gee sighed, her expression pensive. "Well, no. It isn't stupid. You're a Davies, through and through, and we Davies women..." She paused, as if choosing her words carefully. "We've always been sensitive dreamers, you might say."

A sudden chill sent goose bumps up and down my arms. "It could just be stress," I pointed out. I didn't want to think about it being anything else.

"Maybe," Gee Gee said. She lowered her voice, speaking almost too quietly to hear. "But every single Davies woman has been... intuitive, somehow. Our dreams sometimes tell us things that our waking mind won't. That's true for everyone, you know. We're just a little more in tune with it than most people."

There was a long pause. I took a muffin and turned it around and around in my hands, but suddenly I wasn't hungry.

"It's a blessing and a curse," she finally said.

I nodded, but I wasn't sure. I wasn't sure I could believe what she was telling me—about my dream, about "Davies women." It seemed too out there. What if the cancer was affecting her mind now? How would I know?

Then I thought of the dream again, the girl, all alone, and shivered. The baby had to be Grandpa William, but was the girl supposed to be me? I wanted to ask what it meant, but I felt paralyzed.

Gee Gee reached across the table and gripped my hand tightly. "You listen to me, Olwen *fach*. It will be all right. When you feel afraid, remember..." She trailed off, looking lost for a moment. "Remember this moment. That I'm here with you, holding your hand. You aren't alone."

I wasn't sure whether she was talking about my dream now or the whole situation. Cancer. Death. So many questions were clamoring in the back of my mind, but all that came out was a tiny voice I hardly recognized, asking, "What will I do?"

"You'll understand one day. Some things... can't be explained in words." Not for the first time, I got the strangest feeling that she meant something more than she was saying outright. "But it does get easier. Maybe not right away, and there are always hard times in everybody's lives." She gave me a long look. "It'll be all right, I promise."

I could hear the conviction in her voice. But I still felt lost.

7

Cof a lithr, llythr a geidw.

Memory slips, Letters Remain.

Welsh proverb

Gareth was in the schoolyard with Anita Kessler. She was tossing her hair around the way she always did, telling him she was breaking up with him, which struck him as funny because he hadn't remembered going out with her in the first place. That was when he realized he was dreaming.

He laughed, and was about to let her in on the joke, when the scene shifted to something else entirely. Everything went dark, and he felt like he was falling, his stomach flipping with vertigo. A wind from nowhere whirled around him, buffeting him from all sides. Something that looked like white fabric whipped past his face. The smell of the sea was all around him. Then he was moving more and more quickly while a dizzy whirl of images zipped past like a movie on fast-forward: a cairn, his parents standing together in the distance, an inscribed piece of slate, the huge slabs of the cromlech, a hole yawning darkly into the ground and growing ever closer.

"Slow down," Gareth found himself saying, fear making his voice break. "Stop."

The blurring around him began to resolve into discernible images. The fact that the dream seemed to be obeying him was somehow even more frightening.

When the whirling stopped, he was standing over the dark gray slate plaque. He felt sad, but it was a distant sadness, like the memory of a feeling rather than the feeling itself. Then abruptly he was falling again, for a timeless instant, the cromlech a deep dark pit in front of him, surrounding him with walls of stone he couldn't see. More images flashed past him: the small, frail girl in the white dress; his dad's worried face, seeming tiny and far away. A whispery voice, a song on the wind. Who? Who was it? But everything was slipping through his fingers now, the images disintegrating.

Whispers echoing in his ears, he fell into a deep, dreamless sleep.

He woke up the following morning when the family cat, Fortran, jumped on the bed and meowed loudly, right in his face, five minutes before his alarm was set to beep.

"Okay, okay." Gareth sat up, then dragged himself to his

feet. "Seriously rude awakening." It was unfair that Fortran picked on him just because everyone else had left for the day.

The ginger cat kept meowing frantically at his heels the entire way downstairs to the kitchen. He scooped her some dry cat food and then poured a bowl of cereal for himself. Just to be contrary, he scarfed it down while standing at the counter, since nobody was around to cajole him to sit like a civilized human.

He still had a few minutes left, so he went straight to the computer. It had been nearly five days; maybe the other Olwen—Wyn—had finally answered his message. Or maybe she'd decided to ignore it. Perhaps she hadn't even seen it. Or...

His inbox loaded. A shiver traveled up his spine when he saw *Olwen Nia Evans* at the top of the list of new messages.

"Ridiculous," he said aloud, but he couldn't help the image that flashed into his mind at that moment: Slate plaque. Dead girl. Had he dreamed about it last night, again? He gave his head a shake and clicked on the email. "Real world, Gareth," he muttered to himself.

The email was real, at least.

Dear Gareth,

I'm sorry I was a little slow to answer your email. I just have a lot going on right now. You might have some idea, if you've seen my blog.

I'm still shocked there's anyone reading it, let alone someone in London.

*It's kind of a cool coincidence, though, because my
dad's side of the family is British. Welsh, actually. I
know Gareth is a Welsh name, too, so I'm wondering
about YOUR story. You've been reading some of my
story ... So tell me about yourself.*

—Wyn

Welsh. Wales. Olwen. It was uncanny.

Just in case, Gareth refreshed the page. Yes, it was as real
as his hand in front of his face. And now it was his turn to
reply.

The question was, how much of *his* story did he want
to tell?

———

Gareth stared unseeingly out the window of the bus as it
pulled away from the stop near his school. All day he'd been
trying to figure out how to word his reply to Wyn. He didn't
want to sound like a stalker, but he'd read through several
of her blog posts and he felt so strangely as if he knew her.
Her love of writing. Her great-grandmother's cancer. Her
uncanny dreams, with their scenes that sounded so familiar. The fact that she was actually coming to Wales. *Wales.*
Of all places. That was the biggest coincidence of all, next
to the name thing. But how did you bring that up when
you hardly knew someone? He wanted to seem friendly,
not pervy, but the messages he composed in his head never

56

looked quite as good onscreen. They all made him sound desperate somehow. And he wasn't trying to flirt, not really.

Anyway, she probably had a boyfriend already. No doubt a tall, tanned California surfer with bleached-blond hair and huge Arnold Schwarzenegger pecs. The diametrical opposite of what he saw in the bus window reflection: a lanky, pale boy with glasses and an unruly mop of curls. He looked down at his hands gripping the top of his rucksack.

None of that mattered, he told himself. They'd established a connection. Now he had to keep up his end. It was only polite.

It had nothing, of course, to do with the coincidences. Nothing to do with the eerie familiarity that washed over him every time he looked at the tiny picture of her on *Born to Wyn*, her long dark hair framing anxious eyes that stared off into the distance.

Nothing to do with the strong tug he felt from somewhere deep inside his brain, like the pull of a magnet.

He jiggled his leg, annoyed at himself. That was irrational, woo-woo stuff, just like the impulse that had led him to find her website in the first place. He didn't understand it, but that didn't mean anything. He didn't understand a lot of things, and it didn't mean there wasn't a reasonable explanation.

The bus rolled to a halt near the Underground station. Gareth stared out, watching the people climbing on and off the bus and milling around the junk shops, antique stores, pubs, and coffeehouses that lined the streets near the Camden flea market. He saw it every day, but now, he couldn't help imagining it through Wyn's eyes, the throngs of shoppers and buskers and loiterers, the dirty sidewalks he no longer noticed.

He was definitely getting ahead of himself, picturing the two of them wandering the streets together as if they already knew each other, him showing her around like a tour guide as she rushed excitedly from place to place. Her family was probably going straight to Wales, anyway. If so, he'd never even get to meet her.

He was surprised at how disappointed that made him feel.

Of course, that was one place he could start his reply: asking her about her trip. Offering some travel advice. Then he'd just have to see what happened.

The bus cruised past a long block of old-fashioned-looking storefronts: tailors, chip shops, a barber. Gareth's stop was coming up, at the corner next to the Harp and Lion, and he rang the bell before getting to his feet. Slinging his bag over one shoulder, he thudded down the narrow aisle and reached the doors just as they opened into the crisp air and patchy sunlight.

He felt lighter, stepping off the bus. *That's right; shake it off, Gareth*, he told himself. The weather was nice, and it was Friday, and school was over for the day. And, most importantly, he'd figured out what to put in his email to Wyn.

He walked faster, turning off the main road and into his neighborhood—street after crisscrossing street of brick houses that were nearly identical except for the front gardens and the occasional yard gnome. At St. John's Road, he took a brief detour past the park, checking for Amit.

At the other end of the grassy square, a crowd of his school mates were shouting gleefully. Gareth watched from the sidewalk as Dan Dobbs dribbled the ball toward Amit, the goalkeeper, who was standing in front of two trees that served as the goal. Dobbs fired the ball right at Amit's head.

"Oi!" Amit ducked and the ball went right between the trees, bouncing off the fence behind him. He laughed sheepishly as the others snickered.

"You fell for it again," Gareth said, walking over to the group.

"Hey, Lewis," said Dobbs. "We should substitute you in for Patel over here."

"No way. I'm not giving up my post." Amit was sweat-drenched and still grinning. "I have the perfect job for you, Gareth. Highly important. It's called Ball Boy. Let me explain it to you."

"Thanks, but no thanks," Gareth said. "I've got something to do."

"Eh? It's an honor to fetch my balls," Amit said. "I'm offended."

The rest of the players hooted and Gareth smirked. "I was just on my way home," he explained. "I have to ... get some work done on the computer."

"No problem, man." Amit grinned and clapped him on the shoulder. "Say no more. Alone in front of the computer. I know what that's all about."

"You don't know anything about anything." Gareth rolled his eyes. He waved at Amit and crossed the street, the players' yells fading with distance. They were funny, but he wasn't in the mood to hang around and joke. His steps quickened. He might have been heading back to the computer, but he suspected he wouldn't be alone. Not quite.

———

Dear Wyn, Gareth typed, and stopped. This was harder than he'd thought. He just wasn't good at this kind of thing. And Wyn obviously was, which made him even more nervous. She was the writer. He was just…

> *You asked about me. Well, okay, but my life is not that exciting, haha! I'm not a writer like you, but here goes. I take the bus to school every day. I like playing football (or as you call it, soccer) and computer games.*
>
> *You're right about Gareth being a Welsh name. We moved here four years ago from Swansea. That's right, we used to live in Wales, so if you have any questions or need travel advice, just ask. We could Skype sometime if that's easier.*
>
> *What else? … I want to be a programmer, maybe for computer animation. I live in Camden, which is in North London. Me, my dad, my mum, and my little brother Tommy. My best mate Amit lives a few blocks away. What's your family like? Do you still have family here? (Sorry if that's a nosy question.)*
>
> *—Your friend, Gareth*

He leaned back in the swivel chair. That seemed okay. He'd offered to be helpful. And he'd asked about her family. It was kind of indirect, but he was still wondering about Olwen Nia Evans, about whether maybe Wyn had some family connection to her. That would make the most sense.

He didn't know what else to put. He didn't want to sound too eager.

The front door opened with a rattle of keys and his parents' voices filtered in, Tommy shouting over them about wanting roast chicken for dinner.

Gareth sighed. He should probably just hit *Send*, right now.

No, he should wait and re-read it later, when he'd had some time away from the computer.

This was ridiculous. He reached for the mouse just as Tommy came running in and put cold hands on his stomach.

"Aaagh! Get away." Gareth elbowed his brother in the ribs.

"What're you doing?" Tommy peered at the message. "Who's Wyn? Do you know her at school? Do you fancy her?" The boy snickered. "I bet you do! You like her!"

"You're jumping to conclusions," Gareth said, annoyed. "She's just this girl. You don't know her." He quickly clicked the *Send* button before he could second-guess himself anymore—and before Tommy read any further.

"Eww, are you going to kiss her?" Tommy danced around Gareth's chair. Gareth aimed a kick at his brother's shins but missed.

"Why do you even care?"

"I hear arguing," their dad shouted from the front hall.

"It's nothing, Dad," Gareth said loudly. He glared at Tommy, who just laughed again and ran out of the room. The door to the garden slammed a moment later.

It was probably just as well that he'd sent the email. There really wasn't any reason to dither, not if Wyn was going to be coming in just a few weeks, or whenever their summer hols started. The sooner they made plans, the better.

Plans! There he went again. Gareth shook his head, a bit surprised at himself. *Moving a bit quickly, are we, Lewis?* Amit would no doubt approve, but to Amit, girls were a serious pastime. Gareth usually stayed on the sidelines, watching. Amit tried to fix him up with girls from school every once in a while, but it always ended awkwardly, with Gareth realizing that he and the girl had nothing in common.

At least that wasn't the case with Wyn. He already knew they had *something* in common: being Welsh. Partly Welsh, anyway.

A sudden thought struck him, then, and he sat up straight, the springs of the office chair squeaking in protest.

He knew he'd have to wait to find out whether Wyn had any connection with the other Olwen Nia Evans, but what if *he* was connected? What if that was the reason his parents had chosen that hiking spot in the first place? To visit that gravesite? And they didn't tell him for some reason? He felt stupid for not thinking of it before.

Gareth could hear his mum in the kitchen, rattling dishes around. He got up and walked in, his steps purposeful.

"Mum, I've got a question."

"Yes, my love." Her blond hair was flying out of its bun as she bustled around the room, setting a package of chicken on the counter and pulling things out of the fridge.

"I was wondering...we don't have any relatives named Olwen Nia Evans, do we? On the Welsh side?" He lingered in the doorway, watching her work.

"That family tree again? Well, I'm sure I don't know every single relative of your father's, but if it's not on the list he gave you, then it's not likely." His mum smiled at him distractedly and started scrubbing the potatoes. "There are loads of Evanses in Wales, you know that." Her tone lifted, a bit proudly. "Our English side has got Huxleys, going back for centuries on my dad's side."

"Right. Okay." Gareth started pacing back and forth, trying to figure out what this meant. Apparently Olwen Nia Evans *wasn't* a relation—neither of them, actually. But that didn't explain why he was so convinced there was a connection—why he felt so much like he knew Wyn already.

He shook his head. There wasn't any rational reason for there to be a connection. Yes, it was all a major coincidence. Coincidences were a matter of statistical probability—they were bound to happen from time to time.

Right. At this point, he'd done all he could do. He was unlikely to find out any more information.

Finding Wyn's blog—well, that *was* an amazing coincidence, but she was just a girl, an American girl, who happened to have Welsh family, and...

No. Stop it. This was the problem. He just kept going round and round in circles. No, from now on, he was only going to think about programming and his animation project, and reasonable everyday *normal*—

It started as a tingle in his toes. Gareth looked down, surprised, and shifted his feet as if they'd fallen asleep.

But it didn't stop there. The odd tingling began to spread, on up his spine and into his head, which began feeling light and strange as if it were lifting off from his body. He leaned back against the kitchen doorframe, his skin prickling. The room started going dim, and he wondered if this was what it felt like to faint.

But apparently not, because after everything went dark, images suddenly appeared, as if on a screen in his mind's eye. With mounting horror, Gareth realized that he was in his own memory, back in Wales, walking along the grass clifftop overlooking the sea. A part of him noted distantly that he must have fallen asleep on his feet, but it was a very small part, and then it disappeared entirely as dream-images flickered past: A lonely cairn of stones. The grave plaque. And then he was standing in front of the cromlech, its huge boulders looming overhead, its yawning cavernous opening descending into darkness. He approached the hole and peered in.

Then he was inside. Black night surrounded him on all sides, but in front of him was a girl. Olwen. He started, bumping his head on the unseen rocky ceiling. The jabbing pain made his eyes fly open.

He was in the kitchen. He was home. He was leaning against the doorframe.

And his mum had turned from her potato-scrubbing

and was peering at him from across the room with a frown. "Did you just fall asleep?"

Gareth swallowed, his throat dry, and felt his head start to throb. "Er. I suppose. Long day," he tried to explain.

"You're looking a little peaked lately. Are you sure you're not ill?" She set the potatoes in the sink and came over to him, putting a hand on his forehead. He pulled away.

"I'm okay," he said. "Just tired."

"If you're tired enough to fall asleep standing up, you'd better have a lie-down before dinner," his mum told him in a no-nonsense tone. "I'll send Tommy to wake you up."

"No! I mean, no, I don't need a nap." Gareth tried not to let his fear show. "I'll be fine tomorrow. I just didn't sleep well is all."

"If you're sure," his mother said, still frowning.

"I'm sure," he echoed. But he really wasn't, not at all.

—————

The next morning, Gareth woke late. The first thing he did was reach for his phone and check his email.

Nothing.

8

Coelia'n llai'r glust na'r golwg.

Believe the ear
less than the eye.

....

Welsh proverb

I was lying in bed reading, not quite ready to get up yet, when I heard the *ping* of a chat notification on my laptop. Probably Rae. Or Bethany, if she was somehow awake before 11 a.m. on a Saturday. I took a minute to throw on appropriate weekend attire—dark gray sweats—and brush my hair into a ponytail before checking the computer.

LewzerBoy: wyn? it's me, gareth

  I drew in a rapid breath. This was happening. *Right now.*
In my head, I didn't feel prepared, but my fingers were already
tapping at the keys.

OlwenNia: Oh, wow! I just have a minute.
     Sorry I didn't answer your email yet

LewzerBoy: np

LewzerBoy: it was so weird that i found yr website

OlwenNia: That *was* weird. I never thought anyone
     was reading it. I'm a little embarrassed

LewzerBoy: not embarrassing
      yr a good writer

OlwenNia: Thanks. :) It hasn't been that great lately,
     though. I haven't been getting enough sleep,
     I guess.

LewzerBoy: ah don't worry, cdn't tell.
      why didn't u sleep well? horrible california
      weather? lol
      or a hot date
      sorry, jk

OlwenNia: LOL I wish. I had a nightmare.

LewzerBoy: sorry. read about that on yr blog.

OlwenNia: Yeah, I get them a lot…
They're kind of disturbing

There was a long pause. I realized I was breathing shallowly, nervously. But it wasn't a bad kind of nervous. In fact, despite our topic of conversation, there was a smile on my face. A big one.

LewzerBoy: meant to tell u…
asked my parents if there were any evanses in our family. because i recognized yr name. they said every good welsh family has an evans or 2 in it

OlwenNia: Including yours? :)

LewzerBoy: no evans my mum could think of.
wonder why u seem so familiar then

OlwenNia: No clue. I asked my Gee Gee, but no Lewises in our family.

LewzerBoy: so…

OlwenNia: Yeah, I know. I'm confused, too.

LewzerBoy: it's just that u look so familiar.
coincidence, I guess

OlwenNia: Or something else?

LewzerBoy: what do u mean?
like fate? or karma?

LewzerBoy: wyn, are you there?
hello?

OlwenNia: I'm here. You just startled me.
I was thinking the same exact thing!
Normally I'd say that's impossible
but my life has been weird lately.

LewzerBoy: is everything ok? how's yr great-gran,
is she doing all right?

OlwenNia: Yeah.
she's been talking about her old life a lot,
back in Wales.

LewzerBoy: really, like what?
uh oh, mum's calling me. gotta go

OlwenNia: Can we talk again?

LewzerBoy: yeah, i'll email you. or we could
video chat if you want
bye

OlwenNia: Bye.

I closed the chat window and stretched back in the chair, the hard wooden slats pressing into my back. My smile had grown even bigger, despite our conversation being cut short.

And, of course, despite knowing better about random conversations with strangers online. My parents would freak if they knew.

The thing was, Gareth didn't feel like a stranger. And he was obviously a real person. I hadn't quite believed it until today.

He sounded really British, the way he talked about his "mum" and my "gran." Maybe he sounded like a BBC star. We might video chat next time, and then I'd know for sure. Maybe he spoke Welsh.

I squeezed my eyes shut. I could have *asked* Gareth if he spoke Welsh. I should have asked where his family was from, even if we weren't related. I wanted to ask a lot of things, but maybe it was better to take it slow, especially with someone halfway around the world.

Of course, I'd be halfway around the world myself in a week and a half. Instead of waking up in my familiar old room, the sounds of the city all around me, I'd be sleeping in a cottage in Gee Gee's tiny home village, which probably had nothing going on at night. Would it be too quiet? Would there be the rumble of cars driving past? Would there be crickets, or night birds? Or nothing but the smell of the sea and the sound of the wind?

All of a sudden, I ached to talk to someone, tell somebody about Gareth. I hadn't confided in Rae lately, but...I didn't want to leave things the way they were. I wouldn't see her much this summer. Maybe not until school started in the fall, if Gee Gee hung on for that long. I'd have no way to put our friendship back the way it was, not from a distance. I unfolded myself from the chair and retrieved my phone from the foot of the bed.

"Hi!" she chirped. I could hear voices in the background; her dad's familiar rumbling laugh.

"I'm not interrupting, am I?" I sank down on the foot of my bed.

"Nah. We just finished brunch. What's up?"

"Not much." I shifted to face my laptop, which had already reverted to screen saver mode: a montage of photos. Rae and me. Me and my parents on vacation at Disneyland. Gee Gee from years ago, holding my dad as a baby. "Well, okay. This guy … Gareth. He emailed me about my blog." I paused. "He lives in London."

She squealed. "What? I can't believe you didn't tell me! Did you email him back? Did he send you a picture? Ooh: is he cute? English accents are *so hot*."

"His avatar picture is really tiny. He has glasses. Don't sidetrack me!"

Rae gave an evil chuckle.

"Anyway, I was trying to tell you we talked on IM," I said. "Just now."

"You *did*?" She drew in a sharp breath. "That's, um, wow."

"Yeah, I know."

I gave her a quick recap of the conversation. "We thought we might be related. He said my name looked familiar."

"Total pickup line," Rae said.

"You *would* say that." I felt kind of annoyed, even though that was what I'd thought at first, too. "He was serious, though. *He* reads my blog posts," I pointed out.

"Oh, so maybe he's a stalker!"

I chose to ignore that possibility. "I did ask Gee Gee about it. Whether we had Lewises in the family. She said no, though, so I don't think we're related."

"Great. It won't be incest if you guys hook up."

"Thanks for that," I said.

"So what now?" Rae asked.

"Well, we decided we should talk on Skype sometime, face-to-face. Then he had to go help his mom. His 'mum.'"

"Ooh, Skype." Rae laughed, then went quiet, as if waiting for more. "Is that it?"

"Yeah, but ... " I didn't know how to explain it to her, because I didn't know how to explain it myself. But it felt like Gareth and I were supposed to find each other, somehow. If I said that aloud, I knew Rae would laugh. Not in a mean way, but she and I looked at the world very differently. She didn't seem to have the same sense of ... the magic in the universe.

When I was little, I used to believe everything. I believed the Greek gods and goddesses were real, and the Easter Bunny and Santa Claus, and of course all the stories Gee Gee read to me, of King Arthur and Taliesin the Bard and the mythological Olwen. I wanted them all to be real.

I wanted *this*, this one small good thing in my life, to be real.

"Are you there?"

"Yeah."

"Is everything okay? How's your, um, family stuff? You know, just because you don't like to talk about it doesn't mean I don't care."

"Oh, Rae, I don't know." I felt my throat tighten. "I'm

glad we're going to Wales, but this is so hard." It wasn't just that I wouldn't be home this summer. Watching Gee Gee dying was the hardest part. But I couldn't get those words out. I could write them, but I couldn't seem to say them.

"I know it's hard," Rae said quietly. "But you're strong. I know you. You'll manage."

That was another way we were different, I thought after we'd hung up. Rae was the strong one, the one who took charge, the one who kept me from tripping over cracks in the sidewalk because I was too busy daydreaming to watch where I was going. On my own, I wasn't sure I *could* manage.

I hunched over on the edge of the bed, hugging my knees. Rae could sound certain because she had no idea what was going on under the surface of all this. And there was no way I could explain it to her—no way to tell her that it wasn't just the near future that worried me, the things that I knew were inevitable, like Gee Gee dying.

How could I explain the insistent feeling that there was more going on than even *I* knew? And that somehow, soon, I needed to find out what was real and true?

———

In the dream, I'm walking by the sea, along the softly rolling hills. Grass is under my feet, stretching away to either side. The ocean crashes against the rocky cliffs far below, and the faint sting of salt spray needles my skin. It's just like before, but this time, there's more. On one side is an old abandoned church, moss and leaves pushing through cracks in the crumbling stone. I'm moving as if propelled, stiffly, like a marionette.

I pass the church, and the ocean cliff grows nearer. Then I see it: a group of huge rocks stacked on top of one another like a low, sunken doorway. A strange electricity gathers in the air under the gray, overcast skies, and suddenly I'm beyond the stones. In the grass a young woman is kneeling, her back to me. Her long dark hair spills over her shoulders, which are heaving, shaking. Over the loud pounding of the sea, I hear quiet, keening sobs.

The hairs on my arms stand up, as if the atmosphere is charged with static, and then abruptly there's a profound silence, the sounds of the ocean receding into the distance. In the stillness, I hear the young woman let out an anguished cry.

A shiver crawls up my spine. Her voice, low and rich and rough with sorrow, seems somehow familiar. "Olwen," she cries again.

Then the dream is slipping away and my eyes are opening.

———

Someone was calling my name. It was Gee Gee.

"Olwen ... Wyn, are you here?"

Her voice drifted down the hall, quavering but insistent. I hauled myself out of bed, glancing at the clock: 6:27 a.m. I turned off the alarm I'd set for 6:30 and padded quickly in my slippers to Gee Gee's room. Inside, it was dim, the curtains blocking most of the early morning light, and all I could see was a slender, shadowy shape sitting up in bed, surrounded by blankets.

"Are you okay?" My voice was tight with anxiety. I lingered in the doorway; I didn't know what I would do if something was really wrong. "I was just getting up. Do you need me to get you anything? Do you need help up?"

Gee Gee pressed a button, and the back of the hospital bed slowly hummed its way upright. "I should be the one asking you if you're all right," she said with a gentle smile. "I thought I heard you crying out." She started to scoot her legs over the side of the bed.

"No, don't get up." I hesitated. "I'm fine. I was having another nightmare. I guess I was talking in my sleep." I walked in and tucked the blue-and-green quilt around Gee Gee's shoulders, my heart twisting as I felt their fragility, their narrowness.

"Oh, my dear," she said. Her voice was sad, as if she felt sorry. I wouldn't be able to take it if she felt sorry.

"It's okay," I said quickly. "I'm getting up for school now anyway. Are you sure you don't need anything?"

"No, dear, I'm quite comfortable." She patted my hand, her touch papery, ghostlike.

I hated to think about it, but I knew she didn't have a lot of time left. We'd go to Wales, and then... It struck me that I didn't want to be left wishing we'd talked more. Or regretting the fact that I hadn't asked her all the questions I could possibly think of before she was gone.

I sat down at the foot of the bed. "Gee Gee, I know this might sound silly." I swallowed, my throat dry. "Can I tell you about the dream I had?"

"Of course you can, dear." She looked at me, and I could

see the worry lines etched into her forehead. "This dream, though. Was it what we talked about before?" I tensed up, waiting for her to elaborate. "A sensitive dream?"

"I don't know." I hooked one arm over the bed's metal safety railing and stared down at the quilt. "I saw... I keep seeing a woman who looks like you, but younger. Everything's green, and I know somehow it's in Wales. There's an old church, by the sea. And she's crying, like someone's died." Tears sprang to my eyes. "It's so sad. Was it..." I swallowed hard. "Was it real?"

"Oh, Olwen *fach*." Gee Gee squeezed my hand. She didn't seem surprised. If anything, my dream seemed to have plunged her into her own memories. "You know, life was very hard in those days when I was young. I know I've told you about the times during the war when we had to go without so much." There was a long pause. I opened my mouth to ask how I would even know if it was a sensitive dream, and if so, what it meant—why she'd cried my name in it—but she continued, in a soft voice.

"We were very poor in Cwm Tawel. All the villages were." She was looking somewhere past me now, her eyes vague and half-closed. She seemed to want to talk. And I wanted to know, so I kept quiet. "It was a hard time, with so many gone to fight. The men too young or infirm, of course, had to find other work, in the coal mines and the munitions factories. Dad was older, so he was on night watch with the Home Guard."

Gee Gee stopped, put a hand to her head; started again. "Once—it's funny I remember this so clearly now—Dad's team had to take away an unexploded bomb that had landed in the middle of the Morris's vegetable garden. We were so worried it would go off before they got it to Bomb Disposal. Of course, I had to keep the little ones, Petey and my brothers, from running over there to 'help.'" She let out a small laugh, which turned to a dry cough. I handed her the cup of water from the end table next to the bed and settled back in, lying on my side with my head propped up.

"What about the rest of the time?" I asked tentatively. "You didn't have to take care of the boys all day, did you?" I wanted to know more about the cliffside, the sad young woman; I wanted to know more about *her,* but I didn't quite know how to ask.

"Well, with so many of the men away, a lot of us women had to do factory work. But I *was* at home, yes. It might sound strange to you now, but the truth is I longed for that life, the working life. The parties they used to throw for the war volunteers in the cities. The handsome American soldiers." Her eyes crinkled with humor. "A girl from our village, Mair, she was so pretty, and she knew it. Just a year older than me. She had curly golden hair she was forever tossing about as if she thought she was a movie star." Gee Gee smiled wryly. "The boys called her Jean Harlow. The girls called her...other things."

I snorted a giggle.

"Well, Mair would go to work in Swansea and come home evenings with grease all over her face, looking like she'd been through a war herself, she did! I wasn't so jealous of her after that. And anyway, she couldn't keep *all* of the boys for herself. Still, she was independent." Gee Gee drank a few more sips of water, then sank back onto the pillows and closed her eyes. In a barely perceptible voice, she mumbled, "That snooty Mair. She didn't have children to contend with, did she?"

I frowned. "What?" Was Gee Gee stuck with children? Whose? Her younger brothers, maybe? I searched her face, hoping for an answer, but she had already drifted back into a snooze, something that was happening more and more now.

After pulling up her blankets again, I got up gingerly and tiptoed out of the room. I wasn't sure what she'd meant, or why she'd told me that story, but it was time to get ready for school.

Only later, my boots pounding the dirty sidewalk on the way to school, did I realize that Gee Gee's story didn't fill in the blanks, didn't answer all the questions still brimming inside me. And the more I thought about everything she'd told me, the more questions I had. Why *wasn't* she working in a factory, if she wanted to so badly? And what did that remark mean, about Mair not having children to contend with? Gee Gee only had one child, Grandpa William, and he was born after the war. Maybe Gee Gee was thinking of other women she used to know. Or maybe she was getting confused; I'd heard that could happen. I could feel tears gathering at the corners of my eyes.

There was so much I didn't know. And deep down, the same thoughts kept nagging at me. What was Gee Gee *not* telling me? Why? And why did I keep dreaming about it?

9

Ym mhob cyfyngder y mae adbwys.

There is a lesson in every perplexity.

Welsh proverb

Gareth patted down his hair in the hallway mirror for at least the tenth time. The stiff waves were still in place. In fact, he'd used so much of his dad's hair gel that there was no chance it was going to move. Not that Wyn was going to be able to see his hair that well through the webcam, but at least it was something he could exert control over. Nothing else in his life seemed to be quite cooperating.

He heard the jaunty Skype ringtone and raced over to the computer desk.

"Hello?" There was no answer at first, no image, and

for a moment Gareth was afraid the odd thing that had happened on his phone was now happening on the computer. He sucked in a breath, but finally an image loaded.

Her image, long brown hair and all. The window in the room behind her made it a little difficult to see her, but he could tell she had a sprinkling of freckles across her nose that he hadn't noticed in her photo. She didn't look like the little Olwen, and yet ... she did. He suppressed a shiver.

"I'm here!" she said. Her voice sounded nervous, quiet— not like the other Olwen at all—and she was smiling. "Hi. *Shwmae?*"

Gareth couldn't help smiling back. "*Da iawn, diolch.* Um ... and that's all the Welsh I can remember," he said apologetically.

She laughed, and he kept grinning like a fool, all through their awkward first few sentences. He started to relax as she asked him more questions about himself, about his parents and his childhood in Wales. She was there, and she was *real*. She was so enthusiastic that he wished he did remember the Welsh he'd learned in primary school.

"I guess I was just too young to pay much attention," he said, ducking his head.

"My Gee Gee speaks Welsh," Wyn said. "But she didn't really teach my grandpa. I never met him, anyway. And my dad doesn't speak any."

"Same with my dad," Gareth said. "'Course, he didn't learn much of it in the first place, and then he forgot it all when he went to London for university. And my mum's English." Wyn looked a little disappointed, so he rushed on to say,

"My great-granddad still lives in Cwm Tawel, and he speaks it some, even though he's English. He moved there when he was a boy."

"Cwm Tawel?" Her face went pale.

"Yeah, it means 'quiet valley,'" he said.

Wyn was quiet for a moment. "No, I know. It's just... You're talking about Cwm Tawel in South Wales, right?"

"Only one I know of," he said, tilting his head questioningly.

"Well, you won't believe this," she said, "but that's where my Gee Gee's from."

Gareth blinked, and the world spun crazily around him for a moment. He took a deep breath and things steadied again. "No fooling. You're right, I can't believe it." They both stared at each other silently for a moment. "Do you think they know each other?" he asked, his voice shaking a bit. "His name's Edward Lewis."

"I don't think so. I asked her about Lewises in Cwm Tawel, but she didn't seem to know any." Wyn's voice sounded uncertain, though.

"I'll have to ask my great-granddad about it. It's not that big a town. You'll see." Gareth tried to smile.

There was a long pause, and then Wyn cleared her throat. "Could I ask you something? It's kind of personal... and weird."

"Okay," he said, wondering how much weirder it was possible for this conversation to get.

She looked off into the distance, not meeting his eyes. "Do you believe in things that can't be explained?"

Gareth almost wanted to laugh. "If you'd asked me that a couple months ago, I'd have said there's an explanation for everything if you look hard enough." He leaned back in the desk chair. "But now, I—I guess I'm not sure." He glanced at his phone, lying quietly on the desk next to the keyboard.

"I know the feeling," Wyn said, staring at him as if she could tell what he was thinking. Then, all in a rush, she said, "Listen, what would you say if I told you I have dreams that are true?"

"It depends on what you mean exactly," he answered cautiously.

"My Gee Gee says it runs in our family. Dreams that mean something."

"Don't most dreams mean something? They reflect your unconscious thought processes and all." Gareth had a feeling that wasn't what she was talking about.

"Yes, but... Here's what I mean," Wyn said, her words spilling over each other. "Lately I started having dreams about the past, about my great-gran, but way before I was born. Before she left Wales. I thought it might be a coincidence. But there's too much detail! I dream about this place I've never seen before, but it seems so real I could touch it. And then when I told Gee Gee about it, it's like she avoided answering any of my questions directly. She told me these tangential stories. When she says she doesn't remember something, I don't even know if she's telling me the truth." Her shoulders were stiff, and she looked really sad now. Sad and frustrated.

"Okay." Gareth paused and chose his words carefully. "Whatever it means... do you trust in yourself, in what your unconscious is trying to tell you? Or do you trust in what your gran is saying?"

"Both," Wyn said without hesitation. "I mean, I trust her, but I have the feeling she's not telling me everything."

"Well, she's bound to have forgotten some things by now, right?" he pointed out. "It's been a long time."

"I guess so." She seemed to relax a little, but she was still frowning.

"You know what's funny? I've been dreaming about Wales too. I guess because we visited there over spring hols. Or because you and I have been talking about it," Gareth said. He didn't mention that one of his dreams had happened standing up, or that he'd been wide awake a moment before it happened.

"That's kind of uncanny," Wyn said, staring at him.

"It is," he agreed. He glanced at the clock in the corner of the screen and had a moment of panic. "I'll have to tell you about it later. I've got to go to school."

"Email me about it, then." She sounded intense, interested.

"Will do, cheers." Gareth disconnected the call, then got up from the swivel chair and pounded upstairs to put on his school clothes. It was hard to believe Wyn was really having psychic dreams, or whatever they were. But not as hard as it might have been a few weeks ago.

Then again . . . if her great-gran came from Cwm Tawel, maybe she'd visited when she was small and didn't remember, but the images of Wales were still there in her subconscious and coming back in her dreams. Or, he supposed,

Wyn could be lying. But she really seemed to be telling the truth, and she didn't seem delusional.

Maybe *he* was delusional. He stared at himself for a moment. His eyes looked a bit tired and droopy, but other than that, he still looked the same. Would he even be able to tell if he was losing it?

Gareth shook his head and pulled on his school jacket. He needed tangible proof of what was happening. Whatever *was* happening. If he asked Wyn to describe the Welsh scenes she saw, or better yet to draw them, and something seemed familiar, he'd know she wasn't having a laugh at his expense. Or would he? After all, she could just go online, find pictures of Cwm Tawel, and copy those. But who would do that? Who would pull a prank so elaborate on someone they didn't even know? It didn't seem likely that she was pulling some sort of a hoax.

He'd just have to decide to trust her.

Grabbing his school bag from the floor in front of the bed, he headed down the narrow staircase and back into the front room, pausing just long enough to send Wyn an email asking for drawings, descriptions, anything she could give him. He sounded a bit desperate—exactly what he'd been hoping to avoid—but he couldn't help it. His sanity, and his character judgment, were at stake.

And he refused to believe he was insane. Either Wyn was exaggerating about the realness of her dreams, or...

...or her dreams *were* real, and if they were, maybe Olwen was, too.

The sun was out, and it was a warm early summer day in North London. Gareth took his usual route home past the park, its green lawn scattered with kids playing and people lounging on deck chairs. This time, though, he didn't stop to look for Amit. They all had exams to study for next week.

That was when Wyn was due to travel to Wales.

He walked faster, eager to get home and check his email. He hadn't been able to stop thinking about her. He wondered if he might be getting obsessive, but when he thought about it all, he was convinced it was more than just chance that had brought them together.

As he crossed the threshold of his front gate, his phone began ringing. He fished it out of his backpack and then frowned. Had Amit changed his ringtone as a joke? It was playing an old Welsh folk tune, one he remembered singing at school when he was really little. "Ar Lan y Môr"—"At the Seaside." It was a haunting melody, slow, sweet, and wistful.

After a moment, Gareth realized he was still standing half-in and half-out of the garden. He stepped forward and let the gate swing shut behind him.

The melody was still playing, his phone still ringing. He turned it over to see who was calling.

The screen said *Unknown Number*.

This was getting weird. He knew Amit would definitely not go to the trouble to freak him out like this, especially since Amit had no idea he even *was* freaked out to begin with.

Maybe it was Wyn? Gareth swallowed hard and pressed the *Talk* button.

"Hello?" His voice sounded strange and high.

Nobody replied. He heard a soft sound like the wind, susurrating gently.

"Hello?" he repeated. "Who's there?" Suddenly he heard what sounded like a child's laugh, far away. Maybe somebody was pocket-dialing him by accident. A wrong number. That had to be it. He pushed the *End Call* button and started moving again, up the front walk, shoving his unease away.

The quiet didn't last long. The phone rang again, and again it played the same melody. This time Gareth picked up right away and said, "Who is this? Is this some kind of joke?" Again, he heard the child laughing somewhere in the background. But this time, weaving over the laughter, was a woman singing softly—the same song. The Welsh words sounding ancient and sad. He opened his mouth to say something more, but nothing came out.

He cleared his throat to try to speak, to give the person one last chance to respond, but before he could talk, the line went dead.

"Okay." Gareth took a deep breath and let it out forcefully. It was just a wrong number. They'd finally realized their kid was playing with their mobile or something and hung it up. Or maybe it *was* Amit, and he was home laughing right now. Gareth set his bag down next to the front door and hit the speed-dial button.

"Oi, why aren't you at the park?"

"Did you just call me?" Gareth asked.

"Miss me already?" Amit laughed. "No, I didn't call you, G-spot."

"Right."

"Is that it? Because Dobbs is about to—oof!" There was a muffled thud, as if the phone had fallen. Gareth hung up. If it hadn't been Amit, then it was probably just a fluke, a random pocket dial. He went to put his phone back into his bag, but something caught his eye.

He looked more closely at the screen. Something was off. It took him a second to realize: it was the background wallpaper. His usual photo of a silver Jaguar F-Type wasn't there. Instead, the screen was showing a different picture, one that was all too familiar. But he knew he hadn't put it there.

It had changed. Or somebody had changed it.

It was the cromlech—the standing stones on the grassy green clifftop. And in the photo was a girl. A small girl who definitely hadn't been in the picture before, sitting on top of the huge capstone and dangling her legs above the opening. She seemed to be laughing.

Gareth shoved the phone into his bag as fast as he could and zipped it shut, his hands shaking.

Inside, he switched on the main computer in the living room, feeling an irrational need to tell Wyn what had just happened. Of course, she didn't know about any of it yet— didn't know about the girl, or the cromlech, or the grave. He'd been waiting to tell her until he could prove it to himself that something supernatural was happening.

Today, with his phone … that was not easy to explain away. It wasn't exactly proof, but it was something.

Trouble was, it really made him sound like a loon. A phantom ringtone? Photos that changed when you weren't looking? How did you talk to someone about that in casual conversation? Dithering, Gareth pulled up Wyn's blog in the web browser.

There was a new entry.

Born to Wyn, June 16, 10:02 p.m.

Still having dreams. Still learning more about Gee Gee that I didn't know.

During the war, her family took in evacuated children from London and fed them, out in the country where they were supposed to be safer from bombings. Gee Gee was my age, but she helped take care of the kids. She knitted socks for the army. She tended the vegetable garden. But it feels like there was more to it. Something important.

I hope I find out.

Soon we'll be in Cwm Tawel. We'll be in a vacation cottage on the edge of what used to be Gee Gee's uncle's farm, until he sold it after the war. We leave in a handful of days, after school lets out. Despite everything, I'm excited.

Gareth re-read the post. What if he could meet her at the airport? Then he could *show* her the mutating photos. Assuming there was anything in them by the time he looked at them again. He glanced warily at his bag, which still held his phone.

It hadn't rung again since he'd come inside. But that didn't mean anything. What if it kept happening? How would he explain it?

He'd have to turn off the ringer. He had no idea how to even begin talking about this with his parents.

When he pulled the phone out to silence it, he got another shock. The background image was the silver sports car, a Jaguar F-Type.

It was as if none of it had ever happened.

———

Dear Gareth,

I know it's hard to believe, but the photo you sent of the clifftop, with those stones, is exactly the place I saw in my dream. Exactly.

I didn't see anyone in the picture. But I believe you. This might seem like a stretch, but I wonder if the Olwen you saw is the same little girl I saw in my dream? I think we should try to research Cwm Tawel at the time she lived. Maybe we can find something out. Can you check online records? I'll keep asking my Gee Gee.

We leave in four days. I'll send you a link to where we're staying. Please come if you can. I'm getting a temporary phone, so send me your number.

—Wyn

Gareth closed the email window on his phone. The previous night, he had told Wyn everything. And he was surprised at how much lighter he felt simply because someone *knew*. Someone who didn't laugh or joke or doubt. Someone, in fact, who claimed to be having a similar experience.

Yet another improbable coincidence in his currently unbelievable life.

Wyn was right, though. They only had two potential sources of information about the other Olwen: her great-grandmother, and the collective wisdom of the Internet. At least searching the Internet was something Gareth knew he was good at.

He got up off the sofa and sat down in front of the computer in the corner. It seemed like a good idea to start with a general search and then narrow it down from there; a good history site would probably have regional information. He typed *"Wales history"* into the browser search box and hit *Enter*.

Really? 277,000,000 results? Gareth sagged in his chair. Who knew so many people were interested in Welsh history? He scrolled aimlessly through a few of the pages, then typed in *"Cwm Tawel"* along with *"Wales history"* to see if that narrowed things down. It helped a bit, but he was still faced with thousands of possible matches: The local newspaper. Civil budget proposals. Boring government documents from the last ten years. He rubbed the back of his neck, wondering what other keywords he could use.

Then, about halfway down one of the pages, a site caught his eye: *South Wales Historical Society*. It seemed as good a place to start as any. He clicked the link, and found a short listing of regional subheadings: *Pembrokeshire, Vale of Glamorgan, Cardiff, Newport*. He went straight to the *Swansea* link and clicked.

It was a directory of sites, and the very first listing was Swansea Local History: *Information on the local history of Swansea and its environs, including Gorseinon, Llansamlet, Pontardddulais, Gowerton, and Cwm Tawel*. He grinned to himself and murmured "Yes, thank you, I *am* good." He rapidly clicked into the site, fidgety with anticipation.

He was only vaguely aware of the sound of the front door opening, but seconds later Tommy entered the living room and bounced on the sofa, clarinet in one hand.

"I want to play Angry Birds," he said loudly.

"I was just finishing up," Gareth said. "Five minutes, I promise."

Tommy jumped up and down. "Mum said I could!"

"Give him a minute, Thomas. And sit, please." Mum sat down in the green easy chair with a quiet "aaahhhhh," letting her hair out of its severe bun; Dad sank down onto the sofa and clicked on the TV remote. Tommy climbed down and headed toward the computer.

Gareth quickly bookmarked the link and shut the browser window. He'd have to try again later, or use his phone to check. Stupid Tommy. Annoyed, he spun the chair around to face his brother, who was now creeping toward him with his hands behind his back. His face was cloaked in a rather suspicious smile.

"What have you got there? Give it here," Gareth said with a frown.

"It's nothing. Just something I got at school."

"Show me," Gareth said warningly, expecting the worst. A worm, fuzzy with pocket lint? A wad of used gum? He braced himself for something vile when Tommy opened his hands over the desktop, but all that spilled out was a handful of toffees.

Gareth eyed them, but they looked perfectly normal. "Can I have one, then?"

Tommy nodded, his eyes wide.

Gareth unwrapped a toffee and put it in his mouth. He immediately spat it out again. It tasted like it had been coated in salt.

"Blech! Bloody—what did you do to it?" He felt like gagging. "You little slug. I should have known." He grabbed his brother around the middle and dangled him upside down, thinking about how satisfying it would be to pummel him into the sofa cushions. Tommy shrieked and laughed. "I'm serious. You are an annoying little twit."

"Gareth! What's going on over there?" Their dad turned the volume down on the television. "Leave your brother alone."

"He did something to this toffee," Gareth said angrily,

but he let Tommy go. His brother scooted over to the couch with a nasty grin.

"I don't care what he did," Mum said, eyebrows raised. "There's no need to be short-tempered."

He closed his eyes for a moment, taking deep breaths. Sweat trickled down the back of his neck. Slowly, his anger dissipated.

His mum made them apologize to each other, which annoyed him all over again. "All I wanted to do was finish researching this thing online, and Tommy won't let me be," he complained. "I have exams coming up, and all of this other stuff keeps happening."

"What other stuff?" his dad asked, glancing sharply at him. "If something's wrong, tell us, but don't take out your temper on your brother."

"But he was the one who—"

"Enough," his mum said. "We're all tired. Tea first."

Gareth's shoulders sagged as he headed into the kitchen after his parents, but in a way, he was relieved. He couldn't believe he'd blurted that out about "other stuff," and then managed to escape a real explanation.

But maybe it was time for him to say something. It was only a matter of time before his parents found out about his phone acting weird, or caught him talking to Wyn. If he actually told them about it—not all of it, but some of it—maybe he could do something more than just search the web. He sat up straight in the kitchen chair. Maybe, if he didn't botch it up, he really *could* meet Wyn in person.

Hours later, after his brother had gone to bed, Gareth came downstairs in his pajamas and sat in the easy chair. His parents broke off their quiet conversation.

"You look like you've got something to say." His mum's tone was light, but she looked at him intently. Clearly she hadn't forgotten his earlier outburst.

"Here's the thing," Gareth said, swallowing down his nervousness. "I have a friend online, sort of a pen friend, from the USA. Olwen Nia Evans."

"Isn't that a lovely name," his mother said, relaxing a bit into the sofa.

"Her parents must be Welsh," said his dad with a small smile. "Did you ask her about it?"

"Yeah, so, this is really amazing," Gareth continued. "Her great-gran, who lives there with them, is from Cwm Tawel, same as Great-Granddad."

"Is that so?" Both of his parents looked interested now.

"Are you sure she isn't having you on?" His mother looked at him doubtfully. "It could be one of those scams. Like the Nigerian prince."

"It's not," he insisted. "I even talked to her on video chat. She's a real girl, Mum."

"Video chat." His mum closed her eyes for a moment, looking a bit pained.

"Honestly, it's just like that pen friend you told me you used to have in Budapest," Gareth said nervously. "We were just writing to each other at first, and it came up in our emails, the Cwm Tawel connection. That's why I asked if there were Evanses in the family. I thought we might be distant relatives or something. And she's really interested in her family history."

"It's not impossible she's related somehow," his dad said, and Gareth relaxed a little. "But it's so hard to figure these things out. There aren't always records from these small villages, and some of them got destroyed during the war."

"There's more," Gareth said. "Wyn's great-gran ... she's got cancer. It's bad." He crossed his arms, then uncrossed them again. "So their family is bringing her to Cwm Tawel for the summer so she can be in her hometown. They're coming soon."

"That's quite a big decision to make. I imagine their family is feeling quite uprooted at the moment." His mother looked at him questioningly.

"Well, Wyn wants to find out more about her great-gran's life. She's kind of a writer."

"Get to the point, Gareth," his dad said.

He let out a breath. "Okay. I thought perhaps I could meet her there and we could go around getting stories from Great-Granddad and the other old folks in the village. After school lets out, I mean. I could stay with Great-Granddad, have a bit of a visit."

And maybe he could find out something more about the gravesite, about the other Olwen. Maybe he and Wyn could even go to the cromlech themselves, if he could remember where it was. All he knew was that it was near a beach, and they'd driven there.

"Going back to Wales by yourself?" His mum gave him a confused look. "We were just there, and you complained the entire time."

"I thought Wyn might like some company. You know, with her gran being sick. I could take her out hiking."

Gareth's dad winked at him knowingly, and he felt his cheeks go red. "I mean, she's never been here, and she doesn't know anyone besides her family, and—"

"Very charitable of you, yes," his dad said.

"I'll make all the plans. I can research the train schedules and everything," Gareth told them. "I'll even call Great-Granddad and let him know I'm coming."

His mum looked at his dad. "What do you think, Aled?"

"You know, son, there's no Internet in Granddad's house," his dad said solemnly, one corner of his mouth twitching.

"That's okay," Gareth said, inwardly wincing. "I'll have my phone."

His mum got up, turning off the table lamp. "Anyhow, we can talk about the details later." As she walked past, she put a gentle hand on his head. "It's time for bed."

"Okay. Thanks, Mum." He was already halfway to the stairs when something else occurred to him. "Hey, maybe we could meet Wyn's family at the airport when they arrive."

"There's no need to be bothering them when they're trying to get settled in, Gareth." His mother turned back to look at him. "And you have exams coming up and there's no need for extra distractions."

His dad nodded in agreement. "Your mum's right. Exams

first. Don't worry, you'll be on holiday before you know it," he added in an annoyingly jolly tone.

Gareth didn't bother responding to that. Trudging upstairs, he tried to suppress his disappointment. He wouldn't get to meet her for a while yet. But at least he would be able to go to Cwm Tawel. That was the important part.

He closed his bedroom door and climbed into bed. As he reached out to turn off the bedside lamp, he heard a chime from his phone: a voicemail message. Probably Amit. He propped himself up on one elbow and dialed his mailbox.

Silence. And more silence.

"Not again." He sighed loudly, trying to ignore the growing knot in his stomach.

There was a second message. This time somebody did speak.

But it still wasn't Amit. It was a small girl's voice, a familiar voice. Like an echo, a memory: " … promise me that you'll come back to visit me? I'm so lonely."

The voice faded into nothing.

The line was dead.

10

Y boeth ni bbyweb a ŵyr.

The wise will not
say what he knows.

....

Welsh proverb

"Are you still online? It's high time you went to bed, missy,"
Dad said, rumpling my hair as he walked past. From the
kitchen, he called out, "If you're having trouble sleeping I can
make you some herbal tea."

"That's okay," I said. "I'm almost done." I typed the last
lines of my email to Gareth as quickly as I could and hit *Send*.

"What's got you up so late, anyway? More Welsh?" Dad
came back in, holding a glass of water, and hovered uncertainly.

"No, just writing to my friend." It had been a few days

since I'd last opened the Welsh language software and I felt a slight stab of guilt.

"Something on your mind, baby?" He looked a bit down himself; a double frown-line creased the space between his eyebrows, and as he sat down, he sighed heavily.

"You look tired, Dad," I said, avoiding the question. "Are you okay?"

"Sure," he said with a wry smile. "The vacation cottages are going to charge us an outrageous fee for carting in a hospital bed, and your mom is having kittens about only having three days to pack, and I have a kid who's got a computer growing out of her lap. Everything's peachy."

"Sorry." I shut my laptop and set it on the coffee table.

"What about you, though?" he persisted. "I want to make sure you're handling everything okay. What's the scoop these days?"

"Nothing much." But a smile crept onto my face. "I kind of…met a guy," I confessed, not looking at him. "Not really 'met,' I guess. He's been reading my blog. We started writing to each other because he thought he recognized my name. He's got Welsh family, too, and here's the thing." I finally met my dad's eyes, unable to disguise my excitement. "His family's from Cwm Tawel, too! He lives in London now, but anyway, I can't believe it. Maybe I'll get to meet him."

"Hmm," my dad said. He wasn't smiling. "What did you say his name was? I'd like to do a little background checking to make sure he is who he says he is."

"*What?* Dad, come on." I stared at him. "I'm not an idiot. I checked around. Plus, we talked on Skype. I've seen his face."

Dad scowled at me. "I'm sure you were thorough, but Mom has access to all kinds of databases at the law office. I'd feel a lot better if we found more out about this person before you decide to meet him. Which I'm still not sure is a good idea."

"Okay, okay." I relented, but I was still seething at his implication that I could actually be duped by some middle-aged Internet predator. "His name is Gareth Lewis. But I promise you, he's a teenage boy. And not a psycho."

"I'd like you to forward one of his emails to me so I can look at the header data," Dad continued. "And maybe during one of your chats, I can say hello to him."

I let out a wordless noise of frustration. "Fine. I wish you would trust me, though."

Dad's face softened and he shifted toward me, hugging me with one arm. "I do trust you. But you're fifteen years old. I still want to protect you." He squeezed my shoulder. "I can't help it. I'm a dad, and we're about to spend the summer in a place I haven't visited since I was your age. Cut me some slack, man."

I rolled my eyes, but I leaned into him.

"I'm sure Gareth is a perfectly normal kid. Just humor me, and we'll see what happens when we get to Wales."

I sighed. That was probably the best I could hope for. It still wasn't a sure thing, but I was starting to feel a tiny bit excited about seeing Gareth. We would work it out somehow, I was certain. Maybe this was a good sign.

I stood in front of the antique mirror on my dresser, pulling out folded piles of underwear and socks. In the spotted glass, I could see Rae's reflection, sitting subdued on the rumpled bedclothes.

"I can't believe you're leaving." Rae ran a hand through her short, dyed-coppery hair. "You have to email me as soon as you get there. Or I'll worry you were eaten by wolves."

"I'm pretty sure there aren't wolves in Wales." I laughed a little, but at the same time I felt like crying. My face in the mirror looked pinched and pale. "I'll write to you as soon as I can. The main farmhouse has wi-fi but our cottage doesn't."

"What'll I do without you?" Rae wailed, flopping back onto the bed.

I rolled my eyes. "You'll be fine. Don't you have that leadership program for student government?" I asked pointedly. "You'll have Bethany." *And you could have been hanging out with me more this whole time anyway.* But I didn't say that.

"We've never spent a summer apart," she said, her voice still sad. "Can you believe it? We even went to that horrible camp together back in fifth grade, the one where I got eaten alive by mosquitoes and you fell into the river with your shoes on."

I relented, finally. "My purple Converse sneakers. I was so mad I yanked Derek Atkinson into the water after me." Now I *was* crying, and smiling at the same time. I shoved aside a pile of sweaters and sat down next to Rae on the bed. She leaned her head on my shoulder.

"You know, if you end up marrying that Gareth guy, you have to invite me to the wedding." That surprised me into laughing again. "Or you guys can just sneak off and do it behind a bush, but you have to tell me everything."

"God! My parents are scared he's a predator, while *you*, on the other hand, are the actual perv." I shoved her back onto the bed. "Give me some credit. Anyway, at this rate I might never get to meet him." I hated to even think about that possibility.

"You have to, Wyn." Rae was serious now. "You're going to be alone there. You need a friend. It'll make it feel more like home."

Home. Wales would be home for the next month at least. Maybe for the whole summer. I swallowed back a lump in my throat.

"Rae, can you hand me that duffel bag?" I sniffled a little and started stuffing a change of clothes into it.

"Hey," Rae said after a few silent minutes of me packing. "You'll have to learn to drive in opposite land."

"Um, no." I zipped up the green duffel. "I'll take driver's ed this fall instead." I tried to sound like it didn't matter, but I still felt an emptiness in my chest. I'd be missing so much.

A few months was starting to seem like forever.

———

Alone in my darkening bedroom, I pulled my bulletin board off the wall and started unpinning photos: me and Rae as kids, playing on China Beach with the Golden Gate Bridge in the background; me as a two-year-old with my parents at Christmas, Mom with feathery 1980s hair.

A photo Gareth had sent me: the desolate church by the sea, the one that was the same as the scene in my dreams. Just looking at it made me shiver.

And my favorite, an old black-and-white photo of Gee Gee when she'd first moved to the United States: long dark hair swept up into an old-fashioned-looking knot, the expression on her round face somber, almost sad. In the picture, she was wearing a pale, 1950s-style dress and fingering an oval silver locket that hung around her neck. I remembered being disappointed, as a child, when she told me she'd lost that locket.

Last but not least, I pulled off a strip of photo-booth pictures of me and Rae. My throat tightened again, and I shoved all the pictures into the back of my new Welsh dictionary. Before Rae had left, I'd hugged her for what seemed like the longest time. Now she was gone, and I already felt like something was missing from my life. Even if maybe it had already been missing for a while.

———

Moonlight and shadows dappled my bedroom ceiling. I was too queasy to sleep. A cricket emitted muffled creaking outside, and I could hear Dad snoring all the way down the hall. I couldn't imagine what it would be like in a tiny cottage. Not to mention on the flight. I hoped Mom had earplugs.

I lay on my back, idly following the moonlit patterns as my eyelids began to droop. I had no idea what time it was, and I didn't want to know, since my alarm was set for 5:45

a.m. and the airport shuttle was coming less than two hours after that.

When I opened my eyes next, I was sure I was dreaming. The soft beams and the ambient light from a nearby streetlamp had coalesced into one wide ellipse on my ceiling, like a silvery spotlight. I sat up and peered more closely at the pool of light; but when I looked back down, I could see my sleeping form sprawled out on the bed, moving restlessly on top of the covers. Then I was floating up rapidly toward the moonlight, up toward and into it. It spread over my skin like a cool bath, spilling into my eyes so that all I saw was pearlescent darkness.

Before I could see again, I could feel, and I patted my hands around me: grass under my left hand, tree bark under my right. There was a strong smell of pasture and wet sheep, and then a scene blinked into view. In front of me was a small valley, more like a dip in the hilly landscape. The slopes were dotted with cottages, crisscrossed with dirt roads and hedgerows, and bordered by newly tilled farmlands. Though dusk was gathering rapidly, there was not a single light to be seen in any window. All was quiet except for the occasional "baa" of a restless sheep, and a distant roaring, buzzing sound that might have been airplanes. And, a moment later, the low, rippling tones of a woman's laughter, followed by a young man's voice.

"They'll be missing you at dinner—come on!" Two shadows separated themselves from the larger mass of tree-shapes, and I was drawn along in their wake, back toward the gloomy cluster of cottages.

The two figures separated after reaching a main road,

and I floated behind the smaller one, a woman in a dress hastening toward a cottage on one of the side roads. The windows of the cottage were pitch dark except for a line of candlelight showing through the slit of an open door. The woman hurried toward the strip of light and slipped in.

One last insistent whisper escaped into the night.

"Come now, Rhiannon, inside, or the warden will be catching you! There were air raids again tonight, you foolish girl." The door shut and I heard the sound of a bolt being driven home.

Had that been Gee Gee? Before I had time to wonder further, I was drawn backward, irresistibly pulled; but thickly, as if through mud, and buffeted with so many images that I could only discern a few: An older man, ravaged by age but wearing a dented saucepan helmet and carrying a rifle. A young man, handsome and blond-haired, standing in a line outside a shop clutching a fistful of ration coupons in a mud-stained hand. He smiled briefly, a moment of sun in a gray, sad landscape.

A flood of children, mostly alone, but some clutching their mothers' hands, spilling from a train, clutching battered suitcases and gas masks. This last image filled me with such a profound sadness that I began to sob, crying out into the dim pearly light that was surrounding me again as it had at the beginning of the dream.

I awoke with my cheeks wet and throat raw. It had been a dream, but so much more than "just a dream." Much more than ever before. It was far too real.

I sat up and wiped my eyes. What had happened to Gee

Gee back in Cwm Tawel, during the war? I needed to ask her this. I needed to talk to her alone—about the dream, about the things she wasn't telling me. I didn't know if I'd get the answers I was looking for, but I would have to try. I had to find out everything I could; I couldn't think of any other way to make the dreams stop, except maybe sleeping pills. But somehow, I had to make the dreams stop.

I wasn't sure I could handle it otherwise.

———————

Morose and sleepy, I stared out the cold glass window of the airport shuttle at the foggy morning light, the pastel houses of Daly City. I'd be stuck in various sorts of enclosed spaces with my family around me for the next, oh, twenty hours or so, with no escape—and no way to talk to Gee Gee in private. I wanted the chance to be direct with her, even if she was being evasive.

It was interesting ... no matter what she'd told me about her childhood in Wales, it was always like a story, a "once upon a time" where everything was magical and good. But it couldn't have been like that. It was wartime.

I'd already sensed she was leaving some things out. Would she want to remember the rest of it?

If I showed her Gareth's photo of the clifftop, what would she say?

I didn't know what to do next, but I needed to figure it out, before ... what? Before time ran out. Before Gee Gee died. Before I lost my chance. I dug my fingernails into the hard vinyl armrest and let out a loud sigh, then repeated under my breath:

"*Coeden*." Tree. "*Bryn*." Hill. "*Mynydd*." Mountain.

"How're you doing up there, Wynnie?" Dad's voice floated faintly up from the rear seat. "Carsick?"

"I'm fine." I didn't even sound convincing to my own ears. I turned around to give him a weak smile. "Just a little nervous."

From the middle seat of the van, Gee Gee reached forward and gave me a reassuring pat on the shoulder. I could feel her hand trembling, and that made me feel even worse. How could I ask her about something that might be upsetting? I turned back to the front and swallowed hard, fixing my eyes on the San Francisco airport terminal buildings that drew ever closer.

Then the shuttle was stopping at the International Terminal; then we were rolling our suitcases across the walkway to the curbside counter; then the uniformed employee was helping Gee Gee into a wheelchair and we were at the airline check-in desk, hefting the suitcases onto the scale.

"Boarding passes and IDs, please," the woman said briskly, smiling. She clicked around on her computer for a minute or two, then stamped our printouts.

"Enjoy your stay in England," she said.

Gee Gee raised her eyebrows. I stifled a laugh, knowing what was coming next.

"We'll be in Wales, my dear," Gee Gee told her with a tight smile. "And we Welsh may be many things, but one thing we are *not* is English. Not in our blood, not in our language, and not in our hearts!"

"I see," the employee said. She rubbed her temples for a moment, then looked up again. "In that case, enjoy your stay in Wales."

"We will." Gee Gee's voice was gracious now. "*Diolch yn fawr*. Thank you."

I smirked. Her epic takedown was definitely going on my blog.

After we went through the security line, I followed my family down endless hallways crowded with sleepy travelers bearing takeout coffee and plastic bags from the newsstand. Dad pushed the wheelchair, and Mom was pulling along the rest of our carry-on bags. We passed gate after gate before finally reaching G16. Boarding wasn't for another hour, so I sank down into one of the black vinyl chairs in an empty row.

"Gee Gee, take this aisle seat—I'll sit by you," I offered. My mom sat down on my right and pulled out a magazine; Dad sat next to her and started fiddling with his phone.

An hour. An hour to learn as much as I could before we were crammed together on a flight with a couple hundred of our closest eavesdropping friends. I looked around crossly: occupied seats everywhere. This wasn't any more private than the flight would be. Still, even if I couldn't ask about the dream, I could find out *something*.

I leaned closer. "Gee Gee, I had a dream last night that, uh, reminded me of your stories about the village." I paused. "It had to be scary living there during World War II."

With a bit of effort, she turned to face me, her small

hands gripping the armrests. "Yes, of course it was, *blodyn*. So many people lost their lives in the blitz, you see, even in Wales. We were luckier than many, the folk of Cwm Tawel."

I could sense my mom listening in, but I tried to ignore her. She might be interested, but for me, so much more was at stake.

"What was it like? I want to hear the real story. Good and bad." I gave her a tentative smile. "I want to know all about it before we get there. It's ... our history."

"Our history." She sighed, a faraway look in her eyes. "Oh, well, life was hard then, wasn't it. Dad ... well, Dad, out of all of us, didn't take it well. He worked in a factory that made bomb shelters until they let some people go and he went on the dole. After that, he didn't know what to do with himself. Moping about the house. Too old to enlist, they said. So the minute the Home Guard formed up for the villages, he pulled his dad's old tin helmet from the Great War out of the trunk and announced he was joining up."

"Heavens," my mom said. "It's like an old movie."

Gee Gee nodded slowly. "Movie indeed. He and Mum had a big dramatic row. She yelled at him, 'What do you intend me to do on my own, with so many people in the house?' Because of the evacuated children that we took in, you see, and only myself and my older brother Daniel's wife Myfanwy to help. Extra mouths to feed, extra work to do. Three more children, besides me and my young brothers. Everyone had to do it, though. They came in from the cities, some of them without even their mothers."

"That's awful," I said, making a show of jotting down a

few notes in my journal, but my hand was trembling. It was my dream, all right—the children with battered suitcases and gas masks, spilling off the train at the countryside depot. If I were a more skeptical person, I might have remembered all the World War II movies I'd seen and wondered if some of the images had gotten stuck in my head somehow. But that didn't explain the other dream scenes—the ones that had Gee Gee in them.

I sat up straight. The evacuated children. Could one of *them* have been Olwen?

"May I have some water, please, dear?" Gee Gee gave a short, dry cough.

"Let your great-grandmother rest now," Mom said, rummaging in her tote bag for the bottled water. "If you have to sleep, Rhiannon, go right ahead. We'll wake you up when they start boarding." Mom smiled, but as she handed Gee Gee the water, I could see the worry in her eyes.

"I'm quite all right," Gee Gee said, but she did look tired, even though we'd only been up and about for five hours or so. I wanted to know everything she had to tell me, wanted to know who those children in my dream were, but I didn't want to wear her out, either.

"It's okay," I said quickly. Shame welled up inside me, battling with my need to know. "We can talk more later." I stared at my hands, twisting them around in my lap, as Gee Gee sipped at her water and then put it down, closing her eyes.

After a minute, I sighed and pulled out my printout of Mom's uber-organized trip plan. Eleven hours on the plane. We'd arrive in London around eight in the morning, and since we already had our rail passes, we'd just take the subway to Paddington Station and get right on a train for the port town of Llanelli. From there, we'd take a scenic bus ride to Cwm Tawel, arriving mid-afternoon. It was all on the spreadsheet, organized and under control.

It was kind of the only thing we *could* control. I felt a surge of compassion toward my mom, how she tried to make everything run smoothly, and I leaned my head against her shoulder for a moment. None of us really knew what to do, but we were all trying.

Sooner than I expected, I heard the shrilling of the intercom. As we got into the pre-boarding line with Gee Gee, I felt like I was going to throw up. I was excited, but I was terrified. And I was sad. The reason for the trip constantly nagged at the edges of my mind.

While we waited, I could just hear my great-grandmother humming a familiar tune under her breath—my favorite lullaby again. I smiled briefly despite myself.

Then we were handing our passes to the gate agent at the entrance to the boarding tunnel. The tunnel curved so that I couldn't see its end or the door to the plane, and I shivered. The whole journey would be like that—one step at a time, with no way of knowing what lay around the next bend in the path.

———————

The plane's engines roared to life with a subsonic rumble and I double-checked the seat pocket: book, journal, iPod. The flight attendant was doing her perky little demo about what to do in case of catastrophe. She dangled an oxygen mask from one hand, which made me think about my dream again. Those poor children with their gas masks … and had Gee Gee really snuck out during an air raid? I wanted to ask her.

But first there was the stomach-dropping thrill of the airplane taking off, rising higher and higher into the atmosphere until San Francisco looked like a collection of tiny Monopoly houses next to the blue expanse of the bay. Dad, sitting across the aisle, fussed over Gee Gee for at least ten minutes, asking "are you comfortable?" and "do you need another blanket?" until I thought I might go nuts. I plugged my earbuds into the armrest and found a sitcom rerun to block it out.

Finally, Mom leaned back with a crime novel and Dad put on his headset.

Now, I said to myself. I turned to Gee Gee. But she had fallen asleep, breathing heavily and deeply with her head propped up on two of the little airline pillows. She looked so frail, her skin slack and dry and her eyelids fluttering gently. I leaned my seat back and listened to Welsh podcasts on my iPod until I dozed off.

I woke up some time later, neck cramped, when the flight attendants came by with meals on little trays. I wolfed mine down, but Gee Gee only managed a few bites of pasta before pushing it away tiredly. Across the aisle, Mom and Dad exchanged a worried look. The fact that they didn't say anything made the knot in my stomach tighten even more.

I checked the flight tracker on my video monitor and sighed: still six hours to go. I couldn't wait to get off the plane and walk on solid ground, eat some real food: Shepherd's pie, or maybe fish and chips. And tea, real English tea.

I looked over at my parents. They were asleep now. But Gee Gee was stirring, and I immediately snapped to attention.

"Would you help me to the toilet, please?" she asked. *Tŷ bach*, I thought to myself; a very useful word. I kept her arm tucked in mine as we walked the short distance through first-class to the front of the plane. Through the windows, I glimpsed a breathtaking view of jagged, snowy peaks and valleys—Canada, or maybe Greenland.

After helping Gee Gee into the lavatory, I hovered anxiously outside until she came back out. And as we made our way back down the aisle, I seized my chance.

"I still want to hear more about what Cwm Tawel used to be like when you were my age," I began, hoping for more specific information this time. Information about *her*. "Did you do anything exciting? You know, like...go to dances? Or sneak out?"

She turned back to me for a moment, but I didn't meet her eyes. I was afraid she'd be able to see everything just from the look on my face.

"So curious!" She smiled, but there was a fleeting expression on her face that I couldn't read. Then the moment passed and she began to weave a story, speaking softly over the dull thundering of the engines. "Of course, things were very different when I was your age, weren't they. As children we didn't have the kind of freedoms that young people have now, and we didn't have many opportunities, living as we did in a small village."

The rhythms of her voice began to carry me beyond the confines of the airplane cabin until they were all I could hear. "The young men usually became farmers, if they grew up on one of the farms. The rest mostly became coal miners in the valleys, or went north to work in the quarries or the slate mines. Local girls would be expected to get married and have a family, run the household. Or you could become a teacher or a nurse in those days."

"But you were at home still," I said, helping her into her seat.

Gee Gee peered at me for a moment over the tops of her glasses. Then her eyes grew less focused, more faraway. "Yes, but wasn't it nice to be a child in Cwm Tawel, with the sea only a few miles away, and the green hills all round." Those were the kinds of stories she'd always told me when I was growing up—about school in Welsh, about singing in Sunday chapel and growing up on the farm. But now I knew there was more.

I looked at her expectantly. Her expression had grown unreadable again. I listened hard, searching for something—anything—that would help me understand.

"The war made everyone grow up more quickly, you see. Miners were called off to the forces... coal was hard to come by. There were ration coupons for our food and our clothes, though with our gardens and the farms around, we weren't as poorly off as some. And when the evacuees arrived, everyone's lives changed... even at Awel-y-Môr. That was the name of our house. Sea Breeze."

I twisted in my seat to face her. Heart racing, I asked,

"What was that like? Who were the evacuees?" I didn't want to press her in case she retreated again, but I crossed my fingers. Maybe now I'd find out about that little girl.

"Dear me now, let's see … it was 1940, in the dead of winter, when they came. I was nearly thirteen years old. The rain was beating down and the wind was whistling, and in came my mum with three of them. All soaked to the skin and shivering."

I held my breath, hoping for a revelation.

"There was a brother and sister from London, Christopher and Susan. They were eleven and ten years old, the same age as my brothers. The poor things had already lost their father." She thought for a moment. "Then there was the youngest, Peter, who came alone from Coventry, only eight years old … both his parents killed by a bomb that fell in their neighborhood. It was very sad, wasn't it. Christopher and Susan lived with us for almost two years until their mum sent for them; after Cardiff and Swansea were attacked, she felt it was safer back in London! Petey stayed in Cwm Tawel. He lived in our house until he was old enough to move onto the farm, and then he went off to the village of Brynamman to work. He was like a younger brother to me. I did miss him when your great-grandfather and I moved to the States."

I tried to hide my disappointment. I'd been so sure one of the evacuated children would be the girl, Olwen. But then I did a little math, and realized that it couldn't have been possible anyway. Gareth had said the other Olwen lived between 1944 and 1950, and that was years too late to be an evacuee.

So who was she?

"You never mentioned any of this before," I said, trying to find a connection.

"Oh, Olwen *fach*, those stories were so sad, much too sad for a happy little girl like you." Gee Gee's eyes were clouded and half-closed, her voice weary. I sat silently, listening as her breathing grew slow and even as her eyes closed again. If she missed Petey and her life in Wales so much, why had she left at all? After all, once the war ended, things had to have gotten better there. It didn't add up.

I needed Gareth. And I needed whatever information he'd managed to find. I just hoped he'd found something, because, so far, all I'd found were more mysteries.

———

"Flight attendants, prepare the cabin for landing."

My ears popped as the plane descended slowly through the cloud cover. I caught a brief, tantalizing glimpse of houses and green fields as the plane banked and turned, sinking lower and lower toward England. I was more than ready to soak it all in.

I followed my parents and Gee Gee off the plane, into the busy airport, and through the customs line. The most gorgeous English-accented voices were everywhere, as well as a din of other languages: French, German, Chinese, Hindi, and plenty I didn't even recognize.

I felt a swooping in my chest. It was a new morning and I was spending it in London.

Lugging our two huge rolling suitcases, Dad and I navigated the crowded terminal and made our way down to where the trains stopped. Mom was a few feet behind, pushing Gee Gee in her wheelchair. Almost right away we filed onto the express train to Paddington, and I helped settle Gee Gee in one of the cushy purple chairs. The train was modern and clean, and it soon began whizzing along underground at a dizzying speed.

After a half hour, the train emerged aboveground and passed through miles of industrial-looking warehouses and dismal high-rise apartment buildings before pulling into Paddington Station. I wished I could really see London, not just its dirty outskirts, but that might have to wait until ... after. After everything. It might not happen at all.

We hauled ourselves and our luggage onto the platform with forty-five minutes to spare before our train for Llanelli left. According to the porter, it hadn't even pulled into the station yet. I sighed and tilted my head back, looking at the cavernous ceiling and wondering what we'd do in the meantime. Was there wi-fi in the train station?

Suddenly my stomach let out a loud growl.

Dad laughed. "Sounds like your stomach knows what's what," he said. "Let's find some food."

Mom took Gee Gee over to a small seating area in front of the food kiosks and Dad and I scoped out the offerings: a croissant bakery, a McDonalds counter, and a Starbucks. Off to the side was a cafeteria.

"Your mom would hate this," Dad said.

"I know." I, however, was loving it. I took the opportunity to get a full English breakfast, baked beans and all. It took me a few minutes of fumbling with random coinage, but I managed to pay for it and find my way back to my parents without too much trouble.

Gee Gee nibbled at her croissant, her gaze taking in the bustle and activity around us. "You know, the first time I came here was when we were leaving for the United States. I'd never traveled outside of Wales before. It looked almost the same then as it does now." She looked at me and smiled. "It was amazing to be in a train station so enormous, so busy, in a city thousands of times bigger than my village. I was stunned, wondering about the life ahead of us." She trailed off. Then I heard a quiet whisper, almost drowned out by the hubbub of the station: "And trying to forget what we'd left behind."

I leaned in. "What did you leave behind, Gee Gee?"

She looked at me in surprise, her eyes clouded. "Pardon?"

"You said something about what you'd left behind." I peered closely at her.

"Did I?" She seemed confused, and I felt a stab of anxiety. "Well, it's true, we left behind a lot of memories of hardships, but as they say, life presents you with no more than you can bear, doesn't it?" She waved vaguely. "And things were so much better when we moved to California. We made a good life for ourselves and William. Made sure your grandfather had everything that she—that we didn't have back in Wales."

She. Gee Gee said "she." I'd heard it; I knew I did. But I didn't know how to frame my question, and then Gee Gee was speaking again.

"But you'll love it in Cwm Tawel. It looks just like the coast up in Northern California, only instead of forest you have green hills and valleys."

"Wyn, let Gran eat," Dad said, nudging me lightly with his shoulder. "You finish up, too. We've only got a few minutes." I scarfed down my last slice of toast and stared up at the giant signboard listing all the train times and destinations. There was ours: the 10:45 to Milford Haven, stopping in Llanelli, where we'd catch the bus to Cwm Tawel.

Dad had to be just as eager as I was, since he hadn't been back for ages—not since Great-Grandpa John died. I only had a few blurry memories of Great-Grandpa John, like fading photographs. He'd taken me to the Oakland Zoo and held me up so I could see the foxes hiding in their den. But he'd died when I was a child. Dad had flown back to Wales for the funeral with Gee Gee, and Mom had stayed home with me.

And for as long as I could remember, Gee Gee had always seemed to have an air of sadness. Because of losing Great-Grandpa John? Not to mention Grandpa William in the Vietnam War. It would make anyone sad.

Or was it something else?

"Time to get going," Dad said, throwing our trash in a nearby bin. "Rail passes?"

"Right here." Mom pulled a black leather folder out of the side pocket of her suitcase. I got up and grabbed my duffel bag, which I was positive had gotten heavier somehow.

"Let's go, Gran." Dad helped Gee Gee to her feet. I took one last look up at the high, arcing ceiling of sooty glass panels, the daylight shining weakly through, and followed my family along the platform to the train car.

———————

The train rolled through suburb after suburb, rows of houses in brick or stone punctuated by the occasional church steeple or factory. After a while, the swaying of the train made me drowsy, and I leaned my head against the window. My parents were talking quietly in the seats across from me, Mom shuffling through guidebooks, and my mind drifted until I began to doze off.

At some point, the sound of flipping pages changed to the sound of lapping ocean waves. I was walking along a sandy shore, seagulls crying overhead and a chilly breeze blowing. I heard an eerie wisp of song on the wind, teasing my ears with its familiarity. Then I was on a path, on a grassy cliff overlooking the shore—a cliff I'd recognize anywhere. Only this time I walked farther than I had before. I saw the crumbling, abandoned stone church, the one I'd dreamed of before, the one in Gareth's photo. A few ancient headstones leaned at odd angles around it. The music was getting louder. It was "Ar Lan y Môr." The same song Gee Gee always used to sing to me, the same song that I kept hearing in every dream, night after night.

Past the church was the cromlech, and everything else Gareth had described to me: the cairns, the plaque. I drifted closer to the cromlech and its giant ancient boulders, and then felt myself floating gently down into the dark interior.

All was dark and silent for a moment, and then a frail little girl appeared, her long hair glimmering in the faint light.

"My name is Olwen," she said, her eyes sad.

Then I was rising up again, out of the cromlech, out into the air where the seagulls were crying and the waves were crashing against the rocks below.

I woke quickly and scrambled to get my duffel bag from the overhead rack. I had to tell Gareth. There was something important about that place—the cromlech, the hillside over-looking the sea. I knew something strange had happened to Gareth there, and I was dreaming about the area even though I'd never even been to Wales. And now, Gareth's Olwen was talking to *me*.

A tiny spark of fear made me move even faster. I pulled out my laptop, located the train's wi-fi network, and logged into my email. I started a new message to Gareth without even looking at my inbox, writing down every last detail of the dream before I forgot. *You have to take us back to this place*, I wrote. *I have to know who she is.*

We were both seeing it in our dreams. It had to mean something.

"Are you online already?" Mom gave me a look. I nodded but didn't reply.

"You're missing some gorgeous scenery," she said. "Look at those lovely rolling hills—the tour book said we might pass one of the famous chalk figures carved into the hillside. Keep an eye out." She turned to my dad. "Rhys, put that down on our sightseeing list—it's in the left-hand pocket of the travel folder."

They totally sounded like tourists and I cringed, trying to hide behind my laptop. When we got to Wales, I planned on sticking as closely to Gee Gee as possible. When I wasn't with her, I was more than ready to do some exploring on my own.

And maybe—I hoped—with Gareth.

11

Mwyaf y brys, mwyaf y rhwystr.

The more the haste, the greater the hindrance.

Welsh proverb

… Have you ever heard the song Ar Lan y Môr? My Gee Gee used to sing it to me. I keep hearing it in my dream.

Gareth's skin crawled. "Ar Lan y Môr." How was it possible that they were hearing the same song now? Maybe it shouldn't have surprised him at this point, but still… "Highly illogical," he mumbled in a Mr. Spock voice, then grimaced.

He set his phone aside and went back to his notes for his upcoming Literature exam. Amit was sitting next to him at the library table, frantically re-reading *The Tempest* with panic in his eyes. Books and notes were everywhere.

Dan Dobbs was across the table, squinting at a maths review packet. All over the school library, students hunched over textbooks and laptops, notebooks and old homework assignments, in preparation for the exams that started tomorrow. The atmosphere was hushed, with just the occasional rustle of paper or spate of whispering.

All Gareth could think about was getting to the other side of it all. Just a few more days and then he'd be *there*, with Wyn, and they'd figure it all out together. He wanted to help her; she sounded so desperate and sad. He wanted to help the other Olwen, too. And he wanted his life back. But right now, there was nothing he could do. Absolutely nothing.

He picked up his pen, sighed, and opened his own copy of *The Tempest* to the page he'd bookmarked.

How appropriate. *"We are such stuff as dreams are made on, and our little life is rounded with a sleep."* He read it silently to himself, and shivered.

————

A raucous spill of students overflowed from the brick buildings into the cement schoolyard and out onto the street, rapidly shedding school jackets and ties on the way, rolling up shirt sleeves and letting down ponytails and screaming about the summer holidays. Gareth caught sight of Amit already waiting at the gate and navigated toward him through the crowd. Yells and conversation surrounded him in an almost overwhelming wall of noise.

"Going to Brighton this weekend?"

"Come visit me at work—the Starbucks in Westminster!"

"—seeing Gemma's band at the music festival next week—"

"Who are you taking to the dance tonight?"

This last question sounded right in his ear. Gareth glanced at the speaker: a sixth-form girl with the tips of her brown hair dyed pink, pushing past him without a glance and waiting for a reply from her friend. They were talking about the end-of-year dance, held at a nearby rented hall for everyone in year 10 and higher. He should have been more excited about it, but as he trudged out of the gate and onto the crowded sidewalk, all he felt was exhausted.

Amit fell into step beside him, grinning.

"What?" Gareth shot him a suspicious glance.

"I've got you all taken care of, man, don't you worry." He clapped Gareth on the back. "I knew you'd be too busy to get a proper date for tonight, so I made some arrangements, worked a few connections."

Gareth swallowed apprehensively. "What do you mean?"

"I knew you'd put it off, so while *you* were studying, *I* was texting away and finding you a date, my friend. You've got to have a date. It's compulsory."

"It is not. Mr. Thorrington said it was perfectly fine to—"

"It's an unspoken rule," Amit explained slowly, as if Gareth were daft.

Gareth sighed. "So who is it?" They stopped at the back of the long line of students queuing at the bus stop.

There was a dramatic pause.

"Anita Kessler."

Gareth almost choked. Anita was sporty and popular; definitely not part of his crowd. "How did you manage that?"

"Easy peasy," Amit said with a smug smile. "Our dads work together; they're both programmers. Actually, we used to play together as toddlers. I'd have asked her myself, but I felt sorry for you. Figured you could use a good time."

"Eh? I'm fine," Gareth said, frowning.

"Sure you are." Amit slung an arm around his shoulder. "Moping about all day is perfectly normal."

"I'm not moping. I've just been … occupied. There's this girl," Gareth admitted. "You don't know her."

Amit put him in a momentary headlock. "Then why didn't you invite *her* to the bloody dance? I could be with Anita right now! Stroking her long blond hair. Putting my hands on her—"

"She lives in the U.S., okay? She's more like a pen friend. I met her online." Gareth ducked out from under Amit's arm as the bus finally pulled up.

Amit rolled his eyes. "Online. Riiiight."

"Seriously." They boarded the crowded bus and stood near the front, hanging onto ceiling straps. With a jerk, the bus swayed into motion.

"Sure," Amit said. "Anyway, Anita. She'll meet you right outside the hall."

Gareth shook his head. "Anita Kessler. I never would have imagined." It was hard even to imagine now. In fact, it was a bit frustrating that he was responsible for a date, after all. What if he had one of those weird standing-up dreams while he was at the dance? He couldn't help worrying this was all going to end in disaster.

He put his free hand to his head, rubbing the back of his aching neck and trying to picture the flirtatious, famously large-chested Anita somehow agreeing to go to the dance with *him* instead of with Dobbs or some other beefy footballer. There must have been a bribe involved. It was impossible to believe otherwise.

And it was hard to bring himself to care, actually.

Strangely, in his mind, Wyn seemed a lot more solid, a lot more real.

———

Even as he got ready for the dance that evening, Gareth continued to feel remote and unfocused. He put on his blue dress shirt and pants and went downstairs, barely noticing as his mum fussed with his hair and lapels. His hair, as usual, refused to lie neatly, preferring instead to curl down over his ears and interfere with his glasses. His mum fluttered about behind him, trying to mush it down with one of her styling products that smelled like berries.

"Mum!" Gareth ducked out of the way of her descending hand, full of something foamy and pink. "It's fine. I don't want to smell all fruity."

"I don't see what's wrong with smelling nice," his mum said, but she relented, smiling at him in the mirror. "You do look handsome."

"Oh cripes, Mum!" Gareth retreated to his bedroom and

checked his mirror one more time; all seemed to be in order. His clothes were non-wrinkled, his shoes were clean, and he looked...well, older than he usually did. He tried an experimental smile, then a more serious expression. They both looked a bit strange to him.

He thought he caught a glimpse of motion reflected in the corner of the room and whirled around.

Nothing. He shook his head. He'd have to get some more sleep now that exams were over.

Fortunately, Anita didn't seem to notice he was tired. When they met in front of the hall to make their entrance into the disco, she tottered over to him on ridiculously high heels and let out a squeal, throwing her arms around his neck and surrounding him with a cloud of jasmine scent. Momentarily, Gareth wondered if the squealing was part of the deal and, if so, what Amit had promised her in return.

He wasn't about to question his good fortune too closely, however. Especially since Anita was wearing a very low-cut mini-dress. And she did look quite nice. Her long, curly blonde hair was swept up on top of her head, and her wide, lipsticked smile flashed around at their classmates as they entered the hall. The huge main room had been cheerfully festooned with gold and silver balloons and haphazardly thrown streamers, and electronic dance music was pulsating from the speakers.

Amit waved at him from the crowded dance floor and gestured toward a table at the side of the room, already heaped with jackets. Gareth made his way over with Anita. As she dumped her shawl over the back of a chair and adjusted her dress, Gareth felt his phone buzzing in his pocket and pulled it out.

New Picture Message, Unknown Number, it said. A strange feeling began fizzing in his head.

"Let's go dance!" Anita shouted over the music. "Amit and Caroline are already out there!" She pulled on his arm just as he opened the message, bouncing up and down a little. Her cleavage bobbed in time with her jumping.

"Hang on." Gareth dragged his gaze away, back to his phone. On the screen was a photo he'd never seen before.

Darkness. Light filtering down from overhead. And, faintly, a small girl illuminated by the pale glow, her face bearing a sad smile.

Olwen.

His entire body went cold for a moment.

Quickly, Gareth closed the message, only to have a new one pop up on his screen almost right away. *Text Message, Unknown Number.* Now the ghost was texting him? What sort of ghost left text messages?

"Hurry *up*." Anita grabbed the phone out of his hand. She was just putting it on the table when she took a second look at the screen. "Wait, who's Wyn?"

Gareth looked over her shoulder. *It's me, Wyn. Now you have my number. Call or text any time!*

Oh.

Oh.

Anita's expression was rapidly morphing into an annoyed frown, the flashing strobe lights making her face even more severe.

"This is so tacky," she said, almost flinging his phone onto the table. "You're texting other girls during our date. Amit told me you were—*ugh*. I don't know why I agreed to this."

"But it's not—"

She let out a loud groan and turned away from him. "I'm going to go dance. I really don't care what you do."

Wonderful. Gareth sat heavily in one of the vinyl-cushioned chairs. Hopefully nobody would remember any of this by the time school resumed.

Whatever. It hadn't been his idea to go to the dance with Anita anyway. Yet another bright idea of Amit's that had failed spectacularly. Gareth sighed and leaned back in the chair, staring at the ceiling. The room was hot and crowded, the strobe lights were refracting off his glasses, and his dance moves were reminiscent of a spastic monkey. This was not his environment of choice.

For a moment, he was back on the clifftop in Wales, the breeze ruffling his hair, surrounded by green and the quiet crash of waves.

Not long now.

———

"Oi!" Someone jostled Gareth's chair and he jerked upright. "What's your problem?"

"Eh?" Gareth looked up to see Amit hovering above him, his eyebrows merging in an almost comical scowl.

"I got you a date with Anita, man. Why aren't you out

there dancing with her?" Amit wiggled his eyebrows. "Get some action."

Gareth shrugged. "She got mad about a text I just got. From that girl in America. She's in Wales for the summer. Dunno why it was such a big deal."

"Because you're a twat. You don't text imaginary girl-friends while you're out with a real one." Amit smacked the side of Gareth's head.

Gareth looked over at the dance floor. Anita was jiggling around and smiling at Francis Okafor, who looked like he had a perma-grin affixed to his face. Gareth couldn't bring himself to care. In fact, he was feeling a bit lightheaded.

"You know, I think I'm going to just head home, if Anita's already ditched me." He stood up and straightened his clothes.

"Poor bloke. I'll tell her she was too much woman for you. Maybe she'll give you a second chance."

"Whatever." Gareth shrugged again.

"Sure you're all right?" Amit looked more closely at him for a moment.

"Yeah, fine. Just tired."

"Go sleep it off, then." Amit gave Gareth's shoulder a shake and sauntered back off to the dance floor with a wave.

The cool air outside at the bus stop made Gareth feel marginally better, and he wondered what he'd tell his parents about why he was home so early. It had just gotten dark an hour or so before, and the streets weren't even full yet with the usual evening club-goers. He didn't want to reveal the real story, that Anita had abandoned him because he'd been texting Wyn. Or Wyn had been texting him, rather.

He boarded the bus and stared out at the lighted windows rushing past as the bus made its way toward his neighborhood. His faint reflection in the glass had a sort of haunted look, and the passengers around him seemed just as faint and spectral. Businessmen on their way home after working late, couples dressed for dinner. It was all so normal, yet everything had an unreal cast, like an old colorized photograph. His recollection of the little girl, on the other hand, was clear and vivid, as though he could slip back into the scene at any moment. Thanks, of course, to the new photo.

He wondered whether, if he looked at it again, she would even be there, or if it would just be a picture of darkness.

Gareth squeezed his eyes closed, then opened them again. The bus was pulling to a stop. He stomped hard down the metal staircase and into the cold night air, soaking in the *realness* of it all.

———

After managing to get past his mum without incident, Gareth hung his jacket and tie on the coat rack and went into the living room. His dad was lying on the sofa watching an action movie and nodded at Gareth absently.

Gareth sat down at the computer and jiggled the mouse. It was past time to look up some Cwm Tawel history and find out if there was anything useful there, something that might help Wyn figure out what her dreams meant. Something that might lead them closer to Olwen.

Not that he really wanted her any closer, but if she was a ghost, then she might have unfinished business. That was what all the pseudoscience telly programs said. And somehow, that unfinished business had something to do with him, and with Wyn.

Against a rather disconcerting aural backdrop of kicks, punches, and muffled groans from the television, Gareth loaded the Swansea Local History page and clicked on the Cwm Tawel link. He was brought to a simple, sparse site: a black-and-white photograph of some old-fashioned-looking folks standing in front of the town chapel, which he vaguely recognized from his last visit. Underneath the photo was a menu of about eight links, most of them useless to him. He didn't need *Places to Stay*, *Traeth Tawel Caravan Park*, *Cwm Tawel in 1900*, or *Getting to Cwm Tawel*.

Then he saw exactly what he was looking for: *World War II Memories*. He clicked. A long, dense page of text flooded the screen, and he scanned it eagerly.

Below all the general information about who'd fought in the war, how many people had died and whatnot, he found anecdotes from residents of the town. Pages and pages and pages of them. Stories about dads joining the Home Guard and mums hoarding ration coupons. Land Girls tilling plots of vegetables and older brothers who never came home. Bomb shelters in back yards. The terror of air raids. His head began to throb. How would he even know where to start, or what was important? He didn't even know Wyn's great-gran's full name. Something Evans.

Frustrated, Gareth spun around in the office chair, and then stopped. Wyn would have a much better idea of what to look for. He got his phone out and texted her. Now that she had a mobile number, there was no reason why they couldn't be in contact in real time and tackle the problem together.

Check your email, he wrote. *Sending you a link in just a sec.*

He turned back to the computer and was about to send the email when he remembered one more thing.

Yeah, I do know that song. I've been hearing it too. I don't know what it means. I always thought it was a sweet song, but it's getting a bit creepy.

Not much else he could do for now. It was getting late.

Up in his room, he changed into a pair of pajama pants and a *bow ties are cool* T-shirt, then flopped down on top of the covers.

One last time, he looked at the messages on his phone and opened the photo that had appeared during the dance. The little girl was there still, but as he stared at it, he realized that something was different. The other times she'd appeared in his phone, Olwen's figure had been blurry, or faded, or frustratingly dim. But he could see her vividly now, almost as though she'd posed for the photo.

Almost as if she was *trying* to get him to see. But what?

It didn't make sense—it sounded crazy just entertaining the idea. But he couldn't help swiping his fingers across the screen, zooming in just a bit more. He saw nothing but darkness around her, but he saw her face more clearly than ever, brushed with the misty light filtering down into the crom-lech from the sky above. He scrolled around, zoomed in even closer. Her long dark hair was smartly combed, and she was wearing a lacy white dress that hung large on her tiny, frag-ile frame. Over the dress was a silver, oval-shaped locket. Her eyes were surrounded by dark, sickly looking smudges, huge in her gaunt face. Yet she was still a beautiful child.

A ghost. A real ghost. And it wasn't at all like the ridicu-lous ghost-hunting shows on the science fiction channel.

It made his breath catch, the tragedy of it all. He didn't know how on earth he could help. But he would keep trying.

12

Tecaf fro, bro mebyd.

The fairest place is the neighborhood of one's youth.

....

Welsh proverb

When the train rumbled past a huge white suspension bridge across a river, we were really, officially, in Wales, according to the signs. The blue-gray sea, now tossing, now calm, continually disappeared and reappeared to the south. I followed our progress on the map in Mom's tour book as we stopped at the occasional train station: Port Talbot. Neath. The bustling city of Swansea.

Meanwhile, Mom sorted through her folder of paperwork, getting everything we needed to check in to the cottage. Dad was snoring, jet-lagged. And Gee Gee...like me, she couldn't seem to stop staring out the window, her face rapt. I shifted closer to her and she smiled back at me, her face so serene that I didn't want to disturb her by asking more questions. I just wanted us to be happy, in this moment.

The weather had been bright during much of the trip, but the sun had gone behind clouds by the time we arrived in the quiet little port town of Llanelli.

"Llanelli," I murmured to myself as we pulled our luggage out of the storage area and down the steps of the train car. "Llanelli." I still hadn't quite mastered that double-L to my satisfaction. But the air smelled like the sea, and people around me were speaking Welsh and English, flowing from one to the other without a pause, and I couldn't keep a smile from spreading over my face. We were here.

The bus to Cwm Tawel wasn't a double-decker like I'd been hoping for, so I went straight to the rear window seat for a better view. Once we left the town behind, I could see the white-capped, steel-colored ocean under the gray sky on one side of the bus, and rolling green hills dotted with sheep on the other.

After a few miles, the bus crossed a river and turned slightly inland; the sea receded and then disappeared behind a ridge of hills. About forty minutes later, we arrived at the Cwm Tawel bus stop.

We stepped out of the bus and into the misty air, the driver clambering out of her seat to help us with Gee Gee's wheelchair. I looked around me and swallowed past a sudden lump in my throat. I'd never been to this place in my life, yet it was so strangely *home*. There were farms on either side of the road we had just traveled, with pastures of cattle and sheep that stretched all the way up the vivid green hillsides encircling the little valley. Nestled at the bottom was a scattering of buildings and houses, a few miles square. And then there was the eerily familiar smell—ocean air and grass and the tang of farmland. I had to remind myself to keep breathing.

Gee Gee inhaled slowly, then let out a sigh. "It looks just the same," she said. My dad nodded. She turned to me and gave me a smile that wavered just a little.

Next to the bus stop was a pub, a weathered-looking building of dark wood called the Friar's Folly. Across the street was an old stone post office. A main road, called Cwm Road, stretched to the south toward the barrier of hills that separated the valley from the sea. On both sides of the road were businesses, cottages, and smaller lanes branching off toward the hills. All of it hauntingly familiar.

We hauled our luggage into the cozy warmth of the bus station, which seemed more like somebody's living room than a public building. It held an old-fashioned pot-bellied stove, a ticket desk, several wooden chairs, and a postcard stand.

There was a smiling, rosy-cheeked woman with graying brown hair behind the ticket desk, and as she caught sight of us, her eyes widened.

"You *are* here," she said, coming straight over to Gee Gee and grasping her hands tightly. She had the same lilting accent as Gee Gee, only more pronounced.

"Can that be who I think it is?" Gee Gee smiled broadly at the woman and squeezed her hands in return. "Little Margie Jenkins from Llanfair Street?"

"Indeed," the woman confirmed. Her wide grin dimpled her round cheeks. "Only it's been Margie Robinson for a little while now."

"Well, well. Has it really been so long since I was back?"

"I hardly remembered what you looked like," Margie said, leaning down to hug Gee Gee. "You'll have to drop in for tea soon, all of you. Peter and I got a little place on the new Stryd Myrddin, near the school, since you and Rhys were here last. Much quieter than that flat in Ammanford."

"Peter. Of course I must see little Petey. Not so little, now."

"Elderly, in fact," said Margie, laughing.

"My, how things change," Gee Gee said softly. I shifted my feet and stared at the postcards on the rack, flipping through a few nearly identical scenes of misty green hills.

"Of course," Margie added, "we'll be along to visit you as well. You'll be shocked to see how the farm has changed. English owners," she said with a sniff. "Same couple that owns the caravan park down at Pontfaen Sands. Lovely little beach." She turned toward me with a conspiratorial smile. "Perfect place for a girl your age, I should think. You'll have to catch a bus, though."

My thoughts raced. If that was the same beach I'd seen in the dream, it would be the logical starting point for finding the cromlech. Then again, there were miles of beaches around here, but it seemed like a safe assumption. I'd have to ask Gareth; he was the one who'd actually been there.

"That sounds lovely," Mom said, somehow acquiring

a British accent out of nowhere. "We can all go when the weather warms up."

Dad nodded. "Thank you. *Diolch*," he added.

"Yes," Gee Gee said with a sigh, her eyelids fluttering. "Pontfaen sounds like an excellent idea. But for now, I'm afraid, I'm wanting to get some rest." She slumped a little lower in her wheelchair. Bundled in a huge green coat, she looked smaller and frailer than ever. Almost as though she were shrinking.

Margie went over to her desk, picked up the phone, and spoke a few sentences in Welsh very quickly, then hung up. "Hugh Jones will be along in no time with the cab."

She looked at me again, curiously this time. "You do take after Rhiannon!" she said. "You've got the same eyes. As if you're hiding the mysteries of the world." She smiled.

I froze, my gaze glued to the floor. Yes, I was hiding things. But I wasn't the only one. And soon, I hoped, I'd find out just what Gee Gee was keeping hidden.

———

Before long, a roomy black taxicab pulled up outside the bus station. The front door opened to admit a blast of chilly sea breeze and a stocky, round-faced man who introduced himself as Hugh, doffing his cap. He didn't look that old, but his brown hair was already balding. He had cheeks red from the brisk wind and merry blue eyes. There were introductions all around, and each of the ladies was treated to a great, enveloping, two-handed handshake, including me. As he drew away,

I glimpsed an old blurry tattoo of a little Welsh dragon on the inside of his right wrist.

"Cute," I murmured.

He grinned at me and picked up my suitcase. "Anything you need, anything at all," he said, loading our luggage effortlessly into the trunk of the cab. "You just phone me up and I'll be there in no time. If I have passengers, I'll just chuck 'em out into the ditch."

We all laughed at that, even Gee Gee, whom Hugh lifted right into the front seat as though she were a little girl. Mom, Dad, and I slid into the rear seat of the cab.

I rolled down the window momentarily. "*Diolch yn fawr*, Margie!"

"You know some Welsh?" Hugh looked at me curiously in the rearview mirror.

"I've been learning a little," I admitted, rolling the side window back up.

"I must say, I've never met an American who speaks *yr hen iaith*." The old language.

"Truly a Davies at heart," Gee Gee said. I blushed.

"Me own dad and mum didn't see the need for me to learn it. Said I'd get a better job knowing English," Hugh said, chuckling. "And look at me now! Going to night classes."

"A proper nationalist." Gee Gee grinned.

I smiled. Maybe I could find some of these night classes.

The taxi trundled up a slight hill, taking the road leading east from the bus station. We passed another pub and a few houses, and then suddenly we were surrounded by fields. Hugh turned left onto a gravel road that was bordered on either side by low hedges and drove up to a huge stone farmhouse. Behind it was a handful of more modern bungalows. A faded blue-and-white sign on a post read "Gypsy Farm Cottages."

Hugh pulled the cab up alongside a dirty yellow farm truck with a few bales of hay and some farm implements lying in the back.

"I'll just fetch Mrs. Magee for you and she'll get you settled right in," he said, sliding out of the driver's seat.

By the time we got Gee Gee out and into her wheelchair, Hugh had returned with a tall, reedy woman in a gray pantsuit. Her short dark hair was cut in a severe, jagged bob. She had an air of strictness as she surveyed us all, like she ought to have a pair of half-moon spectacles on a chain around her neck and a blackboard pointer in her hand.

Mrs. Magee led us to the nearest cottage, a low-roofed place paneled in whitewashed wood. Next to the front door, a slate plaque read *Primrose Glen* in large block letters, and *Gypsy Farm Cottages* in smaller script beneath. Hugh followed us in, a suitcase in each hand.

Briskly, Mrs. Magee explained the amenities of the cottage and the times that the farmhouse was open for meals. She handed each of us an old-fashioned-looking metal key.

"So different now," Gee Gee said mildly, turning the key over in her hands. "My uncle once owned the place, you know."

Mrs. Magee's demeanor softened. "Then you'll be wanting to see the old photographs up in the farmhouse, I'm sure.

They were left by previous owners. You can come by later and help us identify them for labeling."

"I'll go too," I said. At least looking at photos would be something I could do with Gee Gee that wouldn't be exhausting. And maybe I'd find something that would help me figure things out, though I wasn't sure what.

Mom and Dad talked to Mrs. Magee for a few more minutes, and then she left us to settle in. Hugh had put our suitcases in the front room, which had a sitting area in the center and an attached kitchenette. There were two back bedrooms, one of which already had a hospital bed set up inside; one bathroom; and a tiny front bedroom. Everything was decorated in dusty roses and blues and greens, with watercolor landscapes on the walls.

"I like the artwork," I said, "but I'm not sure about these doilies." I reached out to touch one; it was made of flimsy paper.

"Good God, they're everywhere," Dad said.

I walked into the front, south-facing room, and my breath caught. It had a gently sloping ceiling, a four-poster bed, and two large windows on the south wall that looked out on the farmlands and village. This room was so mine.

"Dibs on the front!" I yelled, bringing in my suitcase.

"Not fair," Dad complained, poking his head around the doorway.

"What?" I said innocently. "I was here first."

He laughed. "It's fine. We'll take the room across from Gran. We'll be able to help her more easily if something happens." His smile disappeared, and he turned away to put Gee

Gee's luggage into her room. I checked out the one tiny bathroom, which had a toilet that flushed by actually pulling a chain on a wall tank. I pulled it, just to see, and jumped at the sudden roar of water. I took a picture with my new phone to send to Rae.

After freshening up, I helped Gee Gee unpack, putting clothes away in the wooden bureau and hanging up dresses in the tiny closet. Dad was unpacking in the other bedroom, opening and shutting drawers, and Mom was looking around the kitchenette. Gee Gee was lying on her bed, directing me, until she fell into a doze, emitting a light snore every so often.

Every time she snored, my chest tightened with anxiety and I looked at her, checking to make sure nothing was wrong.

Finally, I got to the last of the clothes from the boxes we'd sent ahead. I put a gray raincoat on a hanger and hung it in the closet, and then pulled the last item out of the box—a '50s-style dress in light blue with a lacy white collar. It was the dress Gee Gee wore in my picture of her as a young woman, newly arrived in America. I realized that though she hadn't worn it in years, she'd be able to fit into it again without any trouble. In fact, it would probably hang loosely now.

I stared at the dress for a while, my eyes filling with tears. I swallowed hard, put it on a hanger, and left the room as silently as possible, my throat aching. We had so little time left, and I could already feel Gee Gee slipping away.

———

After sobbing out the last of my remaining energy alone in the front bedroom, I drifted into a deep and dreamless slumber. I woke some time later to the sound of muffled voices. The sun was lower in the sky, the village falling into shadow as a layer of clouds moved in. The digital clock on the wooden nightstand read 6:12 p.m.

I turned on the unfamiliar bedside lamp, fumbling for the switch, and stood up groggily. After digging around in my duffel bag, I finally found my hairbrush and got my hair to lie reasonably flat. Then I rinsed my face at the sink in the corner, drying it on a rose-colored hand towel. At least I'd gotten the best room in the whole cottage.

When I opened the door, my parents were standing in the front room talking to a short, sturdy woman with reddish blond hair pulled back in a tidy braid. Gee Gee was sitting on the slightly worn sofa.

"Wyn," Mom said, "come here for a minute, please, and meet the on-call nurse." The nurse was wearing an official-looking white jacket, and over her shoulder was a navy-blue messenger bag printed with *Valley Local Clinic and Hospice*.

"Lisa Morgan," she said, smiling broadly. She gave me a hearty handshake, then turned back toward my parents. "Just phone the clinic if you need me for any reason. I'll be calling on Mrs. Evans every day at two o'clock, then."

While Mom and Dad walked her out, I rummaged through the small kitchenette cupboards and found a shelf of glass tumblers. I filled two glasses with water from the tap and brought them both over to the sofa.

"Well, what do you think?" I looked at Gee Gee. Her eyes

were bright, but I couldn't read her expression. "She seems nice."

"She seems just fine, yes." Gee Gee sipped absently at her water.

I nodded, feeling awkward. This was so new. And it felt strange to have someone else taking care of Gee Gee, someone who was basically a stranger. Someone who was literally there to help her die.

She saw the expression on my face and hugged me close. "It will be nice to have the extra hands, so that you three can explore the village without worrying about me." She smiled. "Truly."

"I guess it's better than having Mrs. Magee come in every day," I allowed.

Gee Gee's smile grew wider. "Those English. She is a bit stern, isn't she?"

"She'd probably feed you castor oil," I said, relaxing back into the lumpy sofa. Gee Gee leaned against my shoulder and closed her eyes.

"Mmm," she responded. After a moment, she was breathing slowly and evenly. I curled my legs underneath me as carefully as possible and tried not to move, as if I could somehow keep time from sprinting forward and changing everything. But my mind kept hurtling ahead, spinning in circles. My dreams. The cromlech.

Olwen, Gareth's ghost girl.

Gee Gee was dying, and there was no avoiding that reality. But if there were ghosts... restless spirits, somewhere beyond life and death … how could I let Gee Gee go? If she died, who—or what—would be waiting for her?

———————

At dinner, I ate ravenously, finishing off a huge bowl of *cawl*—hearty lamb and vegetable soup—along with two rolls spread with fresh-tasting local butter, and a hunk of cheese. The high-ceilinged farmhouse dining room was nearly empty except for one older couple in the far corner. Mrs. Magee had seated us across the room, near the unlit hearth.

The nearby walls were covered with framed black-and-white photographs. When we stood up to leave, I took another look, searching for faces I recognized. The oldest ones were from the early 1900s: women in voluminous, somber-colored skirts and men in dark suits standing solemnly in front of the farmhouse. There was even a photo of the Romani Gypsies that had given the farm its name— a dark-haired bunch standing in front of a tree with a painted cart and horse in the background. And, of course, there were the family photos. Maybe Mrs. Magee would let me get the pictures scanned.

"That young man is my Uncle Rhodri." Gee Gee pointed at a spindly, dark-haired teenager holding a pitchfork that was quite a bit taller than he was. "This very old one, these are the owners of the farm before my great-grandfather Matthew bought it."

My favorite was an oval portrait of a tiny baby in a lacy christening gown that was Gee Gee herself. Next to it was a photo from World War II showing several women in overalls out in a field with rakes and hoes.

"The Land Girls," Gee Gee said. She pointed to a tall young woman with her pants rolled up to mid-calf. "That one's Margie Jenkins's mother, Marged. I wanted to be a Land Girl, but I wasn't quite old enough. You had to be eighteen."

She turned away from the photo display, her eyes tired. By the time we got back to the cottage, just a short walk down the path, Gee Gee seemed drained. I hoped it was just jet lag. It was only eight thirty.

Dear Rae,

Got to Wales today after what felt like weeks of traveling. We're staying in the most adorable cottage on a farm that used to be Gee Gee's uncle's. It's beautiful here. I wish you could see it. And people are so nice. You'll probably get this way late, but anyway.

—Love, Wyn

I dropped the postcard and pen on the nightstand, called a quick good night to my parents, and pulled on my blue fleece pajamas. I'd have to remember to buy stamps tomorrow. It was kind of funny because I'd already emailed Rae from the farmhouse, but I liked postcards. I couldn't help it.

I crawled into bed, turned off the light, and was asleep within minutes.

After sleeping better and longer than I had in quite some time, I woke up the next morning with energy to spare. The chilly air felt good to me as we walked to the farmhouse for breakfast, but while I downed two poached eggs, a grilled tomato, baked beans, toast, and half a grapefruit, Gee Gee only picked at her eggs and toast. As I pushed her wheelchair down the path back to the cottage, I could hear her breathing heavily.

Inside, I settled her on the sofa with a blanket and went into my parents' room, where they were finishing their unpacking.

"Gee Gee seemed really tired out on the walk back," I said without preamble. I tried to sound calm, but I shifted from foot to foot anxiously.

"We noticed the same thing, honey." Mom folded a sweater into a perfect square and put it into one of the dresser drawers. "We've talked about this, though. It's normal for someone in her condition to get worn out easily."

"What do I do if something happens and you guys aren't here? Should I get Mrs. Magee?"

"Oh heavens no," Mom said. "I made a schedule." Of course she did. "Either Dad or I will be around, unless we have to leave for a short time, and we've posted the number of the clinic next to the phone. Oh, and the emergency number here is 999. You shouldn't need that, though, unless you need to call the police or the fire department."

"Fire department? Not reassuring." It was, though. Not for the first time on this trip, I was glad my mother was kind of a control freak.

Dad said, "Hey, listen—how about coming with me into town? I was going to do some grocery shopping, and thought you might like to have lunch out with your old dad and explore a little." He slid a dresser drawer closed, then pulled an old gray fleece out of the standing wardrobe.

"Okay," I said, willing to be distracted. "Let me grab my camera."

"There won't be much going on, on a Sunday," Mom pointed out. "Tuesday there's a farmer's market, though."

I rolled my eyes. "I *like* scenery. When was the last time I took a picture of a human being?"

"Just this morning, I saw a picture of a sweet little girl on your phone." She smiled.

My forehead wrinkled in confusion.

"Well, maybe you didn't take it," she added. "I was looking at your pictures of the train trip, and the picture just popped up. Maybe it was a message. I'm sorry I forgot to tell you."

Without a word, I ducked out of the room and rushed across the cottage. My phone was on my bed, where I'd left it a few minutes ago. I unlocked the screen and checked my messages.

"Jeez, Mom," I muttered. There was a message I hadn't seen, from Gareth. *The latest mystery photo*, he wrote, and attached was a picture.

The girl.

Olwen.

I hit *Reply*.

I see her this time. Come as soon as you can.

———————

The lane that led down to the main road was about half a mile long, bordered by tall hedges on either side, and Dad and I walked in companionable silence, me snapping the occasional picture. There was hardly any traffic noise, just wind in the trees, occasional snatches of birdsong, and the buzz of a distant tractor.

We walked by the clinic where Lisa worked, which wasn't far at all, just a block from the bus station. Both places were closed, as was the Friar's Folly, though a middle-aged man with spiky blond hair and an apron was hanging around the side door of the pub, breaking down empty cardboard boxes. He waved and smiled, then went back to work.

I snapped a picture of him for my mom's benefit.

On the main road we passed tourist shops, offices, several banks, and regular side roads that branched off into neighborhoods. Some of the side streets were obviously older, lined with quaint bungalows, while others held more modern-style apartment buildings. After walking for another half mile, we found the grocery store; not much more than a corner market. I followed Dad up and down the aisles, pulling the occasional strange item off the shelf to inspect more closely.

Dad laughed at me when I made a face at a jar of Marmite spread. "Just wait till you try the laverbread. It's not even bread."

"I'll stick with beans on toast, thanks." I was becoming less and less sure about British cuisine the longer we shopped, but then Dad found a nearby fish and chips shop and my opinion flip-flopped yet again. We sat on tall stools at the counter and munched away at crispy, greasy, piping-hot fried cod and potatoes, wrapped in cones of newsprint and sprinkled with malt vinegar. Outside, people dressed in church clothes trickled up the street, laughing and chatting. A few came in and out, and I couldn't help listening in to see if anybody spoke Welsh to the elderly man behind the counter.

Finally, one woman said "*p'nawn da*"—good afternoon—and began chatting away too quickly for me to understand.

"Did you hear that, Dad? She talked so fast, though. I need to practice more."

"So you can eavesdrop more effectively?" He stole one of my few remaining chips and popped it into his mouth.

"Hey!" I pulled my cone of newsprint closer. "No, I just thought I could talk to people. Make some friends."

"Speaking of friends," Dad said, his face serious. "I spoke to your mother about this Gareth guy."

"Uh huh."

"We aren't too sure it's a good idea for you to be meeting him right now. With everything that's going on ... " He looked out the window, seeming lost for words. "The thing is, we always want you to be safe, and we don't know him."

"Maybe you could talk to his parents over the phone," I said, trying to keep calm.

"Maybe," Dad said. "But your mom and I have a lot on our plates right now. I can't make any guarantees. And your mother is more cautious than I am. I'm sure he's just a normal kid, but give us some time to work it out."

"But I already asked him to come," I blurted out.

Dad ran his hands through his hair, leaving it a spiky

mess. He sighed heavily, then looked at me. "Then I'll definitely be calling his parents, I guess."

"Why does it matter? He's staying with his great-grand-dad," I said, my voice rising with desperation. "Dad, I don't have any other friends here."

His expression softened and he put an arm around my shoulders. "I know you feel that way. I know this is hard."

I swallowed down tears and leaned against him.

"We'll work it out," he said after a moment. "I promise."

I straightened up and slid off the stool to throw away our trash. "Can I at least walk around a little by myself?"

Dad looked at my face and sighed again. "Be back at the cottage in two hours, Wyn. Let me put Hugh's number in your phone, too, in case something happens and you need a cab." He fiddled with my phone for a second, then handed it back.

"What's going to happen? There is literally no trouble here for me to find."

Dad laughed at that, so I figured things would be okay with Mom, too. He hugged me and headed back down the street.

Sadly, it only took me half an hour of walking around to realize that not much was open on Sundays. None of the cute shops; not even the bookstore, Smyth and Sons. The breeze was starting to get chillier, and I increased my pace, heading south along Cwm Road until the businesses and houses started to thin out a bit. The road was sloping very slightly upward again, and the vivid green hills I could see distantly from my bedroom window looked almost close enough to touch now. I stopped at what seemed to be the last big intersection in town. The road curved to the west and was marked with a worn green sign reading *Heol Owain Glyndwr*. Underneath the street sign was a smaller sign with an arrow pointing left.

Amgueddfa—Museum
Capel Llanddewi Newydd—New St. Davids Chapel
Ysgol—School

A museum. I felt a rush. This was what I'd needed all along—somewhere to look up the history of this place, maybe find out who Olwen was. I trotted down the road and passed the chapel, which was a medium-sized, cheery-looking, whitewashed building with a small steeple in front. Just past it was the Cwm Tawel Museum, a tiny brick building set back from the road. I walked down the front path through neatly tended flower beds and read the sign on the door: *Open Monday–Friday, 10 a.m.–3 p.m.*

I sat down on the step for a few minutes, nonplussed. I'd just have to come back some other time. I'd have to find something else to do this afternoon.

I heaved myself up, trudged back to the main road, and walked north along the quiet street, wondering whether it would be weird if I just walked into some shop that happened to be open and tried to practice Welsh on people. There'd better be more to do in Cwm Tawel on weekdays. It was certainly living up to the name "Quiet Valley" today.

If Gareth was here, I'd definitely be more entertained. And I'd feel less alone, too. But he wasn't. Not yet. I wished

Gee Gee was well enough to show me around, but there was no use thinking about that.

The lane leading back to the farm was empty, but there was a cheery murmur of voices spilling from the open door of the Friar's Folly. Curious, I peeked in just to see what was going on. The dimly lit, wood-paneled room was half full, men and women alike enjoying pints of beer and chatting in Welsh and English.

"Well, if it isn't Miss Olwen Evans," said a booming voice. I looked over to see Hugh waving at me. "*Shw mae?*"

"*Shw mae,*" I said, to which Hugh and his companions responded with an outburst of pleased-sounding laughter. I blushed. "I'm just heading back to the cottage. I'll see you later. Uh, how do you say that in Welsh?"

"*Wela i ti!*" Hugh grinned at me.

"Come back here any time, day or night, if you want to learn more Welsh—you'll find Hugh here *siwr o fod,*" said one woman at the table. She gave Hugh a fond smile.

"Yes, because Annie here won't let me back into our house without buying her a pint," he teased back, kissing her on the cheek loudly.

"Thanks," I said. "Maybe later. *Wela i ti.*" I smiled at them and ducked out the door. Maybe I'd track down Hugh next time I got bored. Getting to speak Welsh with a real person ... it would be nothing like practicing with software, that was for sure.

———

The moment I walked into the cottage, I smelled broiling steak and baking potatoes. My dad hurriedly introduced me to Dafydd, a garrulous older man with graying dark hair and a paunch who turned out to be Gee Gee's nephew. For most of dinner, he talked about his work as a bank manager in nearby Llanelli, flashing nervous smiles at Gee Gee every so often. I felt sorry for him. He obviously wanted to be supportive in some way, and just as obviously didn't know how.

After dinner was over and Dafydd had left, Mom cornered me to help with the dishes.

"You missed Margie and Peter while you were out on the town," she said, handing me a dripping plate to dry. "You know, Peter works in the museum. Did you get down to that end of the village?"

I dried the plate with a dishrag. "Yeah, but the museum was closed. I ran into Hugh in the pub, though."

"Oh, Wyn, you didn't go in that place, did you?" Mom shot me a look. "You're underage."

"I just poked my head in the door to see what it was like," I said defensively. "People were eating in there. It wasn't like it was a bar or anything."

"I know. I just don't want you getting into trouble while you're walking around alone." Mom sighed. "It's one thing to let you run around and explore, but things are different here. Kids grow up faster." She smiled at me tiredly. "I guess I just don't want you growing up too fast."

Oh God. "Okay, okay." I hung up the damp dish towel, exasperated. "I think I'm going to get ready for bed now." I couldn't deal with this conversation anymore.

"It's a little early," she said, raising her eyebrows. "You must still be jet lagged."

I managed not to comment on that, and I said good night.

When I went in to hug Gee Gee, she was already asleep. She was breathing loudly and shallowly, her jaw slack, and that sick feeling of anxiety I'd managed to ignore all day started to come back. Tomorrow I'd spend the day with her, no matter what. The Internet and the post office would wait.

———

I knew I was dreaming as soon as I saw the mirror. It was the carved, heavy wood-framed mirror from my bedroom at home, but it hung on the wall instead of leaning on my dresser, and it wasn't in my bedroom at all but in a living room in a strange house. It was almost pitch dark, but I could make out shadowy shapes of tables, chairs, and other furniture by the slight gleam of the embers in the fireplace. A faint glow was reflected in the mirror, and I could see a small halo of light growing until it revealed itself to be a candle.

I heard a racking cough.

"Can't sleep, Mum," said a soft little voice. Reflected in the mirror was a little girl holding the candle—the same girl I'd seen by the ocean in my other dream, the same girl in Gareth's photo. Olwen.

I whirled around. The girl saw me, or seemed to see me, at the same moment. Her mouth opened in a tiny O of surprise, and she let out a squeak. She clutched at her silver necklace as though it were a talisman and backed slowly away. The candlelight faded as the little girl disappeared back into the darkness of the house, and I felt myself fading too, sinking back into the darkness of sleep.

13

Dyfal donc a dyr y garreg.

Persistent tapping breaks the stone.

Welsh proverb

Gareth shoveled mashed potatoes into his mouth, half-listening to his parents as they rattled off a list of rules he was supposed to adhere to while visiting his great-granddad. Who cared whether he had to help weed the garden or go round the shops? He'd scrub toilets if it meant he had a chance to figure everything out.

" . . . nine o'clock, mind you," his dad said. "Are we clear?"

"Of course I'll be in the house by nine o'clock, Dad. There's nothing to do in Cwm Tawel at night," he pointed out. He served himself another spoonful of potatoes and poured gravy all over them. "What if Wyn's family asks me to stay for dinner?"

His mother raised her eyebrows. "I suppose if it's all right with them. But please, please try not to be a nuisance to Wyn or her family. I know you're excited to meet them, but they're going to be very busy. Her mum told me. And if anything happens to her great-gran … Well, heaven forbid, but they might be grieving, you know." She looked upset.

"I won't be a bother, Mum," he said. "I promise. I'll just make sure they have someone to ask if they need anything. Do we have any guidebooks or maps I could give them? I could show them the walking path we took last time."

"I'm sure they already have plenty of guidebooks, Gareth." His dad gave him a small smile. "But I'm sure they'd appreciate some recommendations. Do you remember Kidwelly Castle, from our trip last year? They might enjoy that."

"Murder holes! Murder holes!" Tommy cackled, looking up from his plate.

"Yeah, that's right," Gareth said. "We climbed all over the place and Tommy got his foot stuck in a murder hole." He jabbed his brother lightly with his elbow. "I'll make sure to tell Wyn about it. But do you remember where we went over the hols? I think she'd really like that."

His dad shot him a look. "Not off the top of my head. But it was just off the beach, Gareth. Don't you remember?"

"He was too busy with his phone," his mum said. Gareth rolled his eyes.

After a moment, his dad added, "We have an old Ordnance Survey map of the coastline there. If you can find it, take it. Maybe there's some GPS app you can download, too. If you go exploring, I don't want you getting lost."

"Cheers, Dad." If his parents had a map of the area, then there was little doubt in his mind the cromlech was on it somewhere. Wyn was expecting him to know where it was, and he didn't want to disappoint. Even worse, he didn't want to admit he hadn't really been paying attention the last time—at least, not until he'd lost his mobile.

"Don't worry, I won't bother Wyn or her family," Gareth added. "But if she needs a friend, at least I'll be there."

His dad gave him a skeptical look.

"Friend … or *girlfriend*?" Tommy said.

"Honestly," Gareth began, but then he sighed and gave up on explanations. Maybe after it was all over, he'd tell them everything. At this point, he still wasn't even sure what was going on himself.

———

The next day, after digging through an old shoebox of brochures and maps in the boot of his dad's car, Gareth triumphantly pulled out a bedraggled copy of an Ordnance Survey Outdoor Leisure Map of the South Wales coast. There were rips at some of the folds, and it smelled musty and ancient. His parents must have used this very same map when they'd taken him out on holiday as a boy; maybe even on their last trip, not that he would have noticed.

At first glance, the map was nearly impossible to read, crammed full of tiny symbols and town names and minuscule boxes for houses and neighborhoods and farms. Not to mention the parks and footpaths and incomprehensible geographical symbols.

On the other hand, everything was on this map. *Everything.* If he could find Cwm Tawel on it, and the nearby beach, then he could trace all the possible paths in the area. That would give them a starting point for exploration, for finding the gravesite. And then ... he didn't know what would happen after that, but hopefully he and Wyn would figure it out together.

Tracing the coastline westward from the Gower Peninsula, he found Swansea on the map, and then Llanelli and Carmarthen, and not far from there, Cwm Tawel itself. The whole area was crisscrossed with trails, bridle paths, cycling paths, and narrow country roads. There was a multitude of sandy beaches, and the area was also positively littered with ancient sites. The historical ruins that dotted the hills and cliffs along the seashore were labeled in a tiny calligraphy font: *Cross, Settlement, Standing Stones, Homestead.* And, to his chagrin, all along the coasts and inland areas too, over and over: *Cairn, Cairn, Cairn.* He didn't see the word "cromlech" anywhere. But the mapmakers would have to note something as large as the one he'd fallen into—perhaps they just called it "standing stones"?

He let out a groan of frustration. Maybe it would be worth it to buy an online map, especially if it was searchable. Or try to find a tourist map when he got there.

He put the map aside for the time being and checked his email. A forwarded joke from Amit; a rather long tirade from Anita about his behavior at the end-of-year-dance. Then a grin sneaked onto his face; there was a message from Wyn at long last.

Dear Gareth,

I'm so glad you're coming. I think my parents are still weird about me meeting you, though.

I can hardly believe I'm here. Everything is really surreal right now. I had a dream about my Gee Gee's old house, so I asked her where it was, but when I went to find it, it wasn't there anymore. Just a block of flats now. But I dreamed about the locket, too, the one Olwen was wearing in the picture you sent. I didn't realize it was a locket in the dream. Not until you said something. It looks familiar... I wonder why.

The museum was closed when I tried to go. Peter Robinson, who works there, was an evacuee as a child in my Gee Gee's house. He has to know something. I'll keep trying to talk to him.

I'll be at the Carmarthen train station with my mom to pick you up on Saturday afternoon.

—Wyn

Gareth felt a prickle of anticipation. It felt like some of the puzzle pieces were finally starting to mesh, or at least like they were on the right track. Maps. Museums. Lockets.

Something had to be significant there. He hit *Reply* and started typing.

———

Gareth's room was a maelstrom of dirty clothes, clean clothes, waterproof jackets, extra socks, and half-filled baggage. His dad's old brown suitcase teetered on the edge of the bed as he put things in various piles. Meanwhile, he was listening to Amit's ridiculous romantic advice, which he had no intention of following at any time in his life whatsoever.

"Remember what I said about pickup lines?" Amit's voice coming out of the speaker phone was tinny. "Did you get that email I sent? With the list?"

"I assumed that was a joke," Gareth said.

"I'm telling you, though, they work! Think of how many girls I've gone with just this year."

Gareth pulled a lightweight yellow windbreaker out of one of the piles and rolled it into a crinkly ball, shoving it into one corner of his suitcase. "I'm not questioning your ability to attract the girls," he said. "Just your ability to keep them."

Amit said an extremely rude word.

Gareth laughed. "Hey, when I get back, let's organize a game with Dobbs and them."

"Are you serious? You, playing football?" Amit asked with exaggerated surprise.

"I meant Halo."

"Figured," said Amit. "Still, you could build up some

muscle while you're there. Chasing sheep around or something."

Something about that annoyed Gareth. "There's more in Wales than just sheep."

"Yeah, there's your American girlfriend!"

"Is that all you can think about?" Gareth packed up several rolled-up pairs of identical black socks and his new dark-blue jeans. He'd miss Amit's usual antics, but he'd only be gone for two weeks.

Would he and Wyn be able to find the gravesite, the cromlech, in that amount of time? They'd have to.

―――――

Gareth was sleeping on top of the covers with the windows open when his phone buzzed. He opened his eyes to see the darkness of his room, faintly lit by a yellowish street light. His first thought was, *Something's happened to Wyn's gran.*

He blinked, then fumbled for his glasses and his phone.

When he squinted at the screen, it showed a new picture message. *Unknown Number.*

He opened it, his hand trembling just a little.

The photo was a close-up: the girl's worried face, pale and thin, took up the left side of the picture, her eyes dark glittering hollows glancing off to the side. Following the direction of her gaze, he focused on the background landscape: green grass going right up to the edge of a cliff. Whitecapped ocean waves, a sandy beach in the distance. A different angle than the other picture, a view without the cromlech.

After a moment, he realized he was breathing heavily. His hair was damp with sweat.

And then he smiled.

Whatever was happening, whatever strange and frightening things were now a regular part of his life, Olwen was helping him. She wasn't one of those vengeful Hollywood ghosts—he hoped. She'd sent him a picture of where she was.

She wanted him to find her.

Of course, what he'd do then—what *she* would do—he hadn't a clue.

14

The best work is hope.

Welsh proverb

Born to Wyn, July 11th, 8:48 a.m.

I slept great our first night here, but not anymore. Groggy in the daytime. Can't fall asleep at night. Waking up at random times, wide awake, only to discover it's the wee hours of the morning.

No dreams.

I'm actually writing this at 3 a.m., by the way. Can't post it until morning. Only the main farmhouse has wi-fi.

This place really IS no-place, lost in time.

I felt less lost the next morning, after going to the farm-house to check email and publish my blog post. I let myself back into the cottage, closed the door against the wind and rain, and flopped down on the sofa, letting out a huge yawn. I slid sideways until I was in a lying-down position and closed my eyes.

"Don't go falling back asleep now," Mom said from the kitchenette. "If you keep to a regular sleep schedule, you'll get used to the time change more quickly."

"I'm fine," I said, stifling another yawn. "I got up on time this morning, didn't I?"

"Yes, but we want you alert." Mom leaned around the doorframe and smiled at me, then went back to clattering dishes around.

I pulled myself upright and got up to get some tea. Caffeine would help. In the kitchen, I filled a mug with water and put it in the microwave.

"Your dad and I are taking a quick trip to the Tesco in Carmarthen to pick up groceries. Will you be okay here by yourself for an hour or two?"

I nodded. "I'll spend some time with Gee Gee."

The rain was sheeting against the kitchen window, a summer storm flinging huge splattering drops everywhere and sneaking cold drafts into the cottage. It had started yesterday afternoon, but today there were brilliant blue gaps in the clouds far off over the hills, above the ocean. I was glad to see some sky. In two days we'd be picking up Gareth, and it would be time to really start the detective work... and I did not relish the thought of hiking the hills in the rain.

Settling back onto the sofa with my mug of tea, I tried to picture Gareth here. I tried to imagine what it would be like to actually talk, in person, to someone who understood how I felt, who would believe the strange things that had been happening to me.

Gareth might be the only one who could help me figure this out. Especially if something happened to Gee Gee. I didn't want to think about that eventuality, but it was an eventuality whether I tried to ignore it or not.

The last few days, I hadn't even been able to pretend anymore. The cold and wet weather, or maybe just the illness, had seemed to weigh on her. She spent all day in bed or on the couch, sleeping or watching news and Welsh soap operas on the small 13-inch television. Her frame seemed smaller than ever, cushioned by a nest of pillows, and her skin was slack and papery. When Lisa Morgan came in the afternoons to bathe her, she lifted Gee Gee with what seemed like no effort at all. But Gee Gee's eyes were still clear and alert, and she didn't seem to be in pain. And she seemed glad to be here, in Cwm Tawel. Sometimes I'd catch her gazing out onto the hills, a slight smile on her face.

Today, as the rain pounded away, she was still in her bedroom. When I went in to check on her, the hospital bed was levered so that her torso was mostly upright. Her eyes were sharp and there was a book in her lap, but she was staring off into the distance, at nothing. This was happening more and more now, like she was just ... somewhere else.

"Gee Gee, do you want tea?" I hovered in the doorway.

"Oh! Hello, dearest. No, I'll just take some hot water, thank you." Her voice was low and a little hoarse-sounding.

"Are you cold? I can't believe it's raining so much in July." I squirted some lotion from the large bottle on a tray next to the bed and rubbed it into Gee Gee's dry, cracked hands, massaging them gently.

"That's lovely, *blodyn*. Just having my family nearby warms my heart." She smiled, though it seemed to take some effort. I pulled an extra blanket out of the closet and lay it over her legs, then climbed onto the bed myself, snuggling up beside her. She didn't smell like lily-scented powder anymore; just soap and lotion and something indefinably hospital-like.

"I hope you're getting out a bit, seeing the village," she said.

"Yeah. I saw Hugh yesterday. He said to say *cofion cynnes*." Warm regards.

"Your accent is improving quite nicely. You'll be speaking Welsh in no time, I'm thinking." She looked pleased, but a little sad.

I bit my lip. "Do you miss it?" I asked, quietly. "Speaking Welsh every day? Having a life here?"

"Well, dear, we can't always predict what life is going to give us, can we. Moving away was what John and I had to do at the time. It was good for William, too, and then for your father. They grew up with so many opportunities we didn't have for … for our families here." She yawned.

"It's so beautiful here, though. I've never seen hills this green." It was true. "And the history. I can't wait to explore some of the ancient sites. Like cromlechs." I looked at her carefully, trying to gauge her response. Hoping for something. But her eyes were faraway now.

"Yes, it's lovely … it is that." She paused and drew a shuddering breath. "Dearest, you must understand—there were things I had to leave behind. Difficult times during the war and after. I was just so afraid that something would happen to little William, or to one of us. It was simply … safer in America. Peaceful, I thought."

I sighed with frustration, tired of being cautious. "But *why* was being here so terrible? I'm sorry, but I just look at all of this"—I gestured around me, outside the window—"and I can't understand why anybody would leave."

She smiled a distant smile.

I didn't want to upset her, but at the same time, I didn't know if I'd have many more chances to ask her this. I had to figure out what in the world I was supposed to do, besides finding the cromlech and the gravesite. Something was still hidden; something important. I just didn't know exactly what, where, or how.

"*Why* did you leave, Gee Gee?" I tried one last time.

"Listen now," she said, a bit of challenge in her voice. "We were all on edge after the war. Things were mostly all right out here in the countryside, but those poor folk in Swansea, their houses and lives destroyed … We could see the planes flying overhead, you know. And we had a few close calls ourselves. Those were frightening times. Many didn't survive. Life was just too hard for some of the little ones. Especially the ones that came in from the cities, leaving behind everything they knew. You can ask Petey about that."

I would, if I could ever make it to the museum when it was actually open. Maybe Petey could show me some more old photos.

I stiffened. Maybe he knew who Olwen was.

Gee Gee's voice had been growing quieter and weaker throughout her brief speech, and now her eyes closed. I stroked her hair, gently, smoothing down the white wisps as if she were a child. At my touch, she stirred slightly.

"Oh, Olwen *fach*, my Olwen, always so curious," she breathed. "Such a clever girl. *Fy merch am byth…*"

My eyes brimmed with tears.

"I'll miss you too, Gee Gee," I whispered. I kissed her on the cheek and silently left the room.

———

That night I dreamed about my great-grandmother.

Gee Gee was standing in front of me in a white dress, the one from my old nightmare. But instead of being overtaken by darkness, she floated in the space in front of me. We were outside. Her figure was translucent; through her and behind her, I could see the hills of Cwm Tawel rising gentle and green. We faced each other for what seemed like several minutes, neither of us saying anything, Gee Gee's face smiling and sad.

"I love you, Olwen *fach*," she said.

"I love you, too, Gee Gee," I answered, my voice breaking. She began to recede, moving imperceptibly farther and farther away.

"Wait!" I reached out. Gee Gee reached out, too, and

in her hand was something silver, sparkling on a chain. I stretched and tried to grab her hand, but everything was fading now, and gradually it all became darkness and I slid into deep sleep.

———

My footsteps echoed along the quiet streets of Cwm Tawel. I'd finished the chores my parents insisted on and gone walking into the village. I hadn't had a set plan, but now I found my subconscious had led me back to the street where Gee Gee's house had once stood. The narrow lane, called Lôn Brynmelyn, was lined on both sides with gray-and-white two-story apartment blocks—nice in their way, with wood trim and colorful hanging flowerpots. No little house called Awel-y-Môr.

I stood back a bit, in the street, gazing at the flats. In a way, I was glad Gee Gee couldn't be here to see this.

Or maybe she'd be glad?

I heard a car rumbling along, growing louder, and then a distant toot-toot of someone tapping on the horn. I stepped back onto the sidewalk, but the car slowed anyway and then rolled to a stop with a faint smell of exhaust. It was a black taxicab, and inside it was Hugh, waving out of the open window.

"Hey, there, *bore da*!" He grinned. "Fine day today, isn't it? *Mae hi'n braf heddiw.*"

"*Ydy, mae hi'n braf heddiw.*" I managed a smile. "What are you doing, out in the taxicab?"

"Oh, just back from taking old Mrs. Williams down

to the bus, out to visit her sister in Tregaron for the weekend." He looked closely at me. "Listen, now, got anything on your social calendar for lunch today?"

"Not really," I said. Social calendar indeed. "We're going to pick up Gareth in Carmarthen this afternoon. Maybe visit a castle beforehand."

"Carmarthen, eh? Well, if you have time, maybe you'd like to join me and Annie at HMS Tasty's—that's the fish and chips shop on the main road. Well, you'd be welcome. We're meeting there in about half an hour."

"Maybe. Thanks," I said.

"Keep it in mind. Sure you need a meal out of the house now and then." His smile was kind. "And we can practice some Welsh conversation if you like."

"That sounds great," I admitted. "Maybe I'll see you."

I waved as he started the car again and drove away toward the main street. I began to head back in the same direction on foot, feeling happier as I walked. I would get to speak Welsh. I would get fish and chips. I would be meeting not one but *two* friends today. Three, including Annie.

I would finally see Gareth in person.

———

I stifled a laugh. Mom's rental car was a blue Ford Fiesta, small and rotund, and of course everything was on the wrong side: the steering wheel, the dashboard, the pedals. When we got going, I couldn't help grabbing the door handle every time she swerved to the side of the narrow lane to allow opposing traffic to pass. Fortunately, it wasn't far to Cwm Road. From there, Mom made a right turn and headed north out of the village. Almost immediately, the now-familiar lanes of houses were replaced by rolling green hills dotted with sheep, cattle, and the occasional farmhouse. The weather was misty and damp; the sun high, remote, and cold.

I stared out the window, thinking about what Hugh and Annie had told me at lunch. I'd finally found out what it meant when Gee Gee said "*fy merch am byth*"—it meant either "my girl forever" or "my daughter forever."

My girl forever—she could have been talking about me. She had been talking *to* me. But a daughter?

The face of the little girl, the other Olwen, surfaced in my mind's eye. But nobody had ever mentioned a daughter in connection with Gee Gee. I squeezed my eyes shut for a moment. These were the kinds of secret things that broke up families, and my family—it was happy, whole. None of it made sense.

The Ford entered a lush valley patchworked in shades of green—deep and emerald and spring green—and my breath caught. I'd never seen anything so beautiful, never seen any place that called to me like this. Occasional forested patches sprang from the turf, shrubby hedgerows meandered across one another, and the ubiquitous sheep were little white dots on the verdant slopes of the hills. This was the Tywi valley, and ahead were the peaceful river Tywi and the small town of Llandeilo along its banks. Only a few miles away was Carreg Cennen Castle, which I'd been dying to visit.

We paid for our admission at a little booth and hiked

up the steep, rocky hill, the cool air seeming warmer as we panted along.

"Thanks, Mom, for squeezing this in." I realized it was our first real sightseeing trip, which made sad for a moment.

"It was on the way," she said vaguely, seeming lost in her own thoughts.

I didn't blame her. I couldn't think about anything except being in this gorgeous place. The early afternoon sun was breaking up the mist. The views were breathtaking from the ancient, carved stone windows with their arched lintels; the castle stood high on a limestone crag, and the whole Tywi valley stretched below us on all sides.

I walked down a stairway that led to a windowed stone passage. Mom stayed behind on the steps, looking out at the landscape. I stepped carefully inside and wandered along the vaulted hallway, mesmerized by the way it seemed to grow smaller and narrower as it sloped downward. It smelled of stone, and damp, and indefinable age. I leaned against the wall momentarily and shut my eyes, picturing myself living here hundreds of years ago.

Then, in my mind's eye, I saw different stone walls, a smaller space, and dimly, in a corner, her. Olwen.

My eyes flew open. For a moment, the afterimage of her spectral form hovered in my vision, then faded so that I was no longer sure I hadn't imagined it. I backed away from the dark hallway and then turned and fled up the stairs, my heart racing.

Back in the car, after a silent hike down to the parking lot, my mother finally broke the quiet.

"What was that back there?"

"Forget it," I said, staring at the road ahead. After a minute or two of just trying to breathe, I said, "I guess I panicked a little. It was dark."

She glanced over at me, then back at the road. "I'm sorry," she said, her voice confused.

"It's fine," I mumbled. I looked down at my lap, feeling guilty. But I couldn't imagine ever being able to explain this to her.

After about a half hour more of driving through hills and valleys, past outlying farms and another ruined castle, the landscape became slightly flatter, and then the town of Carmarthen appeared. It was much bigger than Cwm Tawel, with low industrial buildings and newer houses on the outskirts. I could just barely see the remains of a castle on a slight hill above the river, abutted on three sides by modern buildings.

"The city center is cute," Mom said. "Maybe we can go shopping there later this week. Or... or we don't have to. Maybe you want to spend time with your friend."

"It's okay," I said, fidgeting in my seat. She was really trying hard. "We can go."

Mom pulled into a nearby parking lot and I scanned the sidewalk outside the long, low train station. It was five minutes to four. No sign of Gareth yet, or his train. I tried to compose myself, brushing my ponytail and putting on lip gloss. My cheeks were pink and chapped from the chilly breeze, and my eyes looked tired and puffy, but I couldn't do anything about either of these things.

A distant rumble grew louder, and a minute or two later,

a train slowly pulled in. As soon as people started exiting the station, we got out of the car. Two elderly women smiling and chatting in Welsh passed us, then came several men and women with business suits and briefcases and a handful of college students with huge backpacks. And behind the college students was a tallish, skinny guy with a mop of curly light-brown hair and wire-frame glasses, pulling a wheeled brown suitcase behind him that looked like it had seen better days.

My stomach did a flip of nervousness. Gareth waved at us, lugging his suitcase in our direction. His grin was a little lopsided, and his eyes squinted when he smiled. He looked very...normal. And, like when we'd chatted on Skype before, there was something about his smile that made me automatically smile in response.

"Hello," he said, "I'm Gareth Lewis." His voice was quiet, and he sounded anxious. He stuck out a hand and shook hands with my mom.

"I'm Linda Evans. Wyn's been so excited to finally meet you," Mom said, kind of loudly. I blushed. Gareth met my gaze with a slight smile. His eyes were a clear light blue.

"It is nice to meet you—in person, I mean." Had that been my voice? It couldn't have been. Somebody with a high-pitched squeak was talking.

Gareth's smile widened. "Nice to meet you, too." He shook my hand. My hand was sweaty, but so was his. Strangely, that made me feel better.

"Glad I wasn't late," he continued as we headed for the car. "I almost missed the connection. My first train had to stop for sheep on the tracks."

Mom and I both laughed.

"What? It's true," Gareth said.

As Mom drove us along the winding roads back to Cwm Tawel, Gareth and I chatted a little more, but it was weird with my mom there. And maybe because we'd talked online already, it added another level of strangeness, like déjà vu.

Finally the car descended from the hills that bordered the village, emerging on Cwm Road just above the bus station. Following Gareth's directions to his great-granddad's house, Mom drove down one of the side streets and pulled over in front of a small cottage on a street of nearly identical small cottages.

"You don't have to wait," Gareth said. "I've got a key." He got out and heaved his battered suitcase from the trunk.

I shot him an intense look. We needed to talk.

"You have my mobile number. Phone me up tomorrow and we can, I don't know, walk around the village or something." He flashed me that goofy smile for a moment—his teeth were perfectly straight, unlike the stereotypical depiction of British dental hygiene—and then he waved and let himself into the cottage. The door shut behind him.

Mom had just started the car again and was pulling away from the curb when her phone buzzed. I glanced at it; the caller ID said *Gypsy Farm*.

"It must be Dad," Mom said. "Can you pick it up, please?"

"Hello?"

An unfamiliar female voice spilled out of the phone, breathlessly. "Is this Mrs. Evans?"

"This is Wyn," I said, a horrible queasiness taking root in my stomach.

"This is Nurse Morgan. Are you with your mother? Please, you must come straightaway." Her Welsh lilt stood out even more than I remembered. "I'm afraid poor Rhiannon's gone a bit worse."

15

ᚷᚹᚱ ᛒᛁᛖᛁᚦᚱ ᚣᚹ ᚣᚠᛟᚱᚣ.

Tomorrow is a stranger.

. . . .

Welsh proverb

The car careened up the narrow country lane. Mom's face was pale, her lips pressed tightly together, and I was clutching my sweaty hands together in my lap. Despite our speed, it felt like we were never going to get there. We would arrive when it was too late. Maybe it was already too late.

Mom pulled the Ford into the gravel parking lot, not even bothering to lock the doors as we scrambled out. I stopped for a moment in front of the door to the cottage and wiped the sheen of sweat off my forehead, steeling myself to go in.

Muffled voices came from the back bedroom, Dad's baritone murmur and the nurse's sympathetic, lilting reassurances.

I didn't hear Gee Gee. My skin went cold and clammy, and I walked slowly toward the back room.

Gee Gee lay ashen-faced and brittle in the hospital bed, her eyes closed. She was breathing, but shallowly. Dad and the nurse were holding a quiet conversation near the window. I let out a shaky breath, and they both looked over at me.

"Dad," I said quietly. Words fought to get out of my mouth: *I'm sorry; I should have been here; I should never have left the house.* In the end, nothing came out.

Dad was saying something, but I couldn't seem to parse it out into words. Meanwhile, Gee Gee just kept on sleeping. I wondered if she could hear us. If she could see us in her dreams.

And if it wasn't us she was seeing and hearing, then who was it?

The tiny bedroom began to feel choked with people. I backed into the front room, sat heavily on the couch, and dropped my head between my knees. I stayed there for what felt like a long time, staring at the sea-green carpet fibers, until I saw Dad's white Reeboks out of the corner of my eye and felt him sit down next to me.

Sparse, dark stubble patches made Dad's face seem even more tired and old.

"Hey, Wynnie." He sounded exhausted.

"How is she?" My voice was barely above a whisper. "How much longer?"

"Well, she's stable for now," he said. "But she's been in and out of consciousness. Not very alert." He swallowed audibly. "She didn't recognize me when I came in to bring her lunch. She … looked at me like I was a stranger, and then she called me John. She thought I was Granddad." Dad stared off into the distance, his eyes shining.

"Listen, Wynnie," he continued. "It probably won't happen today, or tomorrow, but we're thinking that sometime this week … " He ducked his head for a moment, then looked at me. "You know, you've always been her favorite. It's good you're here. She may not have long, but just the fact that she knows you're around … Well, anyway." He gave me a quick hug.

I tried to stay composed, but my thoughts turned to Olwen. If the other Olwen had been Gee Gee's daughter … how different would things have been if she'd survived? Would Gee Gee have been happier, now, at the end?

We sat there in silence for a few minutes, listening to Mom talk to the nurse.

"I just didn't think it would come so quickly, that's all," Dad said suddenly, his voice rough. "I thought we'd have more time. But she seems ready."

There was another long pause.

"Tired—she seems so tired," he said in a small voice.

I hated to see him look so lost, but I didn't know how to make it better. I didn't even know how to make myself feel better.

It felt like we were all dying a little, too.

Later that night, I lay wide awake listening to drizzle tickling the window. It seemed like a horrible irony that I couldn't sleep while Gee Gee did almost nothing but sleep. My stomach ached with unshed tears. How could I talk to her now?

I got up and padded in stocking feet over to the chair by the window, staring out at the dark and rain. The green hills were invisible, blanketed by cloud cover and shrouded in mist, but I could feel them surrounding the village nonetheless. They seemed almost alive, expectant. But what was I supposed to do? I couldn't keep Gee Gee from dying. And I couldn't save Olwen. I wasn't even sure what Olwen wanted.

I hadn't even dreamed of her lately. My last vivid dream had been about Gee Gee.

I wondered if that might be our only real goodbye.

My cheeks were wet and cold, but I stayed in the chair until a pale orange dawn came and clutched weakly at the hillsides.

When I pried myself out of the chair the next morning, I felt strange and hollow. It was seven a.m., and the rest of the house was still asleep—Dad alone in the double bed and Mom in the reclining chair in Gee Gee's bedroom.

It took me three cups of Earl Grey to feel a little more normal. Meanwhile, Dad began to stir in the bedroom, quietly opening and shutting drawers. The three of us had a hushed breakfast of toast and juice, and then I got dressed in jeans, a black sweater, and hiking boots. Today I would call Gareth. I wanted to stay close; maybe we'd visit the museum.

First, though, I was relegated to chore duty—washing and drying dishes and sorting laundry—while Mom and Dad took turns on the phone: calling the nurse, updating relatives on Gee Gee's health. I was finally heading to the bedroom to retrieve my own phone when there was a brisk knock at the front door of the cottage.

I opened the door and Margie bustled in. "I was just taking a little jaunt up the road, dear. I was so worried since hearing the news yesterday."

"Oh. Thanks." I wasn't sure what else to say. "Do you want some tea?"

"No, thank you, I've just had some at home. We could bring some to Rhiannon, though, perhaps?"

"Maybe some hot water," I said, still standing awkwardly near the door. "She hasn't wanted any tea for a while now."

"Well, well!" Margie said in a tone that implied things must be terribly wrong if one were to reject a cup of tea. Shaking her head, she followed me into the back bedroom, where Gee Gee was lying in a doze, her eyes half-closed.

"Gee Gee?" I pushed a stray, sweaty lock of hair from her forehead. Her eyes opened, but she was silent, and her expression didn't change. I wasn't even sure if she could see me. "It's me, Olwen."

Her blue eyes opened wide and fixed directly on me, making me freeze in place.

"Olwen?" she asked in a shaky, almost fearful-sounding voice. Her lips trembled.

"It's Wyn," I said, a little more loudly. "Margie's here—Margie Robinson."

"How are you keeping then, Rhiannon dear?" Margie didn't seem to notice the strange moment, and it quickly passed as Margie chattered on about local gossip. Every so often Gee Gee would let out a quiet, hoarse "mmm" in response.

I couldn't stop thinking about the sound of her voice, the look on her face when I'd said "It's me, Olwen." Even if I could ask her about what had happened, I didn't think she'd be able to answer.

If I hadn't been desperate, I wouldn't have asked Margie. But the more I thought about it, the more it made sense— after all, she was married to Peter, and Peter had practically grown up with Gee Gee. And if Gee Gee couldn't talk, I'd have to get information anywhere else I could.

When there was a pause in the monologue, I jumped in.

"Margie, do you remember much about wartime?"

She looked up at me. "Well, let's see now. I was just a baby when it all ended, you know!" She pursed her lips thoughtfully, taking the random question in stride. "I can remember Mam and Dad telling me how they celebrated around the wireless after the announcement that the war was over—that was in 1945, the year I was born. They were so happy I'd been born into peacetime, you see."

"What about Gee Gee? I—I never had a chance to really ask," I said, my voice breaking. "I have so many questions for her. What went wrong, why she left. I wish we had more time."

"Oh, my dear." Margie gave me a sad smile and gathered herself up from the bedside. "To be honest, I don't know why she and John left. I never could. I can't even imagine moving to Swansea, let alone overseas."

I followed her out of the room and waited by the front

door as she said goodbye to my parents. Then I trailed after her, my boots crunching on the gravel path.

Margie finally sighed and turned around, looking about as if someone might be listening. But there was nobody to be seen but a blackbird on a low branch of an oak tree.

She lowered her voice. "To tell the truth, dear, she did seem happy to leave. She and John, I remember now—they always seemed so sad." She thought for a moment. "You know, come to think of it, my mother never would let me near Rhiannon when we were out in the town. How strange! *Duw*, I was only four or five, the one encounter I remember clearly. I was in the shop with Mam, who was buying groceries. Rhiannon was there alone. I remember she looked a bit peaked; sad, maybe; she couldn't have been more than twenty-two, twenty-three. Though she looked like a grown woman to me at the time." Margie's face was pensive, her eyes following the blackbird as it hopped along the branch.

"Anyway, I was curious, and I wandered away from Mam to have a look at this beautiful lady with the long dark hair. Like yours," Margie said, flashing me a quick smile. "And then, next thing I knew, Mam had me by the arm and was rushing me out of the store! 'That Rhiannon Evans,' she huffed, 'lucky that John would have her.' She always thought John should have been with someone more mature—he was a widower, you know, before marrying your great-grandmother."

I hadn't known. I frowned, trying to work out how everything fit. "When did they get married?"

"Oh, I don't know, dear. You'll have to ask your dad about

that," Margie said. "It was long before I was paying attention to things like young lads and boyfriends." She winked at me. "If you're interested in the history, you ought to pay a visit to the museum. My Peter's got some stories to tell. He lived in Rhiannon's house from the time he was eight until he was twelve and moved to the farm to work." She looked at her wristwatch. "Dear me, it's time I went back down the bus station before the eleven o'clock gets here."

Margie ambled off down the lane, apparently not in all that much of a hurry. I stayed there under the trees in front of the cottage for a few minutes, my thoughts in a frenzy. Great-Grandpa John, married and widowed before even meeting Gee Gee. Why hadn't anybody said anything about it? Was it some big family secret?

Was Olwen *his* daughter, from his earlier marriage?

Time-wise, it would make sense. But, I realized, if this was the case, wouldn't I have dreamed about Great-Grandpa John more? If my dreams really meant something.

I shook my head, my hands clenched into fists at my sides. I still didn't see how all the pieces fit together.

I got out my phone and dialed Gareth's number.

———

I tried once; twice. But Gareth didn't pick up. I was desperate to talk to him, so I went inside and scrabbled through my backpack for the number he'd given me for his great-granddad's house. Back outside again, I dialed, waiting as the unfamiliar double-ring on the other end of the line repeated itself several times.

Finally, somebody picked up.

"Hello?" The voice sounded elderly, and grumpy.

"Is this Mr. Lewis? Could I speak to Gareth, please?" I said.

"Who is this? Who is calling?"

"This is Gareth's friend, Wyn. Olwen Evans." There it was again—it was as if being in Wales somehow made it more natural to use Olwen and not have to explain myself.

There was a long, awkward silence on the other end of the line. Long enough for me to start wondering if he thought I was some friend of Gareth's, making a prank call. Then I heard him sigh heavily.

"Gareth isn't available. He's in the shower. Call back later."

"But—can I leave a message?"

"He'll be out in a minute. I'm sure he'll ring you. Goodbye now," he said tersely, and hung up.

What was *his* problem? I thought I'd been downright cordial. Frustrated, I shoved my phone into my back pocket and stalked off down the path toward the farmhouse.

On my way back from checking email, I finally got a text message from Gareth: *Stopping by in a bit.*

I read for about an hour until there was a knock on the door. When I opened it, Gareth was standing there holding a bakery box.

The moment I saw him, I broke out in an uncontrollable grin. "Hi," I said.

"Hi. Er—I brought this cake. It's lemon. From the bakery," he added. His cheeks reddened slightly.

"Oh! Thanks. Come on in." I stepped aside so he could enter.

He wiped his feet carefully on the mat—clearly he was well trained—and set the cake on the table near the kitchenette.

"Are your mum and dad here?" He looked around the cottage curiously.

"They're in the back."

"Hello, Mr. and Mrs. Evans," he called, in the general direction of the back bedroom. After a moment, my mom came out.

"Hi, Gareth, it's nice to see you again," she said, and introduced my dad.

"I brought a cake." Gareth shook my dad's hand.

"That's very thoughtful," Dad said. Then there was a long silence while we all stood around. I couldn't think of how to fill the conversational space, and my parents seemed to be giving Gareth the once-over.

Gareth started to look uncomfortable, and finally said, "Look, I don't go around meeting people online usually. Just Wyn, I guess. I think it's brilliant that your family's so proud of being Welsh."

"Yes, she takes after her Gee Gee there," Mom said.

Gareth looked over at me with a small smile, then looked

back at my parents. "My great-granddad sends his best wishes for Mrs. Evans."

"Thank you," Dad said, his face serious. "I'm sure Wyn will fill you in on how Gran's doing." He started for Gee Gee's bedroom, Mom following behind. "You kids have fun chatting. We've got soda in the fridge."

After they'd gone, Gareth pulled a super-serious face and repeated, "You kids have fun chatting" in what sounded like a cowboy voice.

I raised my eyebrows at him and went to get two bulbous bottles of Orangina from the fridge. "Is that what Americans sound like to you?"

"Well, uh, no," he said, following me into the kitchenette. "Okay, sort of. I can't help it. Sorry."

I smiled. "I'll start butchering some Welsh for you, then you'll be sorry."

I sat down on one side of the table and Gareth sat across from me. I slid one of the sodas over to him.

"Thanks," he said. "Your Welsh is probably better than mine. It's been years."

"I haven't had that many chances to practice on actual people," I pointed out.

"Yeah," he said. He looked away. "Sorry," he said again. "It—all of this—must be difficult."

"Yeah," I said. I stared at the table. Then, suddenly, it all spilled out: Gee Gee's decline, the scare of the previous day, and how frustrated and devastated I was feeling that I would probably never be able to talk to her again, never hear her voice again as she sang to me or read to me. I felt the burning of tears behind my eyelids and blinked rapidly. I would not cry, not now.

Gareth just looked at me steadily, his eyes slightly magnified behind his glasses, letting me talk.

After telling him what I'd learned from Margie about Great-Grandpa John, I finally ran out of words, breathing hard as if I'd been running.

"I can see why you'd be cheesed off, not knowing that," he said. "'Course parents never do tell you what you want to know. They're good at keeping secrets."

"I guess my family's *really* good at it," I said, twisting the Orangina cap around and around in my hands.

"Yeah, well... every family's got 'em. You've got me thinking there's something going on with my family now." He softened his words with a half smile. He ducked his head a little, and a completely unruly and slightly tangled section of hair flopped partially over his glasses on one side. I had the momentary urge to reach out and tuck it back behind his ear.

"Hey," he went on. "Do you think maybe your parents don't *know* about your great-granddad being a widower? I mean, if your great-gran never talked about it, maybe she didn't even tell them. Maybe she just didn't think it was important. It was a long time ago."

"I don't know." I frowned slightly. "I'll ask my dad tonight, I guess."

There was a short silence.

"Oh, I brought this for you," Gareth said, pulling a folder out from underneath the cake box. Inside was a tattered map of the South Wales coast.

"Wow, thanks." I flipped open the map, absently. "You know, I tried calling you earlier. I tried to leave a message with your great-grandfather, but he sounded . . . I don't know. Weird."

"Weird?" Gareth looked surprised.

I considered my words. "He actually sounded sort of mad. Angry. I told him who I was, and he just went totally quiet for a minute. Then it was like he couldn't wait to get off the phone."

A puzzled expression crept over Gareth's face, then a tiny frown.

"I didn't know if maybe he didn't like girls calling you or what," I said, flustered. "But I was really hoping to talk to him sometime. Ask him whether he remembers anything about Gee Gee, or even Olwen."

"Hmm. Well, it's probably not you," Gareth said. "He doesn't like the telephone. He usually sounds a bit like a hermit using the phone for the first time in decades."

I tried to smile.

"It's weird, though," he continued. "He's been cranky since I got here. More than usual, I mean. And quieter. He hardly said a word to me when he gave me your phone message. And I wouldn't count on getting any stories out of him, either," he added with a note of regret. "I couldn't get much out of him for my family tree project."

"What's that? A school thing?"

"Yeah, for history class." Gareth nodded. "That's how I found you—your website, I mean. I was doing research on public records. I was going to interview him about old times, but he didn't want to talk."

I looked at him more closely. "What do you mean?"

"I guess he just wants to forget all about it. Maybe it was really tough." He took a gulp of soda.

"Maybe," I agreed. "Seems like a pretty common story."

"I don't know much about his life. You probably think that's pretty sad."

"No, I—" I was about to tell him what a weird coincidence it was that neither one of our great-grandparents seemed to want to talk about anything, when there was a knock at the front door. I swallowed the rest of my sentence as Mom appeared and let in the nurse for her afternoon check on Gee Gee. Then, not five minutes later, there was another knock, and Hugh and Annie swept in with a huge vase of wildflowers.

Now the tiny cottage really did seem to be bursting at the seams. Nurse Morgan, my dad, and Hugh were all crowded into Gee Gee's bedroom, while my mom exchanged pleasantries with Annie in the front room and Gareth and I sat uncomfortably at the table. There were several conversations going on at once, voices everywhere—Hugh's bass rumble, Dad's slightly more subdued tones, the nurse's bubbly briskness, Annie's cheery alto, Mom's crisp and polite guest-voice, and nowhere, nowhere to be heard but in my mind, Gee Gee.

I put my head in my hands, trying to tune it all out.

"Okay?" Gareth asked.

I nodded, but after a moment I could hear my mom's voice getting shrill.

"Don't get the teacups down; I'll take care of it," she fret-ted, shooing my dad out of the tiny kitchenette. "There's only room in here for one of us."

I shot Gareth a pained look, and he smiled sympatheti-cally. "I should go," he said.

Part of me wanted him to stay, but the other part of me wanted to run into my room and pull a pillow over my head. "Thanks again for coming. I wish we could have looked at the map more."

"Well, maybe tomorrow?" Gareth stood and put on his jacket. "I've got a few more photos to show you."

"Definitely," I said, walking with him to the door. "How about meeting at the museum in the morning?" I hoped Gee Gee would be okay while I was gone, because this was some-thing I had to do, while I was here. I didn't want to live my life tentatively, in fear of what might happen. And I already knew what was going to happen with Gee Gee. It was the past I didn't know about; it was the past everyone seemed to be afraid of.

And I didn't think Gee Gee had ever lived tentatively, no matter how bad things had gotten.

"Right," Gareth said. "See you then." There was a long silence. He didn't seem to want to leave, and I couldn't seem to close the door and go back inside.

Then: "Sleep well," he said, "and pleasant dreams." He looked right at me, intensely, his eyes boring into mine, before turning away and heading back down the path toward the lane.

———

I sat up in bed, not sure what had disturbed me. The next thing I knew I was standing next to my bed, looking down at my own sleeping form.

Watching myself sleep made me intensely, viscerally uncomfortable, so I turned away and opened the door that led into the main room.

When I stepped across the threshold, instead of entering our doily-festooned sitting area I was back in that darkened room with the carved, gold-painted mirror—the room where I'd seen Olwen in another dream. The windows were draped with black, not letting in even a scrap of moonlight.

A very pregnant, very young Rhiannon was sitting in a high-backed chair in the corner. An older woman hissed at her, "If you won't go into the hostel, you'll be having it here like a common whore, and everyone will know what you are!" The young Gee Gee recoiled, cringing away in her unyielding seat.

I backed away, astonished, through the door I'd just opened, but instead of being back in my bedroom, I was in yet another version of the same living room. The dark draperies had been replaced by curtains of some kind of plain cloth. I was facing the mirror, and reflected in it was a cot in the corner of the room, next to a heavy wooden bureau. There was a figure lying on the cot, but not asleep; curled up in a fetal position, shoulders shaking. The bottom drawer of the bureau was pulled out and a toddler lay asleep in it, emaciated and small. At the sound of a muffled sob, I turned around.

The room changed again. I was back in the dream I'd had before, the candle glow from the hall growing brighter as little Olwen rounded the corner. A racking cough shuddered her tiny frame.

I couldn't escape. I was trapped in this claustrophobic little bungalow no matter what I tried to do.

I desperately ran toward what seemed to be the front door—muddily, as if slogging through glue—and then I was outside, gulping in the clean air and sun on a clifftop near the sea. Green swaths of grass surrounded me; a crumbling stone steeple was just visible over a rise to one side. In front of me was Rhiannon, crying silently next to pile of stones, Great-Grandpa John standing behind her. His face was stoic and haggard despite his youth. She was gently placing a series of small objects—papers? trinkets?—in her lap, just out of my field of vision, obscured by her body.

A gust of ocean wind, salty and freezing, blew right through me with paralyzing chill and swirled me up, higher and higher, until I felt myself dissolving into it, the molecules of my being dissipating into nothing.

16

No one is wise but he that seeks.

....

Welsh proverb

Gareth kicked a stray ice-cream wrapper into the gutter, his hands shoved deep into his pockets and his shoulders hunched. He was meeting Wyn at the Cwm Tawel Museum in ten minutes, but he still wasn't sure what to say to her. She'd just picked up and moved thousands of miles to a cramped cottage to watch her great-grandmother die, and she had to deal with all of her parents' issues as well. Everything he came up with sounded like a platitude. Besides that, he was impatient at making so little progress in finding Olwen, and annoyed at his great-granddad for being weird to Wyn.

He turned onto Heol Owain Glyndwr. The street was empty, and his footsteps crunched in the gravel on the side of the road. Owain Glyndwr, the great Welsh hero. Gareth had studied him in school, back when he'd lived in Swansea. Owain had led some kind of revolt that had ultimately been quashed.

Gareth hoped it wasn't a sign.

He rounded a curve in the road and caught sight of Wyn standing in front of the small, brick-fronted museum. She gave him a quick wave, her gray raincoat flapping in the wind. *Don't be daft, now*, he told himself. *Just be normal.*

"Hey," Wyn said, smiling a little. "The museum doesn't open for another ten minutes."

He watched as she tried to smooth down the billowing sides of her coat. Her eyes were red-rimmed and dark-shadowed. "Get any rest last night?"

"Not really." She stepped onto the path of white rocks that led around the neatly manicured little flower garden in front of the museum; Gareth followed. "I couldn't sleep, actually. I talked to my dad about what Margie said." She paused, and stopped to smell a rose from a small tree that had been pruned into a perfect ovoid.

"And?"

"You know, I was so sure that Dad had to know about his grandfather. I mean, how could he not?" Wyn didn't look at him, just kept trudging around the short, circular garden path. Gareth stayed quiet, though he was itching to know what had happened. He took off his glasses and cleaned them, the garden and Wyn refracting into blurry versions of themselves.

"When I asked him about John being a widower, he got all weird on me," she finally said. "I guess it's a lot for him to take right now, but I wish he'd told me what he was thinking."

"So he just said nothing?"

"He changed the subject. It seemed like he didn't want to talk about it." Wyn picked up a piece of white gravel and clutched it in her hand. "The strange thing is, I was kind of glad." She looked at him.

Gareth could relate to that. It would be even worse if they tried to explain about Olwen and nobody believed them.

"I'm not really sure how much Dad *does* know," Wyn continued. "It seems like Gee Gee kept everything secret from her life before. In Wales."

Gareth tried a smile. "It's the opposite in my family. My mum's such a gossip, she knows everything even remotely scandalous. Dodgy business transactions, babies conceived slightly out of wedlock—if it happened, she knows about it!"

Wyn smiled at him wryly. "Even if it was your second cousin thrice removed?"

"Yeah. 'Course, I'm not really sure what that even means—'thrice removed.' It's like whoever got removed three times had to have done something really horrible, you know, to get their membership in the family rescinded," he said.

Wyn laughed a little then, a fluttery-sounding thing, and

it was like a tiny spark fired up in his brain. He blushed and looked away.

He'd made her laugh, which was good. But this was all a bit intense, this *thing* between them. Too many coincidences and too much that couldn't be explained, except to each other. That small knot of fear in his stomach that wouldn't go away.

"Well, anyway," Wyn said, serious now. "Gee Gee said how hard life was during the war. So I guess she just wanted to forget about all of that. I don't see how she could, though. Especially if they'd had a daughter who died."

"It must have been a tough time," Gareth said. "My great-granddad doesn't like to talk about those days much either, you know."

"But you'd have to talk about your life to someone, wouldn't you?" Wyn persisted. Gareth had to agree; it seemed odd that nobody was willing to say anything about their pasts. It made him start thinking about conspiracy theories.

"Maybe they were all Jerry spies," he said, half jokingly.

"I'd be ready to believe anything at this point." Wyn shook her head and dropped the white rock with a clatter.

"Well, that's why we're here, isn't it? To get more information." Gareth pointed at the door of the museum, which had just creaked open. A slight blond girl about their age unlocked the heavy iron screen door. "Didn't you say—er—what's-his-name was an evacuated child in your great-gran's house?"

Wyn nodded. "If anyone else still living is going to know what Gee Gee was up to then, I guess it would be Peter Robinson." She looked uncertain.

No, she looked sad. And Gareth found he didn't like it at all. He much preferred Wyn laughing.

He slouched toward the door, hoping this Peter Robinson would shed some light on the subject once and for all. He thought of Olwen—the ghost—and shivered. Maybe they could figure things out without ever needing to go back to the cromlech. Maybe this would be enough.

———

The museum was a tiny, two-room converted house cluttered with period furniture, old photos, and a handful of glass display cases. Wyn seemed fascinated.

"It's so quaint," she said.

Quaint was not Gareth's thing, but he kept quiet. Some of the old artifacts were cool, like the World War II gas mask complete with regulation carrying case. And perhaps the photos would prove useful.

"I'm sure you've been here a million times already," Wyn said, "but I think it's cute."

"Actually, I haven't come here since I was a kid. But it's just the same as I remembered." A bit tedious, he thought.

They both turned as the door at the back opened. A tall, wiry man approached them; he looked at least seventy, with gray hair sticking out of his head every which way. He reminded Gareth of a stork, or maybe a heron. Some kind of gangly waterbird.

"Well now, even if I wasn't expecting you, I'd still know

you were Olwen Evans." The man's serious expression was interrupted momentarily by a crooked smile. To Gareth, it wasn't a reassuring smile—it seemed somehow forced. But Wyn looked pleased, so he kept his mouth shut.

"You've got the same hair Rhiannon did when she was your age. Quite a family resemblance." The man stepped closer. "But I haven't introduced myself. I'm Peter Robinson. Margie's told me about you. And who's this, then?"

"I'm Gareth Lewis." Gareth stuck his hand out and shook Peter's. "My great-granddad lives here in Cwm Tawel. I'm a friend of Wyn's."

"Lewis," Peter repeated, pulling his hand back quickly.

Very odd. Was Peter a hermit? Living out his days in this tiny museum? The thought was somewhat amusing, and Gareth hid a smirk.

As they browsed, Peter hovered behind them, telling them all about the musty old clothes and moldy account ledgers belonging to cottagers and farmers of days past. Finally, though, he did show them something relevant. After going back into the office and rummaging through a huge storage cabinet, he returned with a handful of black-and-white photographs from his own childhood. The one that really stood out to Gareth showed a group of three small children standing with a middle-aged couple in front of a small house. The children were gaunt and hollow-eyed, clutching their bags and gas masks, huge identification labels hanging from their coats like price tags. They looked warily, wearily, at the camera—

an older boy and girl and a smaller, dirty-faced boy wearing shorts and a cap. Peter pointed at the small boy.

"If you can believe it, that was me in 1940 when I arrived at the Davies house. And look here at this one," he said, pulling out a little square photo of the same boy sitting at a wooden table, a spoon poised halfway between his open mouth and a soup bowl. "I gained nearly half a stone that first week. It made the local newspaper! Of course, things had been horrific in Coventry before I left. And here, even with the rations"—he pointed at a ragged coupon book in a nearby display case—"I had so much more than before. And I got a new family. The Davies did so much for the children they took in. It was a shame to leave, but I needed the work, you see. But it was so wonderful. A new home."

Gareth and Wyn peered at another photo of Peter, this one taken a few years later, in 1943. He was eleven years old then, he said. Next to Peter, quite a bit taller than he was, stood a young blond woman holding a cherubic toddler, and a teenage girl who could have been Wyn's sister, they looked so similar.

"That's Gee Gee," Wyn said, her eyes widening.

Gareth felt as if someone had sucked all the air out of his lungs. He knew it was just genetics, but it was still creepy.

"Mr. Robinson." Wyn's voice trembled slightly. "How well did you know my great-grandma?"

Peter looked at her intently. "Let's see now," he said in his breathy voice. "I was eight when I arrived, on the very day that other picture there was taken. I stayed until I was twelve—both my parents were killed, you see, so I had nowhere else to go and it was easier for me just to go on living there. Mr. and Mrs. Davies were like parents to me.

"Rhiannon ... well, she always had a bit of a wild streak. Something of the fey in her, or just rebelliousness, I could never be sure. She was forever doing something that her parents didn't approve of—following the Land Girls around and pretending to be one herself, insisting that her mam teach her how to shoot the family rifle in case the Germans invaded the village, slipping out to meet some young man or other from the nearby farms." Peter chuckled wheezily.

"She had lots of boyfriends, you mean?" Wyn tilted her head, questioning.

"Oh, I can hardly remember now. There was a rumor she'd given Dai, the shop-boy, a peck on the cheek in exchange for an extra week's sugar ration. And then she did sneak out nights, every so often."

Wyn was rapt, and Gareth couldn't help being intrigued himself.

"Most people were convinced she was meeting Dai. But sometimes she told me she would go talk to the other evacuees, or the gypsies at her uncle's farm. I once heard some ladies after church gossiping that she was consorting with a gypsy lad, or worse, an Englishman!" Peter gave us his crooked, birdlike smile. "But I don't believe any of it. No, I know Rhiannon, and nothing of the sort was possible. She was kind and generous with her friendship. That's all."

Wyn looked at Gareth with a slight frown. He shrugged.

"Then, of course, she was ill for a long time—this was just after I moved out to the farm," Peter continued. "And then the baby came into the house."

"What baby?" Gareth asked, nearly in unison with Wyn. His heart beat a little more quickly.

"Why, her cousin's, of course," Peter said. "It was 1944, I believe, some months after I'd left for the farm. There was a little baby girl the family took in. All us evacuees were gone by then, so there was room for the daughter of, oh, Sali, I think it was. I was told that Sali had to return straightaway to the Wrens, that was the Women's Royal Naval Service. I never met her, but saw the child once or twice. Dark hair like all the Davies."

"The cousin's baby? What was her name?" Gareth leaned forward expectantly.

"Oh, I don't remember details like that anymore—can hardly remember my own name, when it comes down to it." That lopsided smile appeared again. "Going senile, Margie says. But once I left for the farm, you know, I hardly kept in touch with the family, I'm sorry to say."

Wyn still had a tiny frown of doubt wrinkling her forehead. And Gareth knew that what Peter was saying was clearly impossible. A cousin's baby. What a load of bollocks.

Every clue they had pointed in the direction of Olwen being Rhiannon's daughter. Wyn's dreams about Rhiannon and Olwen, the plaque Gareth himself had seen … 1944 was when Olwen had been born.

Peter shadowed the two of them to the museum's front door, and Gareth turned back one last time.

"Sir? Do you know of any ancient historical sites near

here? I'm trying to find a place I visited with my parents. It's near an old church." Gareth stopped in the doorway, Wyn a few steps ahead. "I was hoping to visit it again while I'm here."

"Oh, well, I don't get out to the trails much, really," Peter said. "If you hike these coasts long enough, you'll run into all sorts of interesting standing stones and dolmens."

"Do you have any maps?" Gareth asked.

"Margie will have them at the bus station," Peter said. "Now, I must be closing for lunch. Goodbye—*hwyl nawr.*"

"But—" Gareth started, but Wyn pulled him away, and in any case, the door was already shut.

They looked at each other.

"All right?" Gareth asked. "That was weird."

"I'm okay." She kicked at the gravel, crunching it with her shoe. "Peter seems really convinced it was a cousin's baby."

"Yeah," Gareth said, staring up at the sky gloomily. "I don't know, though."

Wyn looked at her phone. "Oh no, I have to go," she said. "I'm supposed to be back by noon."

"Oh. Right." There was a long silence. "Hey, sorry. Tell your parents … " He trailed off awkwardly.

"Thanks," Wyn said, smiling sadly. She gave Gareth a quick hug; he patted her on the back.

Why was this so complicated?

She started off up the road.

———

After running a few errands for his great-granddad—picking up milk and eggs from the grocer, dropping off some mail at the post office—Gareth walked back to the tiny house on the west side of the village. His steps were slow, but his mind raced. Wyn's great-gran. A daughter who died but nobody ever talked about. Olwen. And then there was Rhiannon's family, putting out the story that Rhiannon had had a long bout with illness, passing off the baby as belonging to a cousin. A likely story, but maybe that was what people wanted to believe.

Gareth much preferred the story of Rhiannon sneaking out to meet boys and gypsies and whoever else, despite the danger. Who would have thought Wyn's great-gran would have a reckless streak? Everyone always talked about how much Wyn took after her, too. Was Wyn a closet rebel? Gareth smiled to himself. That could be an interesting avenue of exploration.

Then something clicked, and he stopped abruptly in the middle of the sidewalk on his great-granddad's street, right in front of Mrs. Tilly's yard gnome collection.

Rhiannon sneaked out to meet boys. Rhiannon had a baby. But Rhiannon still lived at home.

Had she and John Evans been fooling around before they were formally married? That would explain a lot. It would explain why the family tried to insist that the baby came from a "cousin." Naturally, they would have wanted to avoid any scandals. And if, perhaps, this all happened while John Evans was still married to his previous wife . . . that would have been quite a scandal indeed.

Gareth felt certain he was right. He hurried down the street to his great-granddad's place, let himself in, unceremoniously dropped the bag of groceries onto the kitchen table, and pulled his phone out of his pocket.

Wyn didn't pick up. He forced himself to take a few calming breaths. She probably just had the ringer off.

He hoped everything was okay.

He didn't want to be that annoying bloke who kept ringing and ringing, so he tried to distract himself by making dinner. Half an hour later, he and his great-granddad were seated at the little kitchen table sharing soft-boiled eggs, a mound of back bacon, and some sliced fruit. It was the most exciting thing in Gareth's cooking repertoire, and in fact it had managed to keep him from checking his phone every thirty seconds.

Now, though, he had it sitting next to his plate. Just in case.

Without realizing it, he was jiggling his foot against the table leg, tap-tap-tap, tap-tap-tap, in a nervous rhythm.

Tap-tap-tap.

"That's enough of that!" His great-granddad glared over at him. "I don't need my eggs scrambled," he said.

"Sorry." Gareth took another bite of egg and bacon, hardly tasting it. What was taking Wyn so long? He couldn't wait to tell her what he'd figured out. She'd be amazed. He couldn't imagine what it would be like to find out something like that about his own dull family.

"You're quiet tonight," Great-Granddad said, peering at Gareth across the table. "Trip to the museum put you to sleep?"

"Not exactly," Gareth said. He hesitated. His great-grand-dad's piercing gaze didn't really inspire one to confide in him. In fact, it sort of made him feel like clamming up, but he forced himself to explain briefly: Rhiannon's illness was worsening. Her family was sad and frantic in their cottage up at the farm. He felt bad for Wyn.

Great-Granddad pushed back the shock of white hair that had fallen over his forehead and kept eating, silently.

Gareth frowned. "I thought you knew Wyn's great-gran."

"Yes... yes," came the irritable response. "It's very sad, of course. Then again, she did have a hard life when she was here. I know it's difficult to think of it this way, but sometimes it's a blessing to make peace with it and leave it all behind."

"What?" Gareth nearly dropped his fork. "Why would you say that?" It made him feel awful, really. It made him feel like maybe his great-granddad shouldn't have been living alone all these years.

"Those war years were not easy, Gareth. Even life on a farm wasn't all leisure and horseback riding the way it is now, you see. I *had* to live out here, me and my mum both, because London was getting bombed. We were in the temporary barracks set up on Rhodri Davies' farm. Milking, sowing, harvesting, everything had to be done, and I had to go to lessons besides. When I was older, I left for the mines. And that's all there is to tell, really. Nothing you haven't heard thousands of times before." He gave Gareth a smile that was more like a grimace.

"Yeah, I know. I guess that would be hard." The conversation seemed closed, but Gareth still had one last question. "It's just that Wyn is trying to find out as much as possible about her great-gran's life, before…you know." He swallowed. "Is that really all there is? Do you remember much about her?"

"Oh, all the young lads liked Rhiannon," his great-granddad said shortly. "High-spirited, very pretty girl. But yes, that's really all there is." He picked up a few empty plates and got heavily to his feet, turning his back and going into the kitchen.

———

Strange, Gareth said to himself later, as he finished brushing his teeth in the house's tiny bathroom. Great-Granddad really didn't want to have that conversation. Or maybe he didn't like Rhiannon. Either way, Gareth couldn't help wishing it was as easy to talk to his great-grandfather as it was for Wyn to talk to her Gee Gee.

He spat foamy toothpaste into the sink, rinsed, then padded back to the guest bedroom. The house only had two bedrooms, so Gareth was sleeping on a narrow twin bed with a squishy mattress that was crammed into the second room along with decades' worth of boxes and files and a wooden desk with old-fashioned pigeonholes along the top. The mess gave him a bit of a headache. If only his great-granddad had been one of those old people who was compulsively tidy.

The flimsy beige curtains were still open, so he went over to the window to shut them, his reflection growing larger in the dark glass as he approached. Suddenly, his reflection disappeared.

He blinked and looked again. His heart thudded. It was no longer his own dim figure in the window glass.

It was Olwen.

The little girl looked sadly at him, a mere ghost of a shape, the dark night bleeding right through her form as if she wasn't there. Which, he supposed, she wasn't. Was she?

Gareth was afraid to look away. He just kept staring at her, and she kept staring back, not moving.

Then his phone rang.

He twitched, then stood perfectly still, his muscles tense. The skin on the back of his neck crawled.

The phone kept ringing. Ringing and ringing, while Olwen just looked at him from the reflection in the window glass.

She opened her mouth. It was moving, but he couldn't hear anything. Of course he couldn't.

Almost as if it weren't under his control, his hand reached out for his phone, lying on the desk. He hit the *Talk* button and held it to his ear.

At first all he heard was the sound of the wind. And then, a voice like a breath, a little girl's voice.

"You promised," she whispered. "I'm so lonely. You promised." All the while, she looked at him, pleading.

He felt as if his heart might break, yet at the same time, he was terrified. He hung up the phone and put it back on the desk. But he didn't look away. Gradually the little girl's form faded, and all he could see through the window was moonlight and the dark shapes of neighbors' houses, his own reflection looking wide-eyed and pale.

He'd said he would come back. When he'd seen her in the cromlech, he'd made a promise. But that fear wouldn't leave him. She was a *ghost*. She *shouldn't exist*.

If he went back there, would he find her? Did she want him to find her? Or was she trying to tell him something else?

He sat down on the bed, heavily, wiping beads of sweat from the back of his neck.

Maybe he shouldn't have hung up. Maybe he should have listened.

17

Y gwir yn erbyn y byd.

The truth against the world.

Motto of the Gorsedd (society)
of Bards of the Isle of Britain

"Why don't you take a break?" Mom said, hovering in the doorway of Gee Gee's bedroom.

I glanced outside. Drizzle was pinging the windows, and a draft seeped in from somewhere. I pulled my crocheted shawl closer around my shoulders and huddled in the armchair. My mind felt dull and my body heavy, too heavy to bother going to the farmhouse to check email.

"I'm worried about you. You've been quiet the last couple

of days." Mom came over to the chair and leaned down, putting an arm around me.

I shrugged and turned my face away. "It's nothing. I'm just tired."

"Well, I want you to know you can talk to me," she said. She knelt next to the chair and put a gentle hand on my cheek, stroking it with her thumb before standing up.

I didn't know what to say. Mom was always the one who did the talking. Even when I tried ... with Dad, for instance. I'd asked him about Great-Grandpa John, tried to start a conversation. But I could hardly get more than a few words out. He'd been abrupt, distracted, as if he wasn't able to deal with anything beyond the immediate situation.

"Mom," I said. And then I stopped. There was a movement from Gee Gee's bed.

I turned to look, and my mother's head turned to follow my gaze.

Gee Gee's eyes were open, staring right at me, her mouth working as if to try to speak. I rushed over to the bed and picked up the tumbler on the nightstand.

"Gee Gee, do you need some water?" I asked. But when I held the cup to her lips, she just shook her head.

"Rhys," Mom called in a strained voice. Dad hurried in from the neighboring bedroom. Gee Gee just continued looking at me, two small tears now running down her papery, lined cheeks.

"My Olwen," she croaked, barely audible. "Olwen, Olwen. *Wela i ti.*"

I sank down on the bed and put my arms around her, but she'd already closed her eyes again and drifted back into sleep, into dreams that made her flutter her eyelids and breathe in rapid, shallow gasps.

"What was that? What did she say?" Mom sounded panicked now. "Do I need to call the nurse?"

"I don't know. She's still breathing. I think she's asleep," I said. I could feel the rise and fall of her chest, the beating of her heart like a small animal.

"She said '*wela i ti*,' which means goodbye," Dad said hoarsely. He came over to me and gently tugged me upright so that we were sitting side by side on the edge of the bed. He leaned against me. "Your Gee Gee loves you very much. You know that, right?"

I nodded, but my throat was too tight to respond.

"She hasn't spoken at all for a day and a half. She—" He paused and took a deep breath. "She must have really wanted to say goodbye to you."

I couldn't move. Gee Gee's words kept ringing in my ears. Olwen, she'd said, not Wyn. And *wela i ti*—it did mean goodbye, true, but according to Hugh, it was more like saying "I'll see you."

Tiny goose bumps appeared on my arms. Of course, Mom and Dad didn't notice. They had no idea there was another Olwen. Only Gareth knew. And Rhiannon, but she wasn't going to tell.

I wanted to tell them. My heart felt like it was going to burst inside my chest, and I clutched my hands into a knot in my lap. But what if they didn't believe me? And why would they, anyway? I had no evidence. I had Gareth's photo of the graveside and the plaque, but they'd probably dismiss that as circumstantial, as coincidence. Plus, I remembered what had happened when I'd tried to talk to my dad about Great-Grandpa John. I didn't want to make him any unhappier.

But I couldn't help feeling that Gee Gee hadn't actually been talking to me.

It felt like she was talking to the other Olwen. To some unseen daughter she hoped was waiting for her somewhere. It seemed plain to me, now, that one of the reasons Gee Gee wanted to come back here was to get some kind of closure, put her mind at rest.

Olwen, though, the little girl—she clearly wasn't at rest. Maybe she was waiting for her mother. She seemed to want us to help her. But why Gareth? What was the connection? Was it just that he'd dropped his phone where Olwen happened to be buried, or was there something else we were missing?

Maybe there was something we had to do, something more we had to find out that would somehow free Olwen. I hung my head and put my hand on Gee Gee's arm, feeling the bones just under the skin. I wanted it all to fit together somehow, to make sense. And I'd have to hope that knowing the truth would set us all free.

I tossed a tuppence coin onto the tiny round table in front of the armchair.

"Ante up," I said. Dad put in his two pence and glared at the cards in his hand. He did not have a poker face. I looked at my hand: a pair of tens, a jack, a four, and a seven. I decided to get rid of the four and seven.

"Are you sure this is a complete deck?" Dad grumbled.

I hid a smile behind my fanned-out cards. "You're just resentful because you already lost a pile of pennies. I bet five."

More coins clinked into the center of the table. It was the only sound in the back bedroom besides our occasional comments, Gee Gee's hoarse breathing, and the droplets pelting the windows. Yesterday's drizzle had turned into yet more rain overnight, covering everything outside with a fine sheen of water. There was a break in the clouds off in the distance, though, and the sun was lighting up the tops of the hills to the east.

We'd been taking turns around the clock watching over Gee Gee since she'd spoken. Mom was out in the front room working on her laptop. Technically it was Dad's turn this morning, but I felt like keeping him company.

"I fold," Dad said.

"Jeez, what a wimp." I grinned and threw my cards down. "All I had was a pair of tens."

"You must get your poker face from your mother," he said. "You should consider a career in law."

Then I heard a small sound from the bed. Gee Gee had shifted slightly, and her breathing suddenly became more ragged and labored. Her eyes were bleary and half-open, and there were tiny beads of sweat on her forehead.

Dad got up and used a soft hand towel to gently wipe her forehead, his face a mask of worry. I patted her neck with the lightest touch of her lily-scented powder, trying to hide the stuffy smell of the room. Her hair hung white and lank against the rose-colored pillowcase. She no longer had the bright-eyed, sharp gaze that she'd had even when we'd first arrived at the cottage, and my heart twisted.

"Gran, do you need to move to a better position?" Dad asked softly. She made a very faint noise in reply, which might have been "mmm-hmm." Together, we gingerly turned her onto her side. At first, her breathing eased, but then it became shallow and rapid, and I looked up at my dad, feeling helpless and terrified.

"Wyn, go get Mom and then call the nurse," he said, his voice too calm. "I'll stay here. Come right back when you're done."

I managed to hold it together long enough to talk to Mom, but my voice trembled as I asked for Lisa Morgan. In the middle of telling her to please come now, tears spilled over my cheeks.

"I'll be there in five minutes," she said. "You did the right thing calling straight away. Take some breaths now and go drink a glass of water and I'll be there in a jiff. *Hwyl nawr.*" Her brisk, lilting voice was soothing, and I managed to pull a few deep, hitching breaths into my lungs before hurrying back into Gee Gee's bedroom.

My parents stood over Gee Gee's bed, silently, watching her breathe. Dad was cradling one of her hands in his own. I joined them, hoping with each inhalation that there would be another breath and another.

I didn't even hear the front door open and close. I looked up briefly when the nurse walked in, but turned quickly back to Gee Gee. Not a moment too soon, because then I heard her sigh, heavily and deeply, as if she were exhaling from every nook and cranny of her body. And then she stopped breathing.

We waited. Nobody moved for what seemed like an eternity, listening for the slightest sound from Rhiannon's motionless figure on the bed. But everything remained silent. She might have been asleep, except there was a strange sort of stillness about her—no breath, no movement. Silence.

I heard a sudden inhalation from my dad, and turned to see his head bowed and his hand clutching Mom's. Mom lay her head on his shoulder, looking smaller somehow.

I felt dazed. Distantly, I realized I should be sad, or maybe scared. But I couldn't seem to muster any emotions except for puzzlement. What was going to happen now?

I opened my mouth, fully intending to ask a whole series of questions, but when I tried to speak, the room tipped and swayed around me. I leaned against the wall behind me and closed my eyes. Maybe I'd just rest here for a minute.

The next moment, Nurse Lisa was supporting my arm, and I heard her as if from far away.

"Better for you to get to bed now," she said, and I didn't protest. I was exhausted.

It was over. It felt like everything was over. I let Lisa lead me to my tiny bedroom and followed her suggestion to lie down on the bed. She tuned the clock radio at my bedside to something soothing. It sounded like folk music in Welsh, and I tried to let the music wash over me, the words flickering in and out of my understanding in a language I'd only half learned, or maybe half forgotten.

I opened my eyes, after a while, when I heard a vehicle pull up outside. My mother opened the door, and I heard her speaking officiously to someone. All I caught was "before the funeral Friday," then a bustle of movement. After that, all was quiet again in the little cottage. I felt an incredible lassitude and closed my eyes again.

The next time I opened them, it was dark. I must have slept, but I had no idea what time it was. After tiptoeing to the bathroom in the dark, I refilled my water glass, put on my pajamas, and slid under the covers. It wasn't raining anymore, but the wind was rustling the leaves right outside my window. It felt like I was in a forest.

Then I thought of my dream about Gee Gee slipping off into the woods with some young man, and my chest ached with tears I was too tired to shed. What really did happen that night? Was the man Great-Grandpa John? If not, then who?

What if I never found out?

———

After I finally dropped off, my sleep kept getting interrupted by dreams: trying to revive Gee Gee as part of a CPR test, and failing; running along the gravel path trying to get to the cottage for some urgent reason but not getting anywhere; trying to explain to Rae and Gareth that I'd had an important dream but they didn't seem to care. I kept shouting Welsh words instead, words that made no sense.

Traeth. Beach.

Cerrig. Stones.

Ysbryd. Ghost.

As I slipped between dreams of anxiety and grief, there was one lucid moment of clarity, almost too vivid to be a dream. I saw myself packing away Gee Gee's things, lifting and folding dresses and pants and shirts. The room took form around me: the empty hospital bed, the profusion of doilies on the furniture. Sadness overtook me like a tide and tears ran down my cheeks. I looked up, trying to force the tears away.

The square of sky visible through the window was pearly gray with a mist that made the village, the whole world, eerily nonexistent. Gee Gee was gone, and maybe everything and everyone else I knew was gone, too.

I shivered, watching myself as if it were an out-of-body experience. I saw myself lifting a metal box, laying the box in my lap, and opening it.

My doppelganger reached into the box as if to draw something out, and then everything dissolved into an incoherent swirl of images. Only one stood out—the little girl Olwen, her expression pleading. It felt more like a dream now, and I had a sudden overwhelming feeling of urgency, that there was something I had to find, or do. I opened my mouth to ask, but I was back in the dream trying to explain to Gareth that I had something important to tell him. We were walking along a grassy path, the sea roaring in the distance. I was urging Gareth to listen to my dream about the metal box, saying something about how we had to find it now because Olwen wanted us to. He was looking at me seriously, nodding, when I noticed that the sky above was darkening moment by moment. I stopped talking, stopped moving forward. One by one, the stars winked out.

There was total darkness. I couldn't even see Gareth beside me. I involuntarily reached out for him and clutched his hand, relieved he was still there. He squeezed back, and then the quality of the darkness changed. The breeze stopped, and I had the feeling we were no longer outdoors but in an enclosed space. I reached out my left hand, the one that wasn't holding tightly to Gareth's, and felt cool, rough stone.

Then I felt an overwhelming loneliness so keen that I nearly dropped to my knees in despair. Somehow I knew it wasn't coming from inside myself, but from outside, and I moved even closer to Gareth, grasping his arm with my other hand. Then the loneliness gained a desperate, wild quality, and a small girl's voice came from everywhere and nowhere.

"I want my mum! You promised, you promised!"

I was scared, really scared. My heart was pounding frantically and there seemed to be no escape. Stone walled us in, all around. But then the darkness started to fade, and gradually I slipped back into a regular dream about home and Rae and scarfing onion rings at the school cafeteria.

For some reason, in the dream, I was crying.

————

The next morning I woke up early, before six. My movements felt mechanical, my limbs like they weren't attached to me, as I pulled on a robe over my pajamas and brushed my teeth at the basin in my room.

When I looked at myself in the mirror above the faucet, I had the odd sensation I was looking at a stranger. I saw a flash of fear cross my face, and then suddenly my dream came flooding back. Along with it came the insistent feeling that there was something I still had to do. Something Olwen wanted from Gareth, from me. My legs felt wobbly and I leaned my hands on the edge of the basin.

The metal box—that had to be important. I'd never dreamed about it before; I was positive of that. Maybe it was something Gareth knew about, something he'd forgotten to tell me. Maybe it was symbolic.

If that was symbolic, then what about the part where I'd clutched Gareth's hand? I knew what Rae would say about it, but Rae wasn't here to tease me. In fact, besides my parents, I didn't really have anyone *except* Gareth.

Maybe that was all the dream was about. Maybe it was my subconscious telling me I did have someone I could talk to. And I did have a phone. This was what it was for.

I glanced at the clock and grimaced. Not at 6 a.m. That would be just plain rude.

I splashed cold water on my face and pulled my hair back into a sloppy bun before emerging into the front room.

Mom and Dad were already up, sitting at the table looking exhausted. Dad had a half-empty bowl of cereal in front of him and was flipping through a newspaper. Mom was working on her laptop, but she looked up long enough to insist I eat something. I took a banana from the fruit bowl and ate it standing up, leaning against the counter.

The banana sat heavily in my stomach as the three of us gathered in Gee Gee's bedroom half an hour later. The room only held objects now—the hospital bed and the clothes and belongings the only reminder that Gee Gee had been alive there just a day ago.

"You're very lucky you had a chance to say goodbye, you know," Mom said softly, running a hand across the quilt before sitting at the foot of the bed.

I shifted uncomfortably. "I know."

"Your mom and I said our last goodbyes before the van came to take her to the mortuary yesterday," Dad said. He sounded matter-of-fact, but the lines around his eyes looked deeper than ever, and my heart ached for him.

"We're going to go through your Gee Gee's things today, maybe box some of them up and see what we want to keep," Mom said, sounding uncharacteristically tentative. She stole a quick look at Dad. "Why don't you spend some time outside and get some fresh air? You probably won't want to hang around all day while we sort through clothes and papers."

A tiny alarm bell went off in my mind.

The metal box. What if it was with Gee Gee's things? I had to find it, or whatever it might once have held. At the very least, I could find something out about Rhiannon's life before.

"I can help," I said. "I don't really feel like going out, anyway."

Dad looked at me with a slight frown and then shrugged. "Okay. We could use another pair of hands."

I tried to explain. "I want to see if she has any old letters or diaries, or anything interesting. Maybe pictures."

"You're welcome to anything like that," Dad said, "but as far as I know she never was much for keeping mementos."

I glanced at the wooden lovespoon, sitting forlornly on the bedside table, and I knew he was wrong.

But after a few hours of packing clothes into bags, and emptying some boxes that Gee Gee had shipped here but never unpacked, we'd come up empty-handed as far as interesting documents were concerned. I had a moment of hope when Mom unearthed a stack of papers from one of the boxes in the closet, but when I dove into it, I only found old utility bills, receipts, and a smattering of random magazine articles about everything from quilting to the Welsh National Assembly. None of it gave me any proof of what Gee Gee had been hiding. If there had been any letters or pictures, she'd hidden them well—or destroyed the evidence.

I couldn't help it; frustrated tears spilled out. I'd been sure I didn't have any more tears left to cry, but apparently I was wrong. Mom and Dad both sat down next to me on the bed and Dad hugged me to his side, letting me cry.

I tried to breathe deeply. *Lleuad.* Moon. *Aderyn.* Bird. *Canu.* To sing.

Gradually, my tears slowed. It seemed like an impossible task, finding something that I wasn't sure existed in the first place. I didn't even know what exactly I was looking for, or if there was even a point to searching anymore.

After a moment, Dad stood up and started rummaging through boxes again. I sighed and stared down at the carpet, trying to focus on the feeling of Mom stroking my hair, tucking escaped strands behind my ears.

The shuffling noises stopped suddenly and I glanced up. Dad was holding Gee Gee's jewelry box, which had been sitting on the dresser.

"Well, I'll be damned," he said, pulling something out of the box. A silver chain glittered as it spilled out of his palm. "Look at this, Wynnie. It's your grandmother's locket. I haven't seen this in years. I thought it was long gone."

That was what Gee Gee had always said; that it was lost. My heart pounded. I reached a hand out, then hesitated.

"Why don't you take it?" Dad said. "She would have wanted you to have it."

"I agree." Mom took the locket from his hand and unclasped it, putting it around my neck and then fastening it carefully. The inch-long silver oval was cold against my skin as it rested on my chest. I looked down at it. It was the same locket from my picture of Gee Gee when she'd first come to the States. I reached up and closed my fingers around it, clutched it as though I could somehow absorb any remaining molecules of Gee Gee from the locket and into myself.

Then I looked up at my dad. He smiled at me, and something inside me loosened.

———————

Later that night, I was lying awake in bed thinking about the funeral. I clenched the bedspread in my hands. I couldn't picture what it would be like; Gee Gee's body had already been cremated. And who would even be there? Would I have to talk to them, these strangers who knew Gee Gee from her former life? If I could steel myself to talk to them, what would they tell me?

I couldn't help thinking that we had to do something more, something other than this funeral for strangers. It felt inadequate.

Dad said Gee Gee wanted her ashes scattered or buried somewhere near the sea; we could take an urn home if we wanted to, but she'd been insistent on a part of her staying in Wales.

I sat up in bed. Really, we *could* do something. We could find the gravesite, like we'd been talking about all this time. We could find that clifftop overlooking the sea. If Gareth and I could locate it, if he could remember where it was, maybe we could bring my parents to the spot and convince them that Gee Gee's ashes belonged there.

That felt right.

I turned on my bedside lamp and picked up the locket from the nightstand. It was silver, tarnished and worn, and looking at it reminded me of when Gee Gee had first moved in with us. I'd looked at her old pictures a lot then, wondering about them, wondering about her. Now I had more questions than ever.

I popped open the hasp and peered at the tiny photograph. It was a black-and-white portrait of a baby wearing a little knit hat. The baby was dark-eyed and solemn, with very cherubic cheeks. Grandpa William? Or someone else? I gingerly pried the photo out with a fingernail, but nothing was written on the back. I replaced it as best I could and closed the locket again.

As the mechanism snapped shut, I thought I heard something rattle inside. Maybe I hadn't put the picture back in properly. I opened it again, but the picture seemed fine. I looked closely, turning it around and around in my hands, and then I noticed something I hadn't seen before: on the inside left door of the locket, the side without the picture, there was another hasp that was barely visible.

There was a second compartment in the locket.

The release button was minuscule, and I pressed it with the edge of my thumbnail so that the little flat door could spring open. When it did, a tiny key fell out. It was about the size of a luggage key, tarnished and old-looking.

I stared at it uncomprehendingly for a few minutes.

Then I thought: *My dream. The metal box.*

It had to be somewhere. I just didn't know where. But I was sure now that it existed, and I was certain that this key would open it.

18

Nid hawdd cuddio rhag amser.

It is not easy to
hide from time.

Welsh proverb

The day of the funeral, the sun came out for the first time in a week. Gee Gee would have been happy to see it, the golden rays painting the hillsides and dappling tree-shadows on the ground. I had to squint against the brightness, look away.

As we arrived at the Methodist chapel, there were already a few people wearing somber colors gathered outside, speaking in quiet, muffled voices. A small group.

Maybe more would arrive soon.

I walked up the path leading through the churchyard, my parents behind me. Unlike the Anglican church on the east side of the town, there was no wooden-roofed lych-gate leading into the yard, no elaborate stained glass or ornate carvings. It was just a simple, whitewashed stone building with square windows and a squat clock tower with a heavy-looking bell inside. The bell was green with patina, and weathered; it looked as if it hadn't been used in decades.

I saw a few familiar faces—Hugh and Annie, Margie and Peter—but even as I said hello, there was an odd, stiff feeling pervading the atmosphere. Not only that, but it seemed like people were staring.

Not at my parents, but at me.

"That's the great-granddaughter!" A stage whisper—it came from a small knot of three gossiping elderly women in old-fashioned black hats.

"No!" another voice said softly. "Oh, yes, I do see it now!"

The women nodded politely as we went by, but they stared hard at me. My parents didn't seem to notice. I felt a surge of anger, felt like ripping their silly hats off their heads and yelling, "She didn't do anything wrong!" Instead, I ducked my head, feeling my cheeks flame. I didn't really know exactly what Gee Gee did or didn't do.

The chapel lawn was bright green, and the grass was dotted with tiny yellow wildflowers that waved in the breeze. At the top of the lawn, on a short concrete stairway, stood Gareth, looking uncomfortable in dress clothes and a loud red-and-blue argyle-patterned tie. The man with him was clearly his great-granddad, a bushy-browed old man wearing a dark suit and a moody expression. I self-consciously smoothed down my long black skirt and quickened my pace. My low-heeled shoes clopped a little on the pavement, breaking the hush.

Just before I reached them, Gareth's great-grandfather abruptly turned and went through the chapel's wooden doors. A faint drift of organ music reached my ears as the doors opened and then shut. Gareth trotted down the stairs to meet me.

"I was hoping to meet your great-granddad," I said. People were being so bizarre. I would have liked to think it was just the situation, the funeral, but it felt like more than that.

"He went in to get a seat," Gareth said, then hesitated a moment. "Um, sorry again about your great-gran." He gave me an awkward hug.

"Yeah. Thanks." My stomach flip-flopped as I remembered my dream, remembered what it felt like to hold his hand.

We pulled apart and stood silently for a moment. I couldn't quite meet his eyes.

"Interesting tie," I finally said.

"I had to borrow one from my great-granddad." A faint hint of a blush reddened Gareth's ears.

"It's ... well, it's a little 1970s, that's all." I fingered his tie for a moment and then straightened it as well as I could.

"Or 1870s," Gareth said, one side of his mouth twitching upwards in a smile. I managed a faint smile of my own.

I moved aside to make room for the gossipy ladies, who were making their way inside the chapel. Behind them came my parents. Dad put a hand on the small of Mom's back as she mounted the steps.

"Hello, Mr. Evans, Mrs. Evans. I'm sorry for your loss," Gareth said stiffly. His ears reddened again as he shook both of their hands. They nodded and thanked him, then went on to greet more people inside the chapel. Mom looked pale and washed out, and Dad's eyes were sad and lined. I wondered if they felt as sick inside as I did.

"I have to tell you … " I put a hand on Gareth's arm, then changed my mind and drew it back. In a low voice, I said, "I had this dream a few nights ago, about Olwen."

"Yeah?" Gareth moved closer, his eyes searching my face.

"It was weird. Complicated. At first, I was in the cottage, packing away Gee Gee's belongings. I found a metal box, and it seemed important, but then the dream changed. You were in it, and we were walking along a path near the sea."

Gareth looked at me strangely, his eyebrows raised and mouth half-open as if to say something. Then the church bell gave a single, deep bong. All the hushed conversations went silent and people began to gather in small groups to file into the church.

"Let's talk after the service," I whispered loudly. Then Mom was taking hold of my arm and gently pulling me up the steps into the dimly lit chapel. Gareth nodded, still staring at me, and followed us in.

Everything inside was either made of dark wood, like the benches, or painted the same stark white as the exterior. Even the walls were lined with dark wooden panels up to the wainscoting, and above that, white paint soaring up to the dark beams of the ceiling. Despite the light filtering in through the small square windows, the place felt dark; it had an air of seriousness, and I felt nervous and exposed.

I was glad Gee Gee wouldn't be buried here, at this chapel. I wanted to see her reunited with the sand and the wind and the sea. Not moldering away inside this oppressive place.

Someone cleared their throat, which echoed around the cavernous room. Then I heard the plink of a piano. All the whispers went silent.

The service began with a hymn, slow and resonant, from a tiny choir up in the balcony that included the three gossips from outside. Soon, scattered voices throughout the chapel picked up the melody, and then the harmonies. There were only about twenty people standing among the worn pews, but it sounded as if there were twice as many, the sound swelling rich and full.

Arglwydd, dyma fi. Lord, here I am.

I couldn't understand the rest, so I just closed my eyes and let the music wash over me. I leaned against my dad and felt the vibrations in his chest as he hummed along. In my mind, I could see Gee Gee, lying there as if asleep, her emaciated face seeming relaxed and relieved. My sadness was a hard knot in my chest, a piece of wood.

Everything after that blurred together. Somebody said a greeting in Welsh, then in English. Dad went up and said a few words—nothing I could remember later. Then Mom. Then the Lord's Prayer, in both languages. Then it was all over, the congregation and choir once again joining their voices in a mournful song called "Aberystwyth." The slow, stately notes sounded timeless, and unbearably sad.

The final verse was sung in English, and chills ran up and down my spine as I heard the words ring out in the dim, dark hall:

"Jesus, lover of my soul,/Let me to thy bosom fly,/While the nearer waters roll,/While the tempest still is high;/Hide me, O my Savior, hide/Till the storm of life is past;/Safe into the haven guide,/O receive my soul at last."

My breath hitched in my lungs. I hadn't prayed since I was little, but as the last notes of the hymn rang in my ears, I squeezed my eyes shut and begged whoever might be listening, out there in the darkness, to help Gee Gee be at rest now.

What about Olwen, though? Could I do the same for her? I didn't know.

———————

Afterward, Mom, Dad, and I took up spots at the bottom of the steps, shaking the hands of stranger after stranger as they passed by, filing out of the chapel. Gareth gave his condolences again, apologizing for his great-granddad, who had slipped out sometime during the final hymn. Hugh and Annie hovered at the back of the line until the crowd died down. Then Hugh grasped Dad's hand in both of his meaty paws, looking like he was about to cry himself. Annie gripped me in a forceful hug.

I scanned the last stragglers milling around outside, trying to find Gareth. After a few moments, I located his conspicuous tie. I hurried over and grabbed him, ignoring the shiver that arose at the feeling of his arm under my hands, and pulled him off to the side a few feet, behind a gnarled old tree.

"We have to talk," I said, loosening my grip on his arm with a conscious effort. I felt that same sense of urgency rising again, the feeling that kept hounding me. "We have to figure out what to do about Olwen."

"Yeah," he said, pushing his glasses up his nose. He looked thoughtful. "And your dream ... I had something to tell you about that."

"Wyn!" My mother's voice rose above the sound of the crowd and the wind.

I sighed. "You're coming back to the farmhouse, right?"

"Should I bring something?" Gareth asked. "Don't people always take casseroles to these things? Except the only thing I can make is eggs and bacon."

"You don't have to," I said, trying to smile. "Just ... please come."

Dad was pulling the car up in the lane outside the gate, so I shot one last forlorn glance at Gareth and walked away.

———

It was only four thirty, and I was already tired of complete strangers coming up to me and telling me how much I looked like my great-grandmother when she was young, then simpering sympathetically and going off to stuff their faces at the food table.

If they'd said anything about the other Olwen, I might have been interested. Instead, I had to plaster on a fake smile as people flowed in and out of the old farmhouse, bringing in covered dishes of food, lingering to talk to my parents where they stood by the old stone fireplace. A chaos of competing smells was making me faintly nauseated: casseroles, pasta dishes, cakes. Mrs. Magee kept flitting back and forth in the background with an anxious frown, and for once I felt like frowning along with her.

I put a hand to the front of my dark-gray sweater and felt the comforting shape of the locket underneath, resting against my skin. *Soon*, I told myself.

After a while, Gareth walked in, wearing the same outfit he'd had on earlier but minus the garish tie. He was alone, carrying yet another cake box and a small grease-spotted paper bag. After he put the cake on the table and politely greeted my parents again, we moved out of earshot and Gareth presented the bag with a flourish.

"For me?" I said, smiling a little. Whatever it was, it was greasy and fried and it smelled amazing. My stomach let out an audible growl.

Gareth grinned. "Onion rings. Still hot. I remember you blogging about eating them with your friend, and I thought you might miss it, so ... "

"Where did you get onion rings here?" I felt like I might cry.

"The fish and chips shop was still open, so I had them fry some up," he admitted. "They don't normally have them, but my great-granddad knows the owner." He ducked his head. "Hope they're okay."

I swallowed, my throat tight. "Let's take them outside."

I took two plastic plates from the stack on the food table and grabbed a fistful of napkins. Dad was busy talking to one of his distant cousins over by the hearth, and Mom was already starting to pack the remaining dishes of food into a cardboard box.

"Can you two help me? I need to take this back to the cottage," she said. I opened my mouth to protest. "Then you'll be free, I promise."

I shut my mouth and nodded. I didn't want to argue. Not today. And even though I didn't feel like I could do one single thing more today, I handed the onion rings and plates to Gareth and took the box Mom handed me.

Soon.

When we stepped outside, the sun was low in the sky, shining orange light through the trees. Birds were making a ruckus in the top branches. I took deep breaths of the crisp, damp air as we walked as quickly as possible down the path.

Inside the cottage, I put the box of dishes on the table and helped Mom load the small fridge. By the time we were done, it was jam-packed with casserole dishes and Tupperware.

"I'll give you some to take home," I told Gareth.

"You don't have to," he said, "but cheers."

"So," I said after a pause. "About those onion rings."

He turned to my mom and held up the greasy bag. "Could I stay for a bit? I brought these specially for Wyn."

She nodded and tilted her head toward the sitting area. "Just for a bit. And take some sodas with you. God knows we need the room in the refrigerator."

Gareth and I sat on the couch about a foot apart, our snacks on the coffee table in front of us. As we ate, it felt like the space between us was charged with static. I tried to ignore the feeling by cramming food into my mouth.

The onion rings were the best I'd ever eaten, and I said so.

Gareth looked inordinately pleased. I felt my face get hot, and I looked away, toward the kitchenette. Mom was at the sink now, the sound of running water mingling with the clatter of dishes.

"Well?"

I turned back. Gareth was looking at me expectantly. I began in a low voice, so Mom couldn't overhear.

"Okay. Here's the thing. You know that dream I told you about, where I found the metal box?" He nodded. "Well, it was like a lockbox, with something important in it. When I woke up, I was so sure it would be here, but I couldn't find anything like it when we went through Gee Gee's stuff. All I found was a key, a tiny key."

"So you checked all her things?" Gareth asked.

"Yes. That box has got to be somewhere," I said. "I just don't know where. This might sound weird, but ... I feel like we're *supposed* to find it."

"I know what you mean." Gareth fiddled with his napkin,

then set it on the table. "Listen, though. I—I think I might know where the metal box is."

"Really?" My heart started beating a little more quickly and I looked up at him. He was pulling his phone out of his pocket, tapping the screen with quick fingers.

"Have a look at this," he said. "I kept staring at my pictures of the clifftop, over and over, wondering if I'd missed some detail." He pulled up a picture and held it out in front of me: the grave plaque, the slate embedded in the ground. "And then I saw this." He swallowed, and I could see his hand trembling just slightly. "I saw it that day, too, but I forgot about it."

I looked at him questioningly and he enlarged the picture, zooming in on the bottom right corner. "At first all you see is weeds and dirt, but look." He pointed.

I saw a glint of something metal, sticking up out of the ground. A corner.

"I wasn't sure what I was looking at, but when you said that about the metal box ... " He looked at me, his face serious. "If we can get back to that spot, we can find out for sure, yeah?"

"As long as nobody's taken it," I said. "But maybe you're right." Then again, maybe it was just a scrap of aluminum can. I was afraid to hope too much, but I said, "So let me show you the key."

I unfastened the locket around my neck, popped open the compartment, and poked at the smaller hasp inside until the second door opened and the key fell out into my lap.

"It must open something," I said.

"Keys usually do." Gareth gazed at it. "We'd just have to try it, of course. But I don't know for sure where the plaque is. My mum and dad said you can walk there from the beach, though."

"Well, we've both dreamed about the place, and you have a map. Why don't we go look for it tomorrow?" I felt like my entire body was humming, and I didn't know if it was excitement or fear or exhaustion.

"Okay, but we should maybe study the map first. And the bus schedule—"

"It'll be fine." I had to know for sure what Gee Gee had been hiding. I had to know who Olwen was. "I know we have to do this. I know we'll find it. If we're meant to."

He nodded, not arguing the point.

We sat in silence. I didn't know what Gareth was thinking, but I was already making a mental list of what I'd need to bring tomorrow.

After a minute, he shifted, scooting to the edge of the cushion. "Suppose I'd better get back."

"Wait." I took a deep breath. "I didn't tell you the rest of my dream."

"Oh—right," he said with an unreadable look. "So tell me."

"After the part about the metal box…" I stopped. I couldn't look at him. "Like I said, you were in it. I dreamed we were walking on a path by the ocean. The two of us."

There was a short silence. Then: "The stars started going out," Gareth said, his voice hoarse.

"Then everything went dark and we were underground…"

"…in the cromlech, listening to Olwen," Gareth finished, staring at me, his eyes wide. "She wants her mum."

Goose bumps rose up all over my arms. It had felt like more than just a dream. It had felt like…like a real place, somewhere we'd been together. In a way, I'd known this since the funeral, when he'd looked at me with that strange expression on his face.

I looked at his hands, gripping the edge of the couch cushion, and felt suddenly shy.

"We have to go there," I said, winding a lock of hair around my finger. "She wanted you to come back."

Gareth looked haunted. "I guess she would have been your great-aunt if she'd survived. But there must be more to the story. Why'd she choose me?"

"You were there," I pointed out. That much seemed obvious.

He nodded, but his expression was full of doubt. And fear.

"We'll find out," I said, trying to sound more confident than I felt.

"Yes. But are you sure tomorrow is good? Don't you want some time to, I don't know, recover?"

"Gareth, I don't have that kind of time," I said desperately. "I don't know how much longer we're going to be here." I looked at him pleadingly. "I'll do it alone if I have to."

"No, I'll go," he said quickly. "I'm the one who's been

to the place, after all. I'll study the map tonight and we can take the bus out there tomorrow and hike around."

"Okay, good." I got up and he followed me to the door, where we hovered awkwardly, carefully avoiding touching each other. It felt like any physical contact might be too much, too intense; or worse, that it might suck me back into the darkness of a dream world.

I wasn't sure I could handle that again.

19

Nid anhawdd ond cael gwirionedd.

There is nothing difficult but to find the truth.

Welsh proverb

Gareth woke to the sound of his phone's alarm beeping quietly at him. He sat up and rubbed the back of his neck, which had a crick in it from the lumpy pillow. It was eight o'clock—an hour before he'd agreed to meet Wyn for their search for the cromlech.

Search for the Cromlech. It sounded like a Star Trek movie.

"Our mission: to explore strange old beaches…To seek out old graves and old ruined churches…To boldly go where all the local teenagers have snogged before," he muttered to no one in particular, trying to psych himself up. The house was empty; his great-granddad had already left for Sunday morning chapel.

It struck Gareth, again, that he and his great-granddad hadn't talked much during the visit. Yes, he'd spent a lot of time with Wyn and her family, but that didn't fully explain it. When his family had visited in the spring, Great-Granddad was his usual opinionated self. But this time … maybe he was getting lonely and shouldn't be living by himself? Or maybe he was more upset about Rhiannon's death than he wanted to admit. Gareth wasn't sure.

After breakfast, he made a couple of sandwiches and threw them into his rucksack along with a pair of oranges and a few water bottles. When he opened the front door to leave, a folded note fell onto the door mat. A flyer, probably. Or a note from Mrs. Tilly asking Great-Granddad to come round for tea again. She was forever knocking at the door instead of just using the phone like everyone else.

Gareth picked up the note and was going to set it on the kitchen table, but his curiosity got the better of him. He unfolded the sheet of paper.

If You Had Any Sense At All You'd Stop Asking So Many Questions And Leave Well Enough Alone. Some Secrets Are Best Left Buried. Stop Disrupting The Peace Of Our Town, Please.

It had been written in generically blocky, hand-printed letters. And it was obviously meant for Gareth himself.

For a moment, he didn't know whether to be worried or burst out laughing. "Stop disrupting the peace of our town, please"? He smirked. Obviously someone didn't want them to find out what happened—probably some gossipy old bat with nothing better to do. But a melodramatic note wasn't going to stop him. He crumpled the note and stuffed it into his jacket pocket with a wry smile.

What about Wyn, though? Had she been threatened, too? A thread of worry made his smile falter. What would they do if she had?

A sea of other what-ifs swirled in his mind as he locked the door and walked down the lane toward Cwm Road. What if Wyn wasn't waiting at the bus station? What if the bus didn't come? What if they couldn't find the place? What would happen if they never found the metal box? What if they were looking in the wrong place?

What if it *was* the right place?

That thought was just as frightening.

At least one of his fears was allayed when he got to the tiny cottage of a bus stop and Wyn was waiting outside for him.

"G'morning," he said, feeling his face flush for no reason.

"Hi." Wyn was shifting from foot to foot in the morning chill. She looked exhausted, and her eyes were puffy and red. She also looked different, somehow, and he realized it was because she wasn't wearing her usual long skirt and sweater, with her hair hanging long and straight. Instead, she wore jeans and a dull beige jacket that was too big for her, and her hair was pulled tightly back.

"Are you sure you want to do this now?" he asked. "We could wait until tomorrow."

"Um, no. It took me half an hour to convince my parents to let me out of the house today. We are definitely going." Wyn frowned.

"Okay." Gareth took a step back. If she was up for it, so was he. He had to be.

They chatted idly while waiting for the bus to arrive, Wyn asking him questions about his family and about his life in London. She didn't mention anything about getting a note, and he decided against telling her. She had plenty to worry about already.

The bus when it arrived was clean and new-looking, and it cruised quietly through the middle of town, then out into the hills to the south, green hulks still cloaked with rags of mist. Gareth was trying not to think about Olwen, but he kept envisioning the ghost girl's ethereal, floating dress and her mournful eyes. He couldn't let Wyn go to the gravesite on her own. Especially after getting that note.

Gareth looked at her out of the corner of his eye. She was staring out the window, one hand playing with the zipper on her jacket. He saw her chest rise and fall in a silent sigh.

Feeling a bit desperate, he reached into his bag for the old Ordnance Survey map he'd rescued from his parents. He carefully spread it out across both their laps and pointed at one of the likely seeming spots he'd circled in pencil.

"I found three possible places," he said, trying to sound optimistic. "There are only three here that have ruins, cairns, and standing stones all together. So I looked for that when I checked over the map last night."

"Wow, that's great," Wyn said, turning to face him. She smiled, but it seemed to take an effort. "Did any of them ring a bell?"

"Well, no," he admitted. "One of the spots seems a bit far, though. A couple of miles away from the beach, it looks like. Here's the one just to the east, and the other one a few miles further." He jabbed a finger at the map and accidentally poked her in the knee. "Sorry. There's also one to the west, right here, but I don't think that's it."

He was more nervous than he wanted to let on, even to himself. He wasn't sure what the cost of failure would be, but if it meant getting phone calls from a ghost for the rest of his life, he wanted no part of it.

"When's the last bus back?" Wyn asked, after a moment of silently staring at the map.

He took his phone out and checked the schedule. "Four o'clock, looks like. Good thing it's not raining today." The sun was still weak but poked promisingly through the slight cloud cover. It would be chilly, but it probably wouldn't be wet. He had a fleeting visceral memory of falling on his hands and knees into the wet grass, his phone flying off into the darkness of the cromlech, and shivered slightly.

A few minutes later, the bus stopped at one end of a small, crowded parking lot. The caravan park was at the opposite, western end, with its orderly rows of trailers; the beach itself was right in front of them. When the bus doors opened, a blast of cool air swept in, smelling of brine and decaying sea life.

Gareth hitched up his backpack and they began to weave through the cars in the parking lot. The beach was thronged with people, and children in sun suits and hats ran everywhere. Most of the people were gathered by the caravans, where the sand formed a nearly perfect beige arc and the water was a clear green-blue. Toward the eastern end, the ocean's surface was darker, the water deeper and constellated with lumps of rock. The largest of these was covered in a clamoring mass of seabirds.

"It really does look like Northern California," Wyn said. "I can't believe so many people are hanging out on the beach in this weather, though."

"Believe me, this is nice for South Wales," Gareth said. "If it's not freezing and raining on you, then it's off to the seaside." They reached the sand, their shoes sinking into the soft surface, and stopped.

"That's true back home, too. The water's usually too cold for me, though." Wyn laughed briefly, then went quiet again.

"I guess we'd better figure out what to do next," she said, staring out at the water.

Gareth nodded and brought the map back out. "I'm thinking we should start with the two areas we're already closer to, on the east side," he said. "First, this one, which should be just up that path—" He pointed toward a trail that led from the parking lot up to a clifftop viewpoint. "And if that's not it, we can hike to the one that's farther away."

"What about the third one?"

"I don't know if we'll have time today. We can always come back and try again."

"My parents are already talking about leaving," Wyn said, her voice soft. She looked down at the sand. "I don't know if I'll have another chance."

"Well, if it helps, I'm almost positive it isn't the one off to the west," Gareth said, trying to sound more confident than he felt.

"I hope you're right." Wyn grimaced. "It's a good thing you brought the map."

Gareth folded it up and put it back in his pocket. "Off that way, then," he said, pointing to the eastern trailhead.

They walked along the beach as far as possible, the breeze occasionally gusting into a salty, misty wind that whistled past his ears. The cries of the seabirds were eerily like those of the playing children in the distance. He could taste the salt on his lips.

Wyn was quiet on their walk up the dirt trail, but he could sense her tension. He was anxious, too, more and more so as the morning wore into midday. Then, without warning, they reached the first of the spots he'd circled on the map.

At least, he thought it was the spot—there was no visible marker, but there was a ruined building off to their left, about halfway up a lush green hillside. But it was wrong. It was nothing but a set of four crumbled walls, with some farmer's sheep grazing all around and even in the middle of the old building. One or two of the woolly, black-faced sheep bleated in alarm as they passed, looking up stupidly.

Gareth knew with an unwavering certainty that this was not the place, and said so.

Wyn's face fell. "I guess I knew it, too," she said. She looked around, then back at him. "I'm just scared we won't find it."

He shrugged. "I guess we should go on. Or do you feel like stopping for lunch? I brought some."

"Let's stop closer to the ocean," she said. They walked down the path a little bit farther, skirting a two-foot sinkhole that led down into crashing surf. Cresting a small rise, they came upon a standing stone.

Gareth sat down, leaning his back against the scarred and pitted surface of the ancient stone. Wyn followed suit, and they watched the tiny people swarming across the beach below as Gareth brought out the sandwiches and oranges he'd packed.

"Here we are," he said. "Cheese and tomato."

"To-MAH-to," she repeated, then raised her eyebrows at him.

"I realize you eat to-MAY-toes over in the States, but we don't get those here."

"Right-o." Wyn laughed, seeming more relaxed than she had earlier, and took the water bottle he handed her.

After a quick lunch, they double-checked the map and set off down the trail to find the other site. Time was getting short, and they set a brisk pace. Up one rise, down the next; looping slightly inland among meadowlike grassy fields, and then back toward the sea, turquoise waters punctuated by lumps of dark rock. They occasionally passed the purplish stack rock that had always fascinated Gareth as a boy, rising up the cliffs in narrow columns like layers of stone flipped diagonally.

The whole time they walked, his sense of familiarity grew, and his unease. A headache began to throb behind his temples. The minutes ticked by. Neither of them spoke. Gareth wondered if Wyn was feeling what he was feeling—creeped out.

The path they were on was just like the one in his dream. *Their* dream.

The main difference between the dream and reality, though, as far as he could tell, was that they were walking along without conversation. In fact, the silence between him and her and the sea was nearly tangible, pushing them apart like an invisible wind.

Also, of course, in the dream they'd been holding hands. Another key discrepancy.

Gareth thought about reaching across that unseen divide. His hand twitched, but he kept it at his side.

Then, the path widened, and it was suddenly just as Gareth remembered it. The sea smell of the wind, the grassy, flower-speckled meadows stretching to either side in expanses of green and yellow and purple. As they panted up a slight slope, the path turned inward—and there, beyond a series of gentle rises, was the ruined church, its crumbling spire just visible above the hillside.

And there was something else: a chain-link fence, stretching as far as he could see in either direction.

Gareth's heart sank. He jogged a few steps closer, Wyn

right on his heels. A large, official-looking sign was attached to the fence, reading in red, angry letters:

Perygl / Danger
Dim Mynediad / No Entry

In smaller print beneath, it said: *Closed for restorations. Please keep out of the construction area. The National Trust and CADW will reopen the Llanddewi Historical Preserve in January. Thank you for your cooperation.*

"January?" Gareth said faintly. "They must be joking." What would they do now? All the awful feelings of nervousness and dread he'd been trying to ignore threatened to come crashing down on him.

"But this is the place, isn't it?" Wyn said in a small voice. "It looks so familiar."

"Yes, it's definitely the right place." Gareth didn't know how to react. A surge of disappointment swept over him and he turned away, away from the sign and the forbiddingly tall chain-link fence that hadn't been there just a few months ago. He put a hand to the back of his neck and stared down at the trampled grassy path.

Several minutes passed, neither of them saying a word. The only sounds were the whooshing of the wind and the occasional cry of a gull. Gareth's brain felt totally empty. He couldn't imagine what to do now.

Then, barely audible, Wyn said, "I think we should go in."

Gareth looked at her. Was she daft? "Er, maybe you didn't see it, but there's a giant fence and a 'do not enter' sign," he said. "That's going to make things difficult."

Wyn stared back at him. The wind gusted around her, whipping her long dark hair around her face in snake-like strands that looked like living things. For a moment, he thought of the old historical descriptions of the druid priestesses of Wales, who'd supposedly screamed furious curses at the invading Roman armies. He leaned back, apprehensive. But Wyn's face was rigid and determined.

"You can do whatever you want. But I'm climbing over."

20

Diwedd y gân yw'r geiniog.

At the end of the song comes the payment.

Welsh proverb

I squashed down my nervousness and stepped up to the fence. Was it electrified? I didn't think so, but I'd find out soon enough.

Gareth just stood there, a few feet back on the trail, staring at me. I hoped he would follow me. I hoped I wasn't crazy.

But he didn't know how desperate I was. He didn't know what I'd dreamed last night—that it had been worse than anything I'd dreamed so far.

I wasn't going to think about that. Swallowing hard, I stuffed my wind-blown ponytail down into the collar of my dad's jacket, reached out, and grabbed onto the fence with one hand.

Nothing happened. I let out a long breath I hadn't realized I was holding. I dug one toe, then another, into the holes in the chain-link and started to climb. Ignoring the pain of the wire digging into my hands, I quickly reached the top. The fence was probably about seven feet high, but it seemed like twenty feet as I looked back down at Gareth. My head swam. I looked back up and focused on the fence—on my hands and feet, secure where they gripped the wire—and took deep breaths.

There was an edging of barbed wire, strung to the tall supporting poles, that extended about eight inches above the top of the fence; three parallel strands of wicked-looking metal that extended outward toward me at a slight diagonal. No problem, I tried to tell myself. You've gotten this far. I took my time, edging to the side so I could hold on to one of the supporting poles and pull myself up, so that I was standing near the top of the chain-link, both hands gripping the post. I clenched my teeth, let my body hang outward, and swung one leg high—up and over the barbed wire. Now I was straddling the top of the fence at a slight angle, my legs bowed awkwardly to avoid the barbs.

Okay.

Now the other leg. I hung on to the post for dear life and swung my right leg over. There was a heart-stopping moment as one of the spiky barbs snagged my jeans, but it didn't penetrate the thick fabric. I closed my eyes briefly, just hanging there, thankful I hadn't worn a skirt. Then I hastily clambered down and jumped the last few feet to the patchy grass below, breathing hard.

"Someone could be in there." Gareth looked at me through the chain-link diamonds, his face scrunched into a worried frown.

"On a Sunday?" The breeze picked up for a moment, gusting past with the eerily familiar smell of pasture and ocean, and I shivered. "I'm going, whether you come or not." My voice sounded a lot more confident than I felt; my hands, sore from clutching the fence so hard, were trembling.

Before I could lose my nerve, I turned and continued walking along the closed-off path. It was so much like my dream with Gareth that I almost wondered if I was still dreaming. The green-and-yellow sweep of hillside was dotted with tiny flowers, idyllic and pastoral, but I knew what would be visible once I topped the next few rises, and nervous sweat trickled down my sides. I turned and looked back. Gareth hadn't moved. I curled my hands into fists, letting disappointment wash over me. But I was here, and there was no way I was going to let this chance go by.

I walked a few steps to the top of the rise and looked back at him again. He was holding something in his hand, his shoulders hunched. He seemed terrified. My heart thudded. What was wrong? The next second, he shook his head vigorously from side to side and clambered up the fence as if something were after him. I winced as he barely cleared the barbed wire, then dropped almost the entire seven feet to the ground with an audible thud, one hand on his glasses.

He trotted up to me, shaking his head again as if his ears were ringing.

"Didn't you hear it?" His voice was rough, his eyes wide.

"Hear what?" All I could hear was the wind whistling past my ears and my own ragged breathing.

"The singing. I could hear her singing 'Ar Lan y Môr'… You didn't hear it?"

"No." I stared at him. He was breathing rapidly and his voice had risen to a higher pitch. Panicked.

"It wasn't in my head," he insisted. "Then I got the strongest feeling that I had to follow you. I—don't know how to explain it. Just look."

He took his phone out of his pocket; I realized it was what he'd been looking at. I came closer, slowly, fear bubbling up from somewhere deep inside me. He tapped on the screen a few times and I leaned in, close enough that I could smell sweat and soap.

"Okay, listen to this."

A recording began to play, a voice message. He switched on the speakerphone and turned the volume up.

For a moment, all I heard was the wind.

And then, a voice. Familiar, but a voice I'd never heard outside of my own dreams. A whisper: *I'm so lonely. You promised.* And then: *My mum. I miss my mum.*

The whisper dissolved again into the scratchy sound of wind crackling out of the tiny speaker. Just for an instant I thought I might have heard a snatch of melody; then it was gone.

"Did you hear it?" Gareth looked closely at me. "I'm not crackers, am I?"

"I heard it," I echoed, my voice sounding faint and hollow.

"She keeps saying that. About being lonely," he said. "About her mum."

For a second, I thought I might faint, and I sat down on the grass, putting my head on my knees. Gradually, the blood came back into my head and all I felt was an aching sadness. I felt scattered, broken into bits, like pieces of me were in my great-grandmother, in Olwen, even in Gareth, and I didn't know how to gather them back again.

The dreams I'd been having...I hadn't told Gareth yet, but I'd seen Olwen still living with her mother—Gee Gee—in the Davies home, sleeping as a baby swaddled in spare clothing in the bottom drawer. I'd seen Gee Gee being slapped by her mother and ignored by her father, given the cold shoulder by girls who had once been her friends, and sneered at by nosy neighbors. I saw Rhiannon smiling at a young man, her eyes alive and sparkling, holding his hand while waiting in line at the shop, ration coupons bundled in her other gloved fist. I saw Olwen, this time as a toddler, trailing behind Rhiannon as she shopped for a meager bag of groceries; another mother shot her a dirty look and dragged her own daughter angrily out of the shop. And, saddest of all, a young but haggard Rhiannon and Great-Grandpa John bent ashen-faced over a bed in which Olwen lay coughing in horrible, painful-sounding spasms. I'd woken with tears streaming down my face, sweat beading my forehead and my breath gasping as if I'd been running.

The tears threatened again now, stinging my eyes.

"We have to keep going," Gareth said, holding a hand out to me. "You were right, you know. We had to come back here. I...I made a promise." He looked down at his feet, blushing. "I told Olwen I'd come back. Let's just go."

Olwen. We had to help her.

Nobody else could.

I swallowed my tears down, reached up, and took his hand. He pulled me to my feet, his hand warm and dry, and squeezed my fingers briefly before letting go.

The moment was like a mild electric shock, and I could swear my fingers tingled.

As we started walking, everything had a bizarre, heightened, surreal quality—the green seemed more vivid than anything I'd ever seen, and the chill wind scoured my cheeks raw. The salt air stung my nose and lips. It seemed more like a dream than reality; yet at the same time, it was more real than anything I'd ever experienced before.

Gareth had pulled ahead a little. His stride was longer than mine, and I jogged to catch up with him. We topped the last rise, and there before us was the ruined church: headstones tilting and the low wall around the churchyard nearly crumbled to the ground, just as I'd seen it in the dream. Nearly, anyway—one of the walls was hung with a bright green tarp, and an empty vehicle that looked like a small dump truck was parked next to it, its shovel filled with rocks.

Gareth stopped so abruptly that I nearly fell over him, my chest bumping awkwardly against his arm. It didn't matter; I grabbed his arm and held tight. We were here; this was it. I could feel his muscles, tense and rigid, and I followed his gaze, out over the crumbling walls of brown-gray stone tufted with grass and weeds, past the leaning, age-blurred headstones, over to where the path picked up again near a haphazard pile of construction tools and rubble.

My heart was racing. "Over there?"

He nodded. Between my dreams and Gareth's photos, I knew what we would find when we went up the low, shrub-covered hill, but my breath still caught. There was the row of little cairns, nearly overgrown now by tall green grass, and a startling spray of lilies that must have been planted some years past. But the small, conical piles of rough, round stones were unmistakable.

I could feel the little hairs stand up on the small of my back, felt the goose bumps rise under the baggy sleeves of my dad's rain jacket, even before looking past the cairns to the ancient standing stones I knew would be there. The slabs of rock seemed as if they'd been set there by giant hands, a colossal child building a house from blocks of stone and earth.

Even when I wasn't looking at it, I could feel its presence, solid and looming.

"So the box is here somewhere," I said, reluctantly breaking the silence.

"Yeah." Gareth looked at me. "Near the plaque." He led me, slowly, to the nearest of the cairns. The stone pile was around mid-calf height, and there, embedded in the ground just in front, was Olwen's grave marker. It was a simple flat rectangle of gray slate, carved with weathered letters that read, uncannily, my own name: *Olwen Nia Evans*. I started to shiver again, uncontrollably, and hugged myself, huddling against the misty breeze. I willed myself not to panic. It wasn't really my name on the grave, after all. It was Olwen's.

Gareth knelt carefully in front of the plaque and used his hands to dig around in the tumbled dirt and pebbles, sifting through the top layer of dirt to either side of the plaque. "Do you see it?" he asked, his voice strained.

"Wasn't there a corner sticking up in that picture you sent me?" I knelt in the dirt beside him.

"Yeah, but it must have rained or something since then. Or the workers disturbed the dirt, maybe." Gareth moved toward the other side of the cairn and started pulling up clumps of grass and earth. I was afraid of digging too deep, but I was determined to keep going, despite a sick feeling like a lump in the bottom of my throat. If we didn't find the box, what *would* we find? I didn't want to think about it. I threw aside handfuls of soil and earthworms, wishing I'd thought to bring a trowel.

Finally, my fingernails scraped against something hard and flat. Something metal. I ignored the feeling of dirt clogging my nails and shoved both hands into the ground, worming my fingers around the top edge of the object until I had enough purchase to cling to it and pull. Slowly, the soil released its hold and the thing came free, dirt raining down on my jeans.

The box was about eight inches square and five inches deep, rusted and battered. Grass and roots clung to its sides, and a tiny padlock held the hasp shut.

Gareth and I stared at it. I realized that I hadn't quite believed, until this moment, that the box truly existed. The silver locket with the key felt cold against my chest. But I didn't want to open the box now; not here. I didn't want whatever it held to blow away, to get lost, after we'd waited so long to find it.

Also, I had something else I wanted to do.

First, though, I set the box to one side and carefully began patting the dirt and plants back into place. Gareth nodded and did the same. When we'd restored the site to a semi-tidy state, I got up, went over to the nearby lily plant, and plucked a single white flower. Kneeling down again, I placed it over the newly tamped-down earth. Then I sat back on my heels.

"So," Gareth said. "Ready to go?"

I took a deep breath. "Not quite yet. I want to see the cromlech. I want to see the place where you ... saw her."

"Want" wasn't entirely accurate. It was more that I felt like I had to. Gareth had been visited by Olwen multiple times—in the cromlech, in his photos. But I'd only ever seen her in dreams.

Maybe if I went inside the cromlech, like he had.... maybe I could tell her we were trying to help.

Maybe then the dreams would stop.

I got to my feet. "Show me," I said.

We walked through the ruined churchyard, past the collapsing walls of the sad little building, and stood in front of the stone burial chamber where, somehow, Gareth had found Olwen. I didn't know if it was luck or fate that they'd ... connected. My dad always said you make your own luck.

Then I cocked my head. I heard a rumble, off in the distance. It was faint but slowly growing louder—the unmistakable sound of a vehicle's engine. It went on for a minute, still some distance away, and then stopped.

"What was that?" I asked. Was there some kind of caretaker? A security guard?

"I think we can safely say it isn't Olwen," Gareth said with a weak smile.

"Your powers of deduction astound me." I tried to smile back. "Anyway, let's hurry."

He looked at me more seriously now. "I'm not sure what you want me—us—to do."

We stood side by side, looking up at the massive granite boulders of the cromlech. They almost looked like a gateway, with the capstone resting on two smaller supporting stones. The space beneath was hollowed out and dark.

It was impossible to see very far inside the hole; the opening only let in a small amount of light.

"I want to look inside," I said. "That's where you saw her."

"I'm not sure I'd recommend that," Gareth said hesitantly. "There's really not much room in there."

"Let me just try putting my head in, then." I got down on my knees in front of the hole, then lay on the ground, stretching out my legs so that most of my weight was outside. I inched forward until my head and shoulders cleared the edge. "Can you hand me the flashlight?"

"One torch, coming up," Gareth said. I clicked the button and shone the beam down into the depths.

My stomach did slow flips, afraid of what I might find. I craned my neck to check every corner and flashed the beam in slow arcs from one side of the dirt floor to the other.

I didn't see anything.

I wanted to see her. And I didn't want to. But I couldn't control the feeling of despair that welled up. What if she was stuck now, roaming around? Or maybe she'd taken up residence in Gareth's phone? I wanted to laugh at that, but it wasn't funny.

I hung my head for a moment, then scooted back out.

"I think she's gone," I said.

"Not gone," Gareth said. His voice sounded strange. I turned away from the cromlech to look at him.

He was staring fixedly at something behind me, just above my head.

I whirled around, just in time to see a flash of a white dress, a small figure, not-quite there, sitting on the giant capstone and dangling her legs. She flickered in and out, visible one moment, gone the next, hardly substantial to begin with, but I could see her smiling like the Cheshire cat. Something inside me wanted to smile back. I stepped closer.

Then I heard ... whistling. Not just the wind past my ears, or the distant scolding of gulls over the ocean. It was most definitely somebody whistling, and little by little it was getting nearer. I whirled around to face Gareth.

"Somebody's coming," I hissed. Somewhere nearby, I heard something drag against the ground, a gate opening and then shutting with a mild clink. The whistling continued, an off-key tune I didn't recognize. I thought I could hear heavy footsteps now, and I caught a glimpse of an orange hard hat past the crumbling walls of the ruined church. It was Sunday, wasn't it? Why would there be a worker here? I started to panic, picking up the metal box and looking frantically around for the backpack.

Then I remembered: Olwen.

I turned again. She was gone. I could swear I heard a bubble of laughter disappearing into the air, but then all I heard was the worker's whistling, his crunching steps.

And then it stopped abruptly and he was standing there on the rise, blocking the only way out. Behind us was the cromlech, and behind that, the clifftop and the sea.

———

The worker was tall, dark-bearded, and frowning. Gareth thought frantically, trying to come up with a plausible explanation for why they were there. The truth was just too weird.

"I'm tired of you bloody kids coming in here all the time and leaving your dirty cigarette butts and worse all over the site. This is a construction zone! It's not lovers' bloody lane." He dropped his toolbox and crossed his arms.

"But we weren't . . . " Wyn began, her voice barely audible.

"Leave this to me, er, baby," Gareth said, shooting her a warning glance. He saw her clamp her lips against whatever she was going to say, looking surprised. He hoped she trusted him. He could be getting them in worse trouble, but he had to take the chance. He needed Wyn to hide the metal box. If the worker saw it . . . what if he figured out they'd been digging around? What if he confiscated it? Or worse, what if he reported them to the police? Gareth took a deep breath and hoped he looked more cocky than he felt; he tried his best to channel Amit.

"Look, sir, I just wanted to have a nice picnic with my girl, you know, out here by the ocean where nobody would disturb us." He winked at the construction worker knowingly. "You know how it is. Come on, Wyn," he said, shooting a darting glance at the cairns off to one side. "Gather our things. We'd better go. We don't want to miss the bus back." He took the backpack off his back and tossed it to her, hoping she'd be able to stash the box in there without attracting too much attention.

The worker came closer, glowering at them. "You bloody English vacationers come in and think you own the place, don't you? Well, the rules apply to everyone," he said, not backing down.

Gareth was infuriated. As if it wasn't bad enough, back in London when people teased him about being a Taffy. He found himself wanting to say, *But I'm Welsh!*

But he held back. He kept his eyes on the ground and stuffed the anger back inside. He had to stay calm, try to talk their way out of this. Meanwhile, Wyn had edged away, toward the cairns, and was crouching down to open the pack. He shot her a look, willing her to stay quiet. Things would get even more complicated if the worker found out Wyn was American.

"Look, we're sorry. We'll just be going now, okay? See, my girlfriend got all our things and we'll head back to the Pontfaen bus stop. We haven't left any rubbish or anything. No trouble, right?"

"No trouble?" The worker sneered at him, but at least he wasn't as threatening. "No trouble? The last bus left a half hour ago," he said with evident satisfaction, "so there's no way getting back now, is there. Unless I ring your families." He took a mobile phone out of his pocket. Wyn looked up from zipping the backpack, alarm written all over her face.

"Please, sir, let me do it," Gareth said, trying to sound placating rather than desperate. He took out his phone. Fate must have been smiling on him, because the construction worker relented and put his own phone away. Gareth steeled himself and dialed the only Cwm Tawel number he knew would definitely have a car: Wyn's parents'.

21

Trech anᵹen na ᵬewis.

Necessity is stronᵹer than choice.

Welsh proverb

This was definitely the biggest trouble I'd ever been in. And the irony was, my parents were madder about what we *hadn't* done than what we actually did.

Dad was sitting in the front passenger seat sighing periodically, and he wouldn't look at me even though I kept trying to catch his eye in the rearview mirror. Mom was driving along the winding road back to the village, utterly silent and tight-lipped. Every time I tried to explain what had happened, she cut me off with "We'll discuss it later."

Obviously, the real explosion was yet to come.

It wasn't fair, though. It was the construction worker's word against ours. I couldn't believe we'd had the bad luck to run into him again, in the parking lot at the beach. He'd seemed to relish the opportunity to chastise us in front of my parents and throw all kinds of accusations around, ranting about smoking and snogging and littering. But we hadn't done any of the things he'd accused us of… except trespassing on the site and getting caught. I couldn't believe we'd been so stupid as to miss the bus back, even after we'd made sure to check the time.

On the other hand, we had Olwen's metal box now. I hoped it would all be worth it in the end.

I nudged Gareth and smiled, pointing silently at the backpack. He smiled back, just a little, and I felt a flash of relief.

———————

"I had a feeling things were getting a little too heavy with you two," Mom said later, after we'd dropped Gareth off at his great-granddad's house and returned to the cottage. "And today—well, I really don't know what to say to you." Her eyes bored holes into me, as if she were trying to peek into my brain.

My face burning with humiliation and anger, I got up from the armchair. "We weren't doing any of those things the guy said," I said loudly. "Mom, do you honestly think we were up there smoking and—whatever? When have I ever expressed any desire to smoke?"

"These European kids all smoke, Wyn. Now be honest. Did Gareth offer you a cigarette? He didn't pressure you into anything, did he?" Mom looked up at me with a slight frown.

"No! Gareth doesn't smoke," I said, sitting back down and sagging against the arm of the chair. I wasn't sure if that was true, but I'd never seen him with cigarettes. He never smelled like smoke. "All we did was miss the bus."

"And trespass on a construction site," Dad put in. "That is so dangerous. I just don't understand." He looked at me as if he'd never seen me before, his eyes weary. "I mean, the worker said you were in an area that's closed to the public. Was it an accident?"

Guilt zinged through me. "No, but—"

"Then are you suggesting that worker was lying?" Mom got up and started pacing in front of me like she was back in a San Francisco courtroom.

"No," I said, defensively. "I just mean, he never bothered to hear our side of the story."

"Well, no wonder," Dad said. "If I were him and I'd just found a couple of kids doing who-knows-what in a fenced-off area, I'm not sure any excuses would matter. I'm just really surprised, Wyn." He closed his eyes and rubbed the back of his neck.

"Don't you even want to hear my side of things?" I gaped at him. I'd always thought I could talk to Dad about anything and he would hear me out. Of course, that was before.

Before everything.

"Later," he said. "For now, just please promise us you

won't go anywhere without telling us exactly where you're going to be."

"Okay," I said.

"And we'd prefer it if you didn't visit with Gareth unsupervised," Mom added.

"What? Mom, that's ridiculous."

She rounded on me. "Those are our terms, Olwen Nia Evans." I jerked. "We are here as a family." Then her voice softened. "I know you've been eager to have a friend your own age here, but your dad and I need some time to discuss how to deal with this … incident, okay? Be reasonable."

I clenched my hands together in my lap and nodded. But I couldn't stay in the same room with them any longer. I got up, walked to my room, shut the door, and dropped heavily onto the bed. They would relent eventually. If they didn't, then they were the ones being unreasonable.

After wallowing for a while, I felt less angry and went over to the basin to splash water on my face and wash the dirt off my hands. Turning back to face the room, my eyes fell on the backpack sitting next to the foot of the bed.

I sat back down. Gently, almost reverently, I unzipped the backpack and pulled out the metal box. It was rusty and dirty; I set it on one of the spare hand towels and cautiously wiped off the worst of the grime.

I couldn't wait anymore, couldn't wait for Gareth. He would understand—he'd been the one to push the backpack into my arms with a meaningful stare when we'd dropped him off.

I reached behind my neck and unfastened Gee Gee's

necklace. The inner clasp of the locket opened more easily this time, and the tiny, age-darkened key fell out into my lap. It looked like nothing special, nothing at all, but at that moment it was the most important thing. I jiggled the little key into the padlock's dirt-encrusted keyhole.

After some jabbing and twisting, the key finally went in and I was able to lift the lid of the box. It was only about five inches deep and maybe eight inches wide, but as I removed each object I was amazed that something so small held so much.

The first thing I took out was a book bound in dark blue, water-stained leather. My stomach flip-flopped and I carefully opened the cover. It was definitely a diary, and I recognized Gee Gee's precise handwriting, though it looked a little different. Younger, maybe. More rounded. Maddeningly, though, it was all in Welsh. I set it aside for the time being and looked inside the box again.

Sitting on top of a stack of yellowed paper was a tarnished locket. On the outside, it was identical to the one I wore. But on the inside, when I forced it open, was a tiny scrap of folded lace. And the photo, instead of being a baby picture, showed two faces—a mother, whom I recognized as a very young Rhiannon, and a little girl.

I knew the little girl right away, too, and I shivered. That thin, sad face. Here it was, recorded in a photograph that really existed. Not a ghost. Not a dream. I touched it, feeling the dry paper under my fingertip. A strange feeling rose inside me, and suddenly I felt certain: the picture of the baby in Gee Gee's locket was Olwen, too.

And this necklace must have been the one Olwen was wearing in my dreams. One for mother; one for daughter.

Someone tapped at my door, and I jumped.

"Wynnie," came Dad's voice, muffled by the door. "Could you come out here, please?"

Now what? I hastily threw a blanket over everything on the bed and opened the door a crack.

"Wyn, we've been speaking to Gareth and his great-grandfather on the phone, trying to get the situation figured out." Dad grimaced. "Actually, we called and spoke to Mr. Lewis earlier, and then Gareth just called back and gave us his explanation for what happened." He sighed. "We're still not sure what to think, but he gave us such a nice apology, your mom and I think you should probably do the same for Mr. Lewis. Okay? Gareth's on the line now; he said he'd get him on the phone for you."

I swallowed hard and followed my dad back into the front room, running through various options in my head, none of them good ones. *I'm sorry, Mr. Lewis, for any worry I caused? Sincere apologies for convincing your grandson to illegally jump a fence?*

I picked up my parents' phone, which was lying on the kitchen counter. Dad sat down next to Mom, who was holding a law journal and clearly trying to look like she wasn't eavesdropping.

"Hello?" There was silence on the other end. "Mr. Lewis?"

An impossibly gravelly voice said, "How dare you spend the Day of Rest snogging with my innocent little great-grandson in the middle of a historical restoration zone? Eh? Eh?"

I opened my mouth, then closed it again. "Um…" I bit the inside of my cheek, trying not to laugh, and turned toward the wall so my parents wouldn't see my expression.

"Uh oh. Are your parents there?" Gareth asked.

"Yes, sir," I said in a contrite tone, glancing back at them. "It really was an accident, and I'm really sorry, Mr. Lewis." My stomach ached from holding in laughter.

"Okay, I'll be sure to tell him," Gareth said, chortling. I would have to get him back for this, someday when we weren't both under house arrest. "Listen, Wyn. My great-granddad just left for the pub. I was hoping you'd be able to talk. Can you get somewhere private? Or call me from your phone?"

"Yes, I'll try… sir," I said. I leaned my forehead against the wall and grinned.

"I have to know what's in the box," Gareth said. "Okay, I'll let you go. Call me later." He switched back to his grumpy-old-man voice. "And see that you don't go corrupting my perfect, angelic grandson anymore."

I hung up, closing my eyes and composing myself before turning around to face the room. Dad got up, smiling at me, and came over to give me a hug.

"You did good, Wynnie," he said. "Listen, why don't we all go out for dinner? As a family?" He sounded apologetic. "I know this hasn't been much of a vacation. Maybe we can try to enjoy our last week here. Next Monday's our flight home."

Our last week. I shrugged out from under my dad's arms and stood there stiffly. It seemed like hardly any time was left.

I had to finish going through the metal box.

"I don't feel well," I said, looking at the floor. I was lying outright and it felt horrible, especially after everything else that had happened today. "You guys go, and I'll come with you some other time. I think I just want to lie down."

"Are you sure, honey? We made a reservation in Carmarthen at one of the restaurants there." Dad put his hand on my shoulder, gently. "We really want you to come."

"I'm not hungry," I said. I actually wasn't. I was too preoccupied by what I might find. "Please, Dad."

"Do you want us to stay home with you?" He felt my forehead. "You feel okay, but it's been a hard few days. Maybe it would be better if—"

"No, Dad. You guys go. I'll be fine here. I'll take a nap."

He looked at me tiredly for a few moments. "Okay, well, I guess your mom and I will let you get some rest, then. We'll call you when we're on our way back. We'll bring you something." His eyes narrowed for a second. "Please don't go anywhere."

While my parents got ready, I upheld the pretense of illness by starting up the electric kettle and getting out some chamomile tea. Once I had the cottage to myself, I hurried back into my bedroom. I threw the blanket onto the floor, revealing the open box, the weather-beaten diary, and the locket, just as I'd left them. I'd already half-convinced myself that I'd imagined it, but there they were.

I sat back down on the bed and eagerly lifted the rest of the papers out of the box—a short stack of folded documents and letters mixed together. I gently unfolded the top sheet. It was a death certificate. It read *Olwen Nia Evans* and gave the

date of death: *19 July 1950.* Though it wasn't a surprise anymore, it still brought tears to my eyes.

Six years old.

Next were two brief letters, both in English and in an
unfamiliar handwriting. I brought them closer to the bedside lamp and read:

20 March 1949

Dear Rhiannon,

*I have enclosed some money for you and Olwen. It
isn't much because I have only just found work at
the Big Pit. Some of the mines have closed down and
there aren't as many jobs as there used to be.*

*It has been very exciting out here. Village life was so
dull sometimes and the change has been good for me.
I was not a very good farmer.*

Please kiss Olwen for me.

All my love,

—E.

5 July 1949

Dear Rhiannon,

*I am happy to hear that Olwen has not been ill
this summer. Still, I have enclosed a few pounds*

*just in case. I have been very busy and tired. But I
am happy and don't think I will need a farm job,
especially not one with sheep. I hardly ever saw live
sheep before moving to Wales—the only lambs I saw
in London were the ones that ended up in my stew.*

*Sorry for the brief note, but I must leave for
breakfast and the pit. My thoughts are with you and
Olwen as always.*

—E.

Who was this mysterious "E"? Maybe he'd been one of
the evacuated children. Looking at the letters gave me the
strangest feeling. His signature ... that jagged, blocky way
he wrote his name.

I set the letters aside and unfolded the last document.

It was a birth certificate: Olwen's birth certificate. But the
more closely I looked at the document, the more confused I
got. The name on the birth certificate wasn't Olwen Nia Evans.

It was Olwen Nia Davies. Her mother's name, of course,
was Rhiannon Davies. So Olwen *had* been born out of wedlock. I let out a shaky breath.

Then, my heart just about stopped when I saw the father's
name: Edward Henry Lewis.

———

Edward Lewis.

Lewis was Gareth's last name. A common-enough last

name. But I remembered: in our first Skype conversation, he'd told me his great-grandfather was Edward Lewis.

I let the birth certificate fall gently onto the bed. My stomach knotted. I had to see Gareth. There was proof here, finally, proof that even my parents would take seriously, but I had to talk to him first. And maybe find a translator, too, if we couldn't manage the diary on our own.

Of course, I'd just promised my parents I wouldn't see Gareth. But I'd never said I wouldn't call him.

I needed to think first, though. I got up and put on my coat and boots, intending to take a walk on the tree-lined path around the cottages and farmhouse. It would clear my head. It would pass the time. I wouldn't leave the property, so technically I wasn't defying my dad. And then I would call Gareth.

Small pools of light shone from the front windows of our little cottage, breaking up the dusk and mist. When I shut the door and moved a short distance away, I could almost imagine that the gentle glow and dark bulk of the small building belonged not to our vacation home but to Awel-y-Môr, the house where Gee Gee had lived, where Olwen had spent much of her short life. I could almost see, in between the black tree-silhouettes, the familiar shadow that had appeared in so many of my dreams about Cwm Tawel slipping back into the house in the preternatural stillness after the air raid siren.

I turned away with a shiver and kept walking. Soon I couldn't see the cottage anymore. One of the old trees had a huge, gnarled root and I sat down heavily, breathing in the damp-pine smell.

I could go see Gareth anyway.

I'd feel horribly guilty. But we'd already come so far, and it felt like we were so close now that we'd found the box. Close to what, I wasn't sure, but I hoped that if we saw this through, it would set Olwen's spirit to rest. And if we wanted to do that, I had to tell Gareth what I'd found and figure out what to do next.

All of this—it had to be worth any amount of guilt. Maybe letting the secret out, no matter how painful, would finally allow all the decades of suffering to dissipate—Olwen's suffering, and Rhiannon's. And then, maybe, my dreams would finally leave me in peace.

So what if I'd be grounded until I reached adulthood.

I wiped a few involuntary tears away and leaned my head back, way back until I could see the glowing outlines of the cloud obscuring the rising moon. The cold evening breeze sliced into my jacket and dried the tears on my face. If I could just get my parents to listen … but they wouldn't, not until they were good and ready and had stopped being upset. I wouldn't be able to win back their trust in a day.

Besides, I felt reluctant to give up my newfound knowledge just yet. It felt too precious. I wanted to hold on to it for a while longer, this special, hidden piece of Gee Gee's life.

There was one person, though, who needed to know.

I got up again and crunched down the path that led around to the front of the farmhouse, lost in thought. The moon came out from behind its cloud and shone palely in the darkening sky. I walked faster and faster, feeling the wind in my hair, not caring if I really went anywhere. My brain just kept mulling over everything: my parents' angry faces, Olwen's frightened one, and the papers I'd found in the box. The implications. Before I knew it, I had walked all the way down to Cwm Road.

The tourist shops were closed and dark; so was the bus station. Everything shone with a pearly cast in the moonlight. There weren't many people out, though it was only nine thirty. If this were San Francisco, there would be people everywhere—fancy-dressed, funky, homeless. The only people I ran into were a bundled-up couple coming out of a pub.

I had a vague thought that I might walk by the site of Gee Gee's cottage again, but my footsteps betrayed me and took me to the opposite side of the village, the side where Gareth was staying. I would just walk past and see if he was home, see if a light was on. If not, I'd go back to the cottage and call him.

When I got to his great-granddad's place, Gareth was sitting on the curb outside, staring gloomily into the sky. He turned to look at me as I walked up, seeming unsurprised to see me.

I stopped and sat down next to him.

"I don't know why," he said, "but I just had this feeling you were coming."

"I guess things like that shouldn't surprise me anymore." I looked up at the sky again. A few bright stars were valiantly shining through the clouds.

After a silent minute or two, I said, "You won't believe what I found in the box." I felt a stab of nervousness and glanced back at Mr. Lewis's house.

"Don't worry, he's still at the pub. He just sort of took off after your mum and dad talked to him."

"I'm sorry," I said. "Really."

"Don't be. He didn't seem all that angry. Just quiet." Gareth crossed his feet at the ankles, then uncrossed them again, staring at his dirty sneakers.

"I can't believe I got my parents to go to dinner without me," I said. "I told them I felt sick. I think my dad felt bad about the whole thing, actually." I tapped my heels in the gutter. "I probably shouldn't have come here."

"I'm glad you did, though." Gareth looked at me, the lenses of his glasses glimmering in the moonlight. He smiled, and I felt a new nervousness. A pleasant nervousness.

I was here for a reason, though. "Gareth, listen. I found some unbelievable things in that box."

"Yeah?" He edged closer, so we were just a few inches away from touching.

"I don't know how to start." I let out a long, shaky breath. I could sense Gareth's attention on me, but I couldn't meet his eyes. "There was another locket, with a picture of Rhiannon and Olwen. There was a diary in Welsh, and a couple of letters from someone with the initial E. And—" I hesitated, then plunged ahead.

"I found Olwen's birth and death certificates. On the birth certificate it said her father"—I swallowed—"was Edward Henry Lewis." I stopped and waited, searching his face carefully.

Gareth went completely pale, his eyes wide. When he finally spoke, his voice was barely audible.

"But ... that's my great-granddad."

22

Ɑbbɛꜰ ɣɯ ʇɛɯı.

Silence is admission.

Welsh proverb

Gareth leaned slowly backward and lay against the cool
sidewalk, staring straight up at the moonlit clouds. The
cement was hard and rough through the thin cotton of his
shirt, but he still felt like the ground had disappeared from
underneath him.

Edward Lewis—his Great-Granddad Lewis—Olwen's
father? Was it even possible?

On the one hand, it would explain so much. It would
explain why he couldn't stop thinking about Olwen,
maybe even why he'd seen her at the cromlech in the
first place. And it would account for his great-granddad's

bizarre, withdrawn behavior ever since Rhiannon came back to the village. But it still seemed so unbelievable. His great-granddad had married, had children of his own, grandchildren and great-grandchildren. He had a *life*. And as far as Gareth had ever known, Olwen had not been in it.

"I have to see those papers," Gareth said. He sat back up and brushed his hair out of his eyes. His brain started working again, went into planning mode. "I can probably get out of the house tomorrow afternoon if I offer to run a few errands. If you can do the same thing, we can meet somewhere, like Smyth and Sons, and look at everything together."

"Maybe. I think I could manage that," Wyn said slowly. She looked at her phone and a worried frown appeared on her face. "But I'd better go." She scrambled to her feet.

"Right," Gareth said. The space next to him, where she'd been sitting, already felt empty. "I hope I see you tomorrow. If you can't make it, ring me in the morning."

Wyn gave him a small smile, moonlight glinting in her eyes, and left.

———

It was stiflingly warm in his great-granddad's house, and the tiny bed Gareth was occupying had seemed to get less comfortable every night. He opened the window to let in the damp night breeze, kicked off the covers, and folded the flat pillow in half, but nothing helped. Eventually he gave up and just sat upright, head lolling back against the wall, staring at the darkness. What if something went wrong? What if they couldn't translate the diary on their own? What was Plan B?

He still couldn't quite believe what Wyn had told him about Olwen's father being named Edward Henry Lewis. It just wasn't something he could picture. It didn't even seem like it could happen in the same universe. And if *he* couldn't believe it, then they hadn't much of a chance of convincing anyone else. He had to see the proof—he had to read those documents with his own eyes.

Letters. An idea began to bloom in his mind. There had been letters from his great-granddad, apparently, in the metal box. So, logically, there ought to be letters from Rhiannon somewhere in his great-granddad's house—that was, if he hadn't thrown them away.

Gareth even had a reasonable suspicion where those letters would be.

Two years ago, his great-granddad had a knee operation, and the whole family had gone to Cwm Tawel for a week to help with cleaning and taking care of meals and everything. The house had been a bit of a mess, and Gareth's mum had forced him to sort out what seemed like hundreds of cardboard boxes. Gareth had thrown away mounds of old bills and receipts. Anything that looked important, he'd put back into boxes and stowed away in the closet, here in this room.

Easing himself up from the bed as silently as possible, wincing at the squeak the old springs made when he moved, Gareth tiptoed to the doorway and closed the door with a tiny click, then turned on the small bedside lamp.

The closet had never really been meant for major storage, just for clothing, so when he opened the door, a precariously leaning tower of boxes nearly tipped over onto him. Probably his own fault. He shoved it back into place slowly and, he hoped, quietly.

His mum had written neatly on each box in felt-tip, labeling them *winter clothes, spare towels, books,* and so on. There were a handful of boxes marked *papers,* and Gareth spent several achingly slow minutes unearthing them. Dust swirled up from the disused piles of boxes, and at one point he had to dive onto the bed and stuff his head into the pillow in order to muffle an uncontrollable sneeze. He paused for a moment after that, holding his breath and listening to make sure he hadn't woken his great-granddad; the house remained quiet.

Of the four boxes of papers, one was full of old newspaper clippings and one was loosely piled with financial information. Gareth set those carefully back in the closet. He rifled through the remaining two boxes, which were haphazardly packed with postcards, canceled checks, local senior citizens' newsletters, and random correspondence. He was sure the letters, if they existed, had to be here. But after searching through them once, he didn't see anything like what he was looking for. The only old letters he found were from some Rhondda Valley mine offering his great-granddad a job, and an unreadable scrawled note from his late great-grandmother Ellen.

Gareth sighed under his breath and searched again, paper by paper, trying not to rustle too loudly. But he found nothing.

He was dumbfounded. Those letters had to exist. Unless

his great-granddad had thrown them away. But he never threw anything away; that was why Gareth's mum had made him clean out all the closets. It didn't make sense. They had to be somewhere else, or they just didn't exist.

There was only one thing left to do now, if he wanted to find the letters. He'd have to confront his great-granddad. And in order to do that, he needed the evidence Wyn had found. It was all starting to feel hopelessly convoluted. She needed him; he needed her. Of course, put that way, it sounded simple.

Gathering up the papers, Gareth put them back into what he hoped were the right boxes. But when he shoved the last box into the closet, onto a tower that was already five boxes high, it leaned dangerously forward before he could do anything to catch it. Three of the boxes toppled down and rained their contents—papers, tatty old slippers, plastic fruit, and an empty biscuit tin—down on his head and shoulders in a dusty, rattling shower. His heart thudded and he leapt for the light switch.

The room plunged into darkness, and not a second too soon. The door flew open and his great-grandfather turned on the wall switch. Light flooded the room, so bright compared to the bedside lamp that Gareth didn't have to pretend to blink in shock. Afterimages soared into his field of vision; a purple blob superimposed itself on his great-grandfather's face when he tried to focus on the doorway.

"What in bleeding hell are you doing in here?"

"I don't know, I just woke up when all these things crashed on my head," Gareth said, trying to sound bleary and confused. "I must have been sleepwalking."

"Sleepwalking? With your glasses on?" His great-grandfather peered at him suspiciously. Gareth reached one hand to his head, as if in surprise.

"I must have fallen asleep while reading, I suppose," he said. "I don't remember." It sounded a load of bollocks, but what could he do? He started gathering up the fallen debris and putting it back into boxes.

"Well, tidy that up and get yourself dressed. It's nearly time to get up anyway." His great-granddad gave him one last suspicious look before shuffling back out. Gareth looked at the clock in surprise; it was five thirty. Certainly not a time he'd ever hoped to be awake at, but only half an hour before his great-granddad usually got up.

In any case, it seemed he'd escaped further questioning. Gareth let himself enjoy a moment of relief, then started shoving everything back into the closet. He'd come awfully close to having to explain everything, when he wasn't sure he was ready.

At least he still had time to figure out a strategy. He needed to plan out how to start this conversation—a conversation he never once in his life imagined having.

23

He who is Faultless
is not born.

Welsh proverb

The next morning, I woke up to the sound of a crow caw-ing loudly outside my window, and I threw my arm over my eyes against the sunlight. I lay there for a few minutes, letting my vision adjust. Today I was going to try to meet Gareth, show him what I'd found.

Correction: today I *would* meet Gareth. No matter what, I was going to be there at Smyth and Sons with the metal box, waiting for him.

Last night had been mercifully uneventful. My parents had called twice to check on me—once when I was still walking home from the village—and had arrived home around ten thirty. They'd been in a better mood, and I tried as hard as I could to not raise their suspicions again. I kept the metal box and its precious contents safely hidden, and spent the rest of the evening cramming as much Welsh language into my brain as I could.

My mom was happy when I consented to eat the slice of quiche they'd brought back for me. As far as Dad was concerned, I seemed to be forgiven, since he spent the last hour before bed trying to entice me with brochures about the Brecon Beacons National Park and the Doctor Who Experience.

I got out of bed and threw on a sweater, a long skirt, and hiking boots. We only had a handful of days left in Wales. My parents hadn't arranged our trip home until Gee Gee passed away, but then they hadn't wasted much time in scheduling the flight after the funeral, and filled just about every day we had left with structured fun as if this were simply an ordinary family vacation. But I didn't complain about having to spend the morning touring around in the Fiesta—we'd be back early, in time for my mom to prepare for a Skype meeting. And I would prepare for my own meeting.

My parents were looking forward to our sightseeing outing. Of course, for them, the hard part was done.

Not for me. The need to see Gareth, to confirm what had happened to Gee Gee, was so strong, the entire morning seemed like a blur to me. I knew I should be riveted by the gorgeous Tywi valley, the impossibly green landscape, and maybe in another life I would have been. I felt like I was just a shadow slipping past on another plane.

When we got back from sightseeing, it was two o'clock. I'd gotten a text from Gareth half an hour before: *At Smyth and Sons. Come when you can.*

I didn't know how long he would wait, but I texted him as soon as I got back into my room. *Leaving soon.*

I carefully wrapped the metal box in an extra sweater and placed it in my backpack, then packed my laptop and Welsh dictionary.

"You look like you're on your way somewhere," Dad said, glancing up at me from the couch when I came out of my room.

"I thought I'd check my email, maybe take a walk down to the village." I tried to sound noncommittal. "Gareth said there's a bookstore on the main road."

Mom looked over at me from where she was working on her laptop at the table. "You aren't meeting him again, are you? I thought we could spend some time together as a family tonight."

"No," I said, my voice sounding strange in my own ears. I'd just lied, right to my mother's face. "I'll be back by dinner, I promise." That part, at least, wasn't a lie. But I felt a crawling sensation between my shoulder blades, as if she was watching me as I went out the door. My stomach felt sick, and again I hoped this would all be worth it.

The metal box clinked in my backpack as I quickened my pace down Cwm Road. The more time I had with Gareth, the better. If we could piece together the whole story, I could explain it to my parents, and then they'd have to understand.

I felt a little sad as I passed the cozy shops and businesses on the main road. I might not get to see them again for years. Maybe Smyth and Sons wasn't anything like the well-stocked, brightly lit bookstores I was used to, but I'd grown accustomed to it—to the hot, crisp fries at HMS Tasty's, the friendly young woman at the post office, the tiny bank branch with one single teller. It felt like I'd been here months, not weeks.

Gareth was waiting at a small table by the window when I walked in the door, and he looked up at the squeak of hinges. Mr. Smyth the Elder was nowhere in sight, though I could hear shuffling noises from the back room. I slid into the wooden chair on the other side of the table and looked around; the table across the room was empty, and a shelf of dated-looking "new releases" formed a convenient barrier between us and the rest of the shop. I drew the metal box out of my backpack and set it down.

"I couldn't find anything at Granddad's house. I'm glad you had more luck." Gareth's voice sounded strained. He looked at me intently for a moment. "All right?" he asked. He flashed me a quick smile.

In that moment, his wavy hair sliding down over one eye and the smile lighting up his face, I had a strong flash of … not quite memory, not quite déjà vu, but something else entirely—a sense of being in a different time, of ghostly shadows of long-gone people all around me, of a different young man, who looked a lot like Gareth, grinning at someone standing next to me.

It felt so real that I turned my head to look, but of course nobody was there, and the moment fled. I was back in the wood-paneled bookshop surrounded by shelves, my chest aching with a sadness that hadn't been there a minute ago.

"Yes, I'm all right." I busied myself with retrieving the key from my locket; by the time I clicked open the lid of the box, I felt a little more composed.

"Let's see, then," he said quietly.

I started by handing him the second locket, popping it open to reveal the picture of Rhiannon and Olwen.

"That's her all right," he said, eyebrows raised. "I wouldn't forget that face in a million years."

Next I showed him the birth and death certificates. He went a little pale, but nodded. "Edward Henry Lewis. That's my great-granddad's name. And the letters—well, that confirms it, doesn't it. They're in his handwriting, more or less. It's changed over the years, but not that much."

I let out a long breath. "I guess we know who Olwen's father was. I just wish Gee Gee had told us." It seemed so sad, and I couldn't understand why the entire village wouldn't have grieved the loss of Olwen. And then there was Great-Grandpa John. How did he fit into the picture?

"I suppose because they weren't married," Gareth reminded me. I let out a frustrated noise. "Hey, let's have a look at that diary." He sounded like he was trying to be confident, but his voice trembled the slightest bit when he said the word "diary." I glanced at him; his eyes were troubled.

I'd known for a while now that Gee Gee had her secrets—Gareth was just finding out about his great-granddad's.

I reached out and squeezed his hand. He squeezed back, and then I let go.

"Here it is," I said, pulling the dark-blue notebook out of the box. I twisted my hair around my finger and waited as he flipped gently through the pages.

"Well," he said, "she's got nice penmanship, but I still can't catch more than a few words here and there. Like this"—he pointed at a sentence about halfway down the page—"'*Dw i ddim yn gallu deall*' ... that part means 'I can't understand.' But I'm not sure about the rest of the sentence," he concluded apologetically. "I guess that's ironic, eh? The only part I can understand is the part about not understanding." He smirked, and I felt the corners of my mouth twitch upward.

I had to know what the diary contained. I had to find the missing parts of the story, the gap between Gee Gee's teenage years and the time when she and Great-Grandpa John moved to the States. The small window of time during which Olwen had lived and died. Then maybe we could confront Mr. Lewis. If he confirmed the details, maybe then I could go to my parents with it and they'd believe me.

I knew I couldn't convince them with ghosts and dreams. But they wouldn't be able to deny the physical evidence.

"What do you think we should do now?" I asked. "My Welsh isn't very good either. Not yet."

"Better than mine, I bet." Gareth gave me a small smile, and for a second I forgot what we were supposed to be doing.

"Know any good translation websites?" he said after a pause.

"Well, I brought my laptop with me." I opened it up, and Gareth did a quick search for "*Welsh English translation.*" It only took him moments to find a site that would translate any text you typed into a box.

"You're good at that," I said.

He grinned. "Hope you can type fast, because I'm crap at it."

Unfortunately, both of our efforts were wasted. The translation engine returned a string of confusing gibberish.

"What's this thing's problem?" Gareth said in disbelief. "'He is being heifer'?" He snorted a laugh. "I never thought I'd be the one to say this, but perhaps computers are not the solution to all of life's troubles."

"Don't blame my poor laptop. Without this very computer, we would never have met," I pointed out, and Gareth laughed. "Why don't we just try the dictionary? We both know a little Welsh, and we can just look up the difficult words." I wasn't ready to give up yet.

"Er—okay." Gareth's voice was uncertain. "But I don't remember much from school, I have to warn you."

I got my Welsh dictionary out of my backpack and put it on the table between us. "Why don't we tackle the first entry, the one that says '15fed Mehefin'?"

We plugged away for an hour, word by word, but by the end, all we'd managed was a single entry, peppered with question marks and blanks wherever we couldn't figure out a word or phrase. I wasn't even sure if it was accurate. It wasn't elegant, that was for sure:

15 June 1943

More evacuees came to our school this week. She (It?) makes me so sad and angry I would like to march there to Germany myself! I truly mean it. Mam and Dad (??) if they knew. Half of the poor things are in their clothes for summer and without their coats. These were from village Bryn Coch a few miles away. Not like all the ones from England who are already settled in our houses and farms—the village children already know Welsh and are not so different. But truly, the ones from England are not so different either, only frightened, no matter what old Mrs. Williams says about them not to be blessed like us because they don't (won't?) go to chapel. Well, they do now, anyway.

I had another dream last night, the ones Mam-gu Davies says I must listen to them. It was only images flashing past, some men working in a (??) coal and then the cromlech there by the old chapel Llanddewi, all (??). I can't understand it (him?). I did hear Mr. Jones talking about the new chapel that they are building on border south of town, but hope they do not stop using the lovely old one.

"Wow," I said, when we'd finished.

"Yeah." Gareth stared at my laptop screen, covered in

notes. "All we've done is one entry, and there's how many still to go?"

I flipped through the pages. "It looks like twelve." I dropped the book on the table. "You're right, this is taking way too long. And it's really frustrating, too. Sorry. Not your fault."

"And old Mr. Smyth keeps glaring at us," Gareth said, glancing over at the tall gray-haired man scowling behind the counter.

I was tired and my stomach was starting to feel nauseated again with worry. "Well, what do we do now?"

"We obviously can't do it in less than a year, so we've got to get somebody to translate it," Gareth said, leaning back in his chair. "There's any number of people here in the village who are fluent in Welsh. We just have to find them."

"I'm not sure who we can trust, though." I thought about those old ladies at the funeral, the ones who'd clearly been gossiping about Gee Gee.

Gareth thought for a moment. "What about that woman, you know, the one at the bus station?"

"Margie Jenkins?" I frowned. "I guess that's possible." But it felt wrong. There was something weird about it, since Margie had said that her mother disapproved of Gee Gee. And then the face of Margie's husband Peter swam into my mind. I wasn't sure why, but I didn't want to talk to him, either.

I really only knew one other person in town I trusted. "Let's go to Hugh! Hugh and his wife, Annie. They've been helping me practice Welsh."

"You're sure? I mean, Hugh's a good sort, but do we want

to drag him and his wife into this?" Gareth looked worried. His fingers tapped on the table lightly, a nervous drumbeat.

"I think it's good that they're not really involved." Plus, Hugh and Annie wouldn't have the same prejudices, the old assumptions that had made life so hard for Gee Gee in the first place.

"Okay. So, then, where do we find him at his time of day? Do we need to call a taxi?"

"Perfect idea," I said, grinning.

———

After we'd waited in front of HMS Tasty's for half an hour, Hugh pulled up in his black cab and parked it around the corner. It hadn't taken more than a few minutes of explanation before he agreed to meet us.

When I saw his balding head and bulky frame rounding the corner I felt like running to him, I was so relieved to see him. Gareth, on the other hand, seemed broody, almost morose. I could understand, kind of, but all I felt was urgency. It was four o'clock on my third-to-last day in Wales. By next week, I'd be gone—but I didn't know if my dreams would be.

"Annie'll be here in a few minutes," Hugh said, breaking into a broad grin. "So there's a mystery to be solved, yeah?" He led us to a table in the back of the tiny eatery, separated from the kitchen by a section of wall. The aroma of fried grease and fish filled the air, and the windows were steamed up from the heat of cooking. Hugh waved at the man behind the counter and bought four orange Fantas, which he carefully placed in front of us as if it were a solemn ceremony.

A moment later, Annie walked in, pulling the door shut behind her. Her short dark hair was tousled from the breeze, and she smiled as she sank into a chair. "Let's see this mysterious document, then," she said, sounding intrigued.

"I can't wait," Hugh said. "They've hardly told me anything, these two."

"Of course not. They haven't sworn you to secrecy yet. You might blab to the nearest gossip," Annie said, kissing him on the ear. "Right then, let's have a look."

I pulled out the diary and my laptop, ready to take notes, and watched as Hugh and Annie bent their heads over the precious book. Annie ran one hand through the gray streak at the front of her hair, and Hugh bit at one fingernail, but they were both quiet, reading intently for several minutes. At one point, Annie raised her eyebrows, and Hugh muttered "Well, now!"

Finally, Gareth broke the silence by clearing his throat.

Both Hugh and Annie looked up, startled. Annie's eyes were shining, teary.

"So," Gareth said, his voice sounding falsely casual. "What's in there?"

Annie blinked a few times and said, "I don't know how to prepare you. I—" She carefully turned the pages back to the beginning of the little diary. I felt my stomach lurch.

"Just a sec now," Hugh said, getting up from the table with a determined expression. I exchanged a confused look with Gareth, and then Hugh came back with a paper plate of incredibly greasy French fries. I felt a momentary pang. Next week I'd be home in San Francisco, sitting with Rae in our favorite taqueria, telling her all about this.

It still seemed far away.

Annie said "Ready?" and I brought my attention back to the present. To the past.

"Right. Well...this part here, this first entry, it starts with 'More evacuees came to our school this week. It makes me so sad and angry that I'd like to march on over to Germany myself. I really mean it. Mam and Dad would—er, '*gwylltio'n gacwn*' doesn't quite translate literally, but it's a bit like 'get angry as a wasp'...'"

I typed until my hands got tired, and then Annie took over for a while, until we had the translation of every entry in the brief diary. By the time we were finished, there were almost fifteen pages of notes, and by then an early dinner crowd of backpacking students had wandered in and filled the place with chatter in various European languages.

What we found in the diary had made my head spin.

"The entries are so sporadic," Annie said, "but you can just piece together what happened. *Jiw, jiw.*" Goodness gracious.

"And it isn't a nice story," Hugh added, sounding apologetic.

At first, it wasn't so bad. There were excited entries telling of Rhiannon's trysts with Edward—Gareth's great-granddad—which were kind of a shock but made me smile at the same time, picturing Gee Gee as a rebellious teenager: *Mam has punished me again for seeing Edward. I'm to stay in my room all day knitting army socks. It's truly unfair. I can't understand*

303

why everybody says he's a shady one, not to be trusted. When he smiles at me I know it isn't true. With that sandy-colored wavy hair just sliding down over one eye, I want to brush it aside, to touch his face... and to tell the truth I often do! That, and more...

I looked at Gareth and saw that same lock of hair that just wouldn't stay in place. That floppy hair that, on a much younger Edward, had made Rhiannon swoon. I fidgeted in my chair, not sure what to think. Trying not to freak out at how similar things were.

But they were different, too. Of course they were.

I'm so happy my Edward is too young to be called away to fight. Just a year off, really, he could go if he wanted, but I think he worries about his mam being alone. He hasn't said so, and that spiteful Mrs. Lloyd with her horrible overpriced yarn called him a dodger, which Dad says is worse than a conscientious objector like Uncle Rhodri.

I could hardly bear to listen when Hugh read the descriptions of how Gee Gee had been ostracized by the community for having an illegitimate child with an English boy. She endured spiteful comments from the villagers and got the silent treatment from her parents: *I can scarcely believe that people I've known my entire life, perfectly decent people, could be so nasty. They gave me looks when I was seeing Edward, but now... they just turn up their noses or say "I knew it would happen."*

Then there were the dreams. I trembled, reeling with a sense of overwhelming recognition as I read over some of the passages: *I had another dream last night, the ones Mam-gu Davies says I have to listen to. It was just images flashing by, some men working in a coal mine, and then the cromlech over by the old Llanddewi chapel, all fenced off. I can't understand it.*

I felt like the world was tilting, like I might fall out of my chair. It was overwhelmingly sad; all the more so because we couldn't fix what had already happened. I wasn't even sure we'd be able to deal with what was happening now. Gareth looked uncomfortable, pushing his glasses back up his nose, but at some point, he had put his hand on top of mine and I didn't pull away.

The most painful parts to hear were about Olwen—her lovely fragility, her chronic illness, the way she and Rhiannon depended on one another after Edward left for the mines ... and after Edward's letters stopped ... and the way both of them depended on Great-Grandpa John. *I don't know if I love him yet. But I know I made the right decision for Olwen. And John was lonely. He and Olwen can help each other. As for me ... we'll see. I can think about Edward now without the same pain that it used to cause. I loved him, but I've moved on.* As Annie read out the translation, I saw Gareth's eyes darken, his expression unreadable. And no wonder—he was the first to actually see Olwen, down in the cromlech.

In a way, this part of the diary felt the most important. Because of Olwen, Gareth and I were sort of related, in a way—a bizarre thought. And somehow we'd found each other online. Again, somehow because of Olwen. If Gareth hadn't seen her apparition, he wouldn't have been prompted to do a search for Olwen Nia Evans. And if he hadn't done that, he wouldn't have found me.

I shivered. She was our connection. But she'd been gone for so, so long.

I feel as if I've lost everything, the final diary entry said, after Olwen had fallen ill and died; after all the heart-wrenching words about Olwen's coughing and Rhiannon's exhaustion, caring for her daughter first alone and then with Great-Grandpa John, who had married Rhiannon and loved Olwen as his own. Edward was still away at the mines, for work, and hadn't returned.

… nobody would give me any help. I feel so completely alone. "Should have known better," said awful Mrs. Lloyd. "Now you've got to live with your troubles, dear. We all have them. Some worse than others, I suppose." I should never have spoken to her. I'm sure she's the cow that has told everyone terrible lies about me and Edward.

Now I could understand why Gee Gee left for the United States and hardly looked back. I could guess why Olwen was haunting us, and why she was so lonely. It was clear why Gee Gee had wanted to return here at the end of her life, despite it all.

But it was obvious that Gee Gee's return alone hadn't been enough. Not enough to set Olwen to rest, nor enough to bring the whole story to light.

We needed both sides of the story.

That, we'd have to do on our own. I couldn't ask more of Hugh and Annie, who had given so much help today on short notice.

"Thank you for sharing this with us," Annie said, putting

a gentle hand on my arm before getting up. "It's truly an amazing piece of history."

"We won't breathe a word to your parents until you say so. Good luck to you both," Hugh said, flashing us a smile over his shoulder on the way to the door.

I exchanged a long look with Gareth as Hugh and Annie bustled out into the crisp air. He looked as ill as I felt, but there was no other choice, no reason anymore for avoiding it. My stomach roiled, making me sorry I'd eaten the oily fries.

The next step was to confront Gareth's great-granddad.

24

Haws bywedyb mynybb na myneb brosto.

JT IS EASIER TO SAY MOUNTAIN
THAN TO CLIMB IT.

Welsh proverb

Cwm Road was busy with foot traffic as Gareth and Wyn walked to his great-granddad's house. Busy and normal, with normal people and their everyday problems. Meanwhile, Gareth's hair was hopelessly windblown, his clothes smelled like fried cod, and his brain was utterly devoid of coherent thought. But there was nothing else for it; Wyn was going home in a matter of days, and he couldn't leave things the way they were—couldn't spend his life getting phone-stalked by the ghost of a six-year-old, couldn't keep being distracted by thoughts of Olwen, whom he somehow had to help. Both

Olwens. It was like someone had gone into his mind, headed straight for the logical and orderly part, and kicked it about until only a shambles was left. An utterly disorganized shambles. He booted a stray paper cup into the street.

He'd been going along with things here in Cwm Tawel a step at a time, hoping with each step that the situation would improve. It was hard to imagine that anything good could come out of a confrontation with his great-grand-dad. But now that they'd translated Rhiannon's diary, they didn't have much choice. That *was* their next step.

The diary. Gareth walked a little faster. It was all so difficult for his brain to encompass. The same great-granddad who used to tickle him until he hyperventilated, who kept his tiny garden neat to the point of obsessiveness but couldn't keep his house organized, who took Gareth and Tommy to the Natural History Museum whenever he visited them in London—he was just a normal great-granddad, yet somehow, he was also the same person who'd seduced Rhiannon with his smile, who'd left her with an illegitimate baby, who'd gone off to be a miner and didn't come back for years. The same great-granddad who'd been so distant throughout this whole visit, even the funeral.

It was nearly impossible to think of his great-granddad as a young man; let alone that he was *that* sort. Amit might want to be a bit of a lad, but it was exactly what Gareth hoped not to be. His muscles tightened until his arms ached and he felt like hitting something.

"What do you think we should say?" Wyn asked suddenly. Gareth looked over at her. Her eyes were large and she looked terrified, but, like him, she was still walking on, still determined. There was a flash of something there that reminded him of little Olwen the first time he'd seen her—some fierce will that kept her going. He felt a sharp stab of remorse. It was because of his great-granddad, in a way, that Olwen had died. If Edward had been there, if he hadn't left Olwen without a father and Rhiannon without his love and support, then maybe things wouldn't have been as bad.

"Say something," Wyn said, her voice pleading.

"He ruined her life," Gareth burst out, quickening his pace even more.

Wyn jogged a few steps to catch up with him. "Gareth!" she said urgently as they turned the corner onto his great-granddad's street. She grabbed his arm and he stopped, pulling away. He could see the hurt in her expression and he immediately felt sorry, but he didn't think there was anything he could say to make any of this better. He was sorely tempted to just grab his things and head straight back to London, and pretend none of it had ever happened. It wasn't like he could do anything about the past, anyway. He started walking again.

Then his phone rang.

He stopped in the middle of the sidewalk. Wyn walked a few more steps before turning back to look at him.

"Is that...?" Wyn stopped. All the color had drained out of her face.

Gareth pulled his phone from his pocket. The ringtone—it was "Ar Lan y Môr." He fumbled with the buttons of his phone but it was playing insistently, louder and louder, until he could hardly hear anything else.

"Aren't you going to pick it up?" he heard Wyn say, faintly, from somewhere beside him. He shook his head, trying to clear the rising sound from his ears, but it wouldn't stop. It wouldn't stop.

He clicked the *Talk* button.

It was like the time he'd blanked out in the kitchen, only this time, he didn't quite lose the scene around him entirely. He sensed the road, the cottages, the fences and blue sky and hills, all becoming insubstantial; the sights and sounds of the village were slowly consumed by a dim, dark miasma—except for Wyn. His stomach roiled and he put one hand on her shoulder to steady himself.

He pulled back as if burned. When he'd touched Wyn, it was like there was an electric crackle in the air all around them, a physical shock like the completion of a circuit. But even when he'd withdrawn his hand, the strange sensation continued, a sense of linkage even when he wasn't looking at her. He was staring straight ahead, but he could *feel* that Wyn was turning her head to stare at him. He knew, without being told, that she too felt that connection; she too now saw what he was seeing.

What he saw was a tiny waiflike figure, limned with light and growing more substantial by the second, materializing in the dim, blurry half-world they stood in.

"Please ... hurry! You mustn't ... " Broken up as if by static, the small, faint voice pierced the unnatural quiet that surrounded them like an enveloping ocean wave. Wyn grabbed his hand, and this time he clutched it tightly. Soon, the little figure became just solid enough that they could see her features, see the tears running down her pointed little chin and the anguish on her face. Then she opened her mouth and a thin, wailing cry came out, the cry of a lonely child. It could only have lasted a moment, but it seemed as if the wail echoed up and down the years, unending.

Gareth couldn't bear it. He let go of Wyn's hand and shook his head violently, squeezing his eyes shut. If it didn't stop, he thought he might start screaming himself. He put his hands to his ears, dropping his phone on the sidewalk with an audible crack.

Then, abruptly, it did stop. The sidewalk was solid and reassuringly hard under his sneakers; the street, the block of little houses, the moist and breezy air—everything was as it had been a few moments ago.

Almost everything. Gareth looked at Wyn. Something unspoken passed between them, a flash of understanding. She had seen it—seen Olwen. She had been there. His tensed shoulders relaxed, just a tiny bit. Just enough.

He picked up his phone and the battery, which had popped out. There was a jagged crack across the screen.

"Mum's going to wallop me," he said. Then he grimaced. Flying phones. This was how it had all started, and here he was again.

Wyn smiled at him sadly.

They started walking again, without speaking. For now, it was enough just to feel Wyn's presence next to him and smell the salty, grassy scent of this town, this patch of land that had silently witnessed so many people's hardships. His mind was lucid now; it felt scoured clean.

As they walked, though, his anger slowly seeped back in. He wasn't going to let his great-granddad off the hook. His actions were, as far as Gareth was concerned, inexcusable. But he felt more ready now, ready to deal with any possible reaction. Anger. Denial. It didn't matter. He'd find out the truth. And maybe that would be enough to end all of this—the drama, the unhappiness, the lingering ghosts of the past that wouldn't rest.

When they arrived at the little house, Gareth let them both inside and then stalked from room to room, Wyn following after him. His great-granddad was in the small living room at the side of the house, sitting in a brown tweed chair reading a newspaper. As he looked up at the two of them, Gareth took a deep breath and let it out slowly, hoping his voice wouldn't shake.

"What's this, now?" his great-grandfather asked. "I understood she wasn't to visit with you unsupervised." He glared at them from underneath bushy, grizzled eyebrows. Gareth felt like backing down, but he thought about Olwen, about Wyn standing close behind him, and he knew he didn't have the option of letting this go on any longer.

"We've got to talk to you about something really important," he said stiffly, his hands clenched at his sides. "Both of us."

"Yes? Well, what is it?"

"We want to talk to you about…well…the thing is, Wyn…" Gareth's brain was a muddle of thoughts all competing to leave his mouth at once. He took another deep breath, but then Wyn spoke.

"We want to talk to you about this," she said, and pulled the metal box out of her backpack. She placed it between them on the dark wooden coffee table and opened it. The first thing she pulled out was the diary, which she set on the table. Next to it she put the locket, the birth and death certificates, and finally the two letters.

"What's this now?" Gareth's great-granddad said uncertainly. His gaze fell upon the letters, his eyes darting back and forth. His mouth opened and then closed again. He still didn't say anything, but his hands were clenched on the arms of the chair. He looked like he was miles away, an eternity away.

Then he seemed to snap out of it. "What do you mean by all this? Where did you find it?" His voice grew louder, and angrier. "Why are you bringing this to me now? It's too late, it's far too late!" He turned his face away, toward the window. "I can't do anything. It's finished. It was over a long time ago."

"It is finished," Gareth said, finding his voice. "So why does it matter? We just want to know what happened." His volume rose as well.

"It's my great-grandmother," Wyn added quietly. "I think I deserve to know."

His great-granddad gripped the arms of the chair for a moment as if he were going to stand up. Then, suddenly, his whole body sagged. He looked older than Gareth had ever seen him look, and the expression on his face was one of sorrow and anger. He didn't look at them; he didn't look at the letters again. But he stayed silent.

"You have to tell us," Gareth urged him. "Please! Wyn won't be here in Wales much longer. And we—we can't leave things like this. You don't know how hard it's been for both of us." His own voice sounded ragged and exhausted. "She won't leave us alone."

Wyn shot him a look and jumped in. "We understand what happened to Olwen, I think, and the diary told us Gee Gee's side of the story. But—what was your part in this?" She drew a shaky breath, and Gareth heard the tears in her voice. "Why did you leave? Why did you let this happen?"

"She's dead now. What does it matter?" his great-granddad said in a quiet, hopeless voice. Gareth wasn't sure whether he meant Olwen or Rhiannon. "I hardly remember those days."

"Please," Wyn said. Gareth turned to look at her. Tears were running down her cheeks, and that made him furious all over again. "I know you remember. Even if you don't want to tell us. But—" She closed her eyes, one hand clutching at her locket. "You're the only part of the story that's missing here, and Olwen isn't going to rest until you come clean. *I* won't be able to rest if I don't stop having dreams like my great-grandmother."

Gareth's great-granddad went pale, and he looked at Wyn almost fearfully.

"You know about Rhiannon's dreams?" His voice was a ragged whisper. "That was the one thing about her I never . . ." Then he closed his mouth and pressed his lips together, as if he'd said more than he wanted to. "No! I tell you I don't remember, and there's nothing more to say than that." But he wouldn't meet either of their eyes.

"Now, please leave, or I will ring your parents and tell

them what you've been about." His ashen face turned toward the window again, dimly lit by the graying dusk.

Gareth was gobsmacked. He felt like punching the wall. They'd told him everything. Now what could they do?

Wyn looked at Gareth, sighed, and put her hand on his arm. "I should go," she said, her brown eyes sad and sympathetic at the same time. "I'll talk to you later, okay? Everything will be fine. It has to be, or Olwen will never leave us alone. She'll be lonely forever." She glared at his great-granddad.

Gareth hated all this, hated feeling like he had no control over anything. Wyn wasn't at fault. She was the only one who still seemed sane in all of this. He turned to walk her to the door, wondering if she felt as unmoored as he did.

His great-granddad didn't utter another word, but as they left the room, Gareth took a quick look back. From his chair, Edward was staring at Wyn, his hands clenched together on his lap.

The expression on his face was one of utter fright.

25

To deceive another is to deceive thyself.

....

Welsh proverb

My feet were pounding the sidewalk on autopilot as I made my way back to the cottage, but my mind was like a video stuck on replay. The way Mr. Lewis's old hands had clutched at the arms of the chair. The way Gareth had looked at me just before I'd explained about Olwen. The sick feeling I got at Mr. Lewis's refusal to talk about anything that had happened. I felt a flutter of panic in my chest and returned to my standby coping mechanism, repeating words with each step.

Tristwch. Sadness.

Gobaith. Hope.

The orange light from the setting sun illuminated the white-painted shopfronts on Cwm Road, and I hurried a little faster. My parents were going to be livid; I was supposed to be home an hour and a half ago. And, of course, I was already on thin ice. I tightened my hands into fists in my jacket pockets. Gareth had tried to convince me he'd sort it all out on his end, but I wasn't so sure. He'd walked me out of his great-granddad's house saying he would make sure to get the full story, and then he'd come over the next morning to explain everything, so we'd have an airtight case for my parents.

I wanted to believe that would work. Oh, how I wanted to. Deep down, though, I wasn't sure if it mattered. Why I was trying to get every last detail before telling them? What if I just showed them the metal box?

But this wasn't just my story to tell. It was Gareth's as much as it was mine; as much as it belonged to anyone besides Edward, Rhiannon, and Olwen. It didn't seem right to tell my parents without Gareth there. It would be like a betrayal of everything we'd already done together.

Once on the grounds of the Gypsy Farm Cottages, I paused under the trees, composing myself before going up the path to Primrose Glen. I had an excuse ready, but Mom and Dad would still be angry, and I would still have to live with whatever the next few hours would bring. I took a deep breath and opened the door.

My shoulders slumped. There were my parents, sitting stony-faced on the couch, Dad's dark eyebrows a hard line, Mom's face pale and set. The room was utterly quiet, and I couldn't break the silence.

"Well? Where were you?" Mom's words were clipped and hard, and I felt them almost physically. "And why didn't you pick up your phone?"

I took a step back but stuck to the plan, futile as I knew it would be. "I'm so sorry, Mom, I completely lost track of time," I said, which was more or less true. "I was with Hugh and Annie in HMS Tasty's, practicing Welsh. I'm really, really sorry." I hoped the worry on my face, in my voice, sounded enough like remorse. They'd find out the truth soon enough anyway.

"Well, that's interesting," Mom said, tapping her fingernails on the end table. "Because we were just over at the pub ten minutes ago and guess who we saw there?"

I blinked. "What were you doing at the pub?"

"Looking for you," Dad said. His voice sounded angry and scared and it ripped right through me. "We asked Hugh and Annie if they'd seen you and they said they'd left HMS Tasty's more than an hour ago. But when we went down there to check, we didn't see you there."

"What were you doing wandering around for an hour? We trusted you to be responsible." Mom got up and paced, and I backed away, toward my room, to get out of the way.

"I—I was walking." I couldn't meet their eyes, so I played with the strap on my backpack.

"We were worried." Dad looked up at me. "Why didn't you just call us?"

"I don't know," I said, truthfully. I should have. I wasn't thinking. I could have avoided this. But it was ridiculous, too. "It was only an hour or so."

"I was just about to call Mr. Lewis in case you'd gotten it into your head to try to see Gareth. I'm glad you were sensible about something." Mom threw that out casually, but it stung.

My temper surged all of a sudden, and I couldn't see the point in lying anymore. I had a right to be doing this, even if nobody else could understand that. It wasn't even for me. It was for Gee Gee. She couldn't very well take care of this from beyond the grave.

I dropped my backpack on the floor, swallowed down angry tears, and steadied my voice. "You know what? I *was* with Gareth. And his great-granddad. And I had a really good reason for it. I know you don't want to hear any 'excuses,' but I'm doing this for Gee Gee. It's *about* Gee Gee. Gareth is going to stop by tomorrow morning so we can explain everything, together, and I really hope … I really hope you can trust me. Please."

My chest was tight, and in the tense, brittle silence, all I heard was my own ragged breathing.

"Yes, I should have called to tell you I was going to be late, and I'm sorry," I continued, my tears spilling out now no matter how I tried to keep them in, my words overflowing one after the other. "I know you didn't want me to see Gareth, and I really am sorry I had to go behind your back. But please just trust me this time, okay? You know I'm not irresponsible. Think about it. I wouldn't even ask if it wasn't important. It means—it means everything."

I met my dad's eyes, then my mom's, suppressing the urge to look away. They both stared at me for a moment, seeming lost for words.

"Wynnie, we do trust you," Dad said with a small smile that seemed hard to force out. "We'll just have to think about this, is all." He looked at his hands, then back at me. "I just wish you'd tell me, if there was something about Gran we need to know."

"Sorry, Dad." I winced. I had kept things from him, things he had a right to know. But soon enough he'd know all of it.

"Wyn, you need to understand that this is not over," Mom said, her voice simmering with suppressed anger. "I am not happy to have to call Mr. Lewis yet again and give excuses for my daughter's behavior."

Lovely. Now I was being referred to in the third person. I breathed in; breathed out. *Bore*. Morning. *Noswaith*. Evening.

Wait a minute.

"Call him? You don't have to call him." My heart sank. What would that do to our plans? What if that just ended up making Mr. Lewis clam up forever?

"I think we do," Mom said. "You made that necessary. If you're going to act like a child, we're going to treat you like one."

"You don't understand, I—" I cut myself off. I was not the one acting like a child. Mom could go ahead and call Mr. Lewis if she wanted to see someone act like a child. "Fine. Go ahead." I turned on my heel and went straight to my bedroom. I could feel my parents' eyes like frigid ice cubes on my back, but I didn't turn around.

Once the door was shut and I was alone in my small room, I finally allowed myself to let go. Today had been too much. I'd tried so hard, was still trying so hard to help Olwen, and it seemed like nothing I did helped. I sank onto the bed and took shaky, gasping breaths. One line from Gee Gee's diary kept running through my head: *Edward is gone and I've nobody left but Olwen.* Not long after that, Olwen had died.

Gee Gee. She was gone now, too.

I inhaled sharply, realizing something. I didn't have anything to lose now. I had nothing to lose except time, and nothing to regret except not trying. It only took a moment— as quick as a little girl's smile, a heartbeat—but I realized I would do whatever it took to make sure Gee Gee could have her Olwen back again, even if it was too late. And it wasn't too late; it wouldn't be too late until I'd left Wales.

I lay back on the bed, my chest rising and falling more evenly now, and I thought about Gee Gee. I'd always known that she'd been the one to suggest my name when I was born; the one to whisper it in my dad's ear when Mom was gasping and laboring, wondering if I would be a boy or a girl. Later, Gee Gee told me she'd had the strongest feeling I would be a girl, and she'd told my dad I should have a proper Welsh name to keep the family heritage alive.

Now, I wondered if naming me after her lost daughter was Gee Gee's way of trying to keep a part of Olwen alive. But I could never take the place of the first Olwen. No matter how many times I'd asked to hear the story behind my name, Gee Gee had never told me the real one.

———

When I finally ventured out of my room the next morning, the atmosphere was still tense and my parents were silent all through breakfast. I nibbled at a piece of buttered toast, trying to make it last as long as possible. Gareth had to come; I'd texted him twice already, but I'd only gotten one reply: *Soon. Promise.*

Mom and Dad sat on the sofa reading while I did the breakfast dishes, but I knew they were just waiting for me to come in so the real discussion could start.

Our last official "family discussion" had been about traveling to Wales with Gee Gee. This one promised to be a thousand times more painful.

After drying the dishes and putting them away, I texted Gareth a third time, my fingers trembling.

But he didn't answer. And he still hadn't come.

26

Nid hawdd gwybod y cyfan.

It is not easy to
know everything.

Welsh proverb

"Why won't you tell us what happened?" Gareth's voice was nearly a shout and he was shaking with rage. A nearly sleepless night hadn't helped clear his head at all; in fact, he could hardly think straight. All he could think about was Olwen.

"I'm an old man. I have a right to my privacy after all this time, don't you think?" His great-granddad's voice was laced with sarcasm as he strode across the kitchen, dropping dirty breakfast dishes into the sink. "Do you really think it's any of your business?"

"It might not be any of my business, but Wyn's got a right to know what happened to her great-gran." Gareth thought he could see sadness in his grandfather's face, behind all the anger. "Maybe it's painful for you to remember Rhiannon, but Olwen needs her!"

His great-granddad's face was thunderous, as was his voice. "I've spent a lifetime trying to forget."

"Well, Wyn and I don't look forward to a lifetime of nightmares and ghosts," Gareth retorted, enunciating each word clearly. He leaned against the kitchen wall, his head aching.

His granddad stopped in his tracks. For a long moment, he stared at the floor, arms folded across his gray wool sweater.

"What would you know about nightmares and ghosts?" he said quietly.

Gareth didn't let up. "You know, when you found me with the boxes on my head, I was looking for her letters. I know you've still got them—they have to be here." Unless his great-granddad really had wanted to forget, completely and finally. He wiped beads of sweat from the back of his neck.

Then his anger faded as he saw his great-granddad's stricken expression. The old man closed his eyes and put his head in his hands; his elbows rested on the kitchen counter and he looked thin and exhausted. Some of the tension drained out of the room. In the morning sunlight streaming through the window, they formed a sad tableau: Gareth, breathing heavily and trying to stay calm, and his great-grandfather, leaning forward, head down.

Then the man drew in a ragged breath and began to speak, in a barely audible voice, not moving from his hunched position.

"I was only seventeen," he said thickly. "I didn't realize what would happen. She was so lively, so pretty, and I was lonely. I'd been here just a few weeks with my mother when I saw her for the first time. I didn't know anything then."

He paused. Gareth was afraid to speak. A car door slammed outside and birds sang nearby, but the stillness in the house was complete. Finally, his great-granddad continued.

"I didn't know," he said again. "I thought I loved her, but ... everything was so hard. I was too young to have a baby. I was far too young to deal with the way people treated us after everything happened. They never liked me then. They wanted to ruin it for me—for us. It was different when I came back here, after I'd been working in the mines and married a Welsh girl from Swansea—your great-gran, Ellen. We had two little boys and another on the way. We were a respectable, hardworking family, and they couldn't take that away from me." He finally straightened, leaning against the sink and facing Gareth.

"But did Great-Gran know? About what happened before?" Gareth was afraid of the answer.

"No, I never told her." Edward sighed heavily. "And nobody else ever did either. We had a good life here that way. Things were changing, then—more and more English moving in, and I didn't feel so much like I was an unwanted stranger. I started to feel at home here. I could send my sons to an English-speaking school, where they'd have more advantages in the world. It was better that way."

He looked at Gareth, his eyes pleading. "Look how well your father has been able to provide for you, Gareth. I wanted things to be better for my children and grandchildren than it was for me, leaving my ruined shell of a home in London with almost nothing in my suitcase, going to a place where I knew nobody." His eyes looked distant again, and sad, but he didn't seem angry anymore. Gareth realized that he wasn't angry, either, though he still felt deeply disappointed. He wasn't sure that would ever change. He wasn't sure he'd be able to forgive.

Now, though, at least he could understand.

"I never wanted Olwen to die, you must believe that," his great-granddad said, taking a step closer. "There wasn't anything I could do. I did everything I could for my children after that. Everything!"

"I know," Gareth said. "It's okay." He wasn't actually sure it was okay, not yet anyway, but it would be, probably. He felt a surge of emotion for his great-granddad. Pity. Fondness. Love, despite everything. He straightened up, walked to the doorway and turned around one last time.

"Listen … would you … would you come with me to visit Wyn? I think we owe her this explanation. Her mum and dad, too," he added. "Please?"

"Well." His great-granddad raised his head, looking worn-out and defeated. "Well. There's nothing else for it, is there." Then he added, in a barely audible voice, "I can't hide forever."

"What was that?" Gareth couldn't help a small, self-satisfied smile. He'd heard his great-granddad perfectly clearly, but he had to hear it again, just to be sure.

"Well, it's about time everybody knew the whole story, isn't it. It isn't fair to … Wyn … to have her parents punish her when you two were just trying to do right. You'll have done more for Olwen than I ever have, if you can set this whole matter to rest." He sighed. It was the first time he'd mentioned Wyn by name, as far as Gareth could remember, instead of just calling her "the girl" or "her."

"But … I don't know," he added. "Maybe it would be better if it was just you who went there."

"No," Gareth said, his voice a little shaky. "Please. It would … mean a lot."

His great-granddad shook his head. "I hardly know them, Gareth. What—"

There was a sharp series of raps at the door. They both jerked.

"Don't worry, I'll get it," Gareth said. Was it Wyn? Had she somehow managed to get out of the house this morning? He went through the kitchen and opened the front door, blinking into the morning sunlight.

A tall, scrawny figure was backlit against the bright rectangle of doorway, leaning inward at an alarming angle.

"You, boy!" said a whispery, brittle-sounding voice.

Gareth backed up a step, squinting into the light. This

was odd. It was Peter Robinson, from the Cwm Tawel Museum. Peter had given him the creeps a bit that day at the museum, but now he felt a stirring of fear deep in his gut.

"When are you going to learn to leave well enough alone?" Peter rasped, eerily echoing Edward's words of a few minutes before. Had he been eavesdropping through the window somehow? "You and the girl insist on dragging the past out into the light, past that should stay past!"

The words echoed in Gareth's head, sounding disturbingly familiar. Then he remembered the anonymous note from several days ago and felt his anger rising again. He was tired of people telling him not to do things he had a perfect right to be doing. His first instincts had been spot-on; there had been something odd about Peter when they'd talked to him about Rhiannon.

"Don't you think there are some things that need to be out in the open? Some secrets need to be told," Gareth said calmly, but his voice was strained. "It's so far after the fact now. What's the harm?"

"Who is it, Gareth?" His great-grandfather's voice drifted around the corner.

Gareth opened his mouth to reply, but Peter shot out a hand and grabbed his forearm, painfully wrenching him outside into the front garden.

"Harm?" Peter hissed, his eyes bulging. "Don't you think you've done enough harm already? We'd all forgotten about Rhiannon's—mistakes—until you and *she* came and stirred things up again. Those sorts of things can't happen here."

Gareth pulled his arm away and rubbed it. "But you weren't even around then! Wyn said you were living on a farm in Ammanford. How did you even know what happened?"

"Oh, everyone knew what happened. I came back and found out soon enough." A strange expression overtook the anger on Peter's face; it was almost like disappointment. "Rhiannon was like my older sister. More than…" He trailed off, rubbing his head. "And then she went and did…that. With an outsider—an Englishman." He seemed to have forgotten the fact that he himself had come from Coventry, a war evacuee just like Gareth's great-granddad.

Then his face grew dark and he looked back at the house. Edward Lewis stood there in the doorway; neither of them had heard him approach.

"If it hadn't been for you," Peter said, his voice low and frightening, "none of that tragedy would have happened. She wouldn't have gone astray. She would never have left us." He almost looked like he was going to lunge at Edward, his lanky legs in a slight crouch and his fists clenched at his sides.

"What's all this now?" Gareth's great-granddad frowned, standing his ground.

"We don't want you here," Peter growled. "We've put up with you for far too long, for the sake of Ellen and your little ones, but those times are long past. Can't you see you don't belong? We were happy before! We—" He broke off, and Gareth could almost see the scared little boy he must have been, eyes huge, entering this place for the first time to find himself doted upon by his new family.

"Who's 'we'?" Edward asked. "I've been here nearly as long as you have, Peter. We both chose to make our lives here, for better or for worse. There comes a time when you have to let the past go," he added slowly, quietly. At some point, he had edged surreptitiously toward Gareth, and now the two of them formed a barrier between Peter and the little house.

"'Who's we?' Well, myself, of course, and there's Cati Lloyd, and Marged Jenkins—Margie's mum." He drew himself up to his full height, which was considerable.

"That makes three of you, then," Gareth's great-grand-dad said dryly. He didn't seem fazed at all; in fact, he seemed much more relaxed now that he'd admitted the truth. "I think I can live with the negative opinions of three individuals in a town of four thousand, especially when two of them are daft old women. Now, would you please clear off my property?"

Gareth didn't bother to hide his smile.

"I won't clear off! Why won't you stop making things worse?" Peter stepped closer and loomed menacingly over the two of them. "All these years, and you have to go reminding us all again."

"Don't make me ring the police." Edward turned toward the house and then stopped, abruptly, staring off behind Gareth. Peter, too, was staring, an expression of horror on his narrow, birdlike face. He backed up several steps. Finally, he turned away and almost ran back down the street.

"I thought he'd never leave," Gareth said, looking at his great-granddad. Edward still stood there, his face drained of all color.

Something was wrong. Gareth whirled around.

Quickly, almost too quickly to see, he thought he saw a flash of white dress, of long black hair. But then there was just garden and rosebushes and white lilies swaying in the breeze, casting their black shadows onto the side of the house.

"Did you see—?" Gareth stopped, not knowing exactly what to say that wouldn't sound daft.

"I thought I saw—yes." His great-granddad's voice was shaking and barely audible, and he didn't look at Gareth for a moment. Then, just as quietly, he said, "Let's please just go in and have some tea."

They didn't speak as they went back into the house, but something had changed between them. His great-granddad had seen at least a glimpse of what—who—was driving him.

He hoped.

After they'd had a cup of tea in the sunny, mercifully ordinary kitchen, Gareth tried again.

"Please come with me to see Wyn and her parents," he asked. This time, he didn't beg. He just hoped.

There was a long silence. Gareth jiggled his legs, cleaned his glasses, and resisted the urge to repeat himself.

"All right." Edward looked at him across the table. "But you can do all the talking." He managed a small smile, and Gareth tried to smile in return.

The atmosphere still seemed fragile as they readied themselves to go, Gareth putting on his jacket while his great-granddad got the car keys.

"Wait," Edward said as they were about to go out the front door. "Before we go." He walked slowly toward the back bedroom. Gareth heard a cabinet open, and some rustling, and then his great-granddad returned with a handful of yellowed envelopes.

"Take these. I don't need them anymore," he said.

27

Teg edrych tuag adref.

It is good to look homewards.

Welsh proverb

"All right," my mother said in a tight voice. "Time to talk."

I brought the tea I had just made into the front room and sat down on the easy chair, hoping my parents wouldn't notice how tensely I was gripping the mug. My parents sat on the sofa on the other side of the coffee table. Mom looked like her usual self for the first time in days, her cream-colored cardigan spotless and her dark hair immaculately blow-dried and styled. Dad, on the other hand, looked like he hadn't slept very well. He had serious bed head and his shirt was rumpled.

"Now that we've had a chance to sleep on it," Mom continued, "why don't you explain to us what, exactly, you were doing with Gareth yesterday when we specifically told you not to see him without our permission?"

"So you didn't call Mr. Lewis?"

"Answer my question, please." Her voice was cold, and I started to really worry.

Not only that, I still hadn't heard from Gareth since his one short text. I began to wonder if something was wrong with my phone.

Or his.

I trusted him. I knew he would do what he could. But every muscle fiber in my body felt as tense as a harp string.

"Well?" Mom just kept looking at me, her lips pressed together in a straight line. If this was how defendants felt when she was cross-examining them, I didn't envy them one iota.

But it wasn't about me this time. It was about two people who could no longer speak for themselves.

"I guess I'll start from the beginning," I said. I crossed my legs, smoothed down my navy-blue dress, cleared my throat, and took a sip of tea. Finally, I turned to my dad. He was the one who really needed to know. He was the one who was connected, like I was.

"I started having nightmares not long after Gee Gee moved in with us," I said without preamble. That was where this had all started. "I talked to Gee Gee about it. She told me that all Davies women were sensitive dreamers."

Mom gave me a look but I kept going, and to my parents' credit they didn't interrupt, although Mom looked extremely skeptical. I didn't go into too much detail, but I told them I'd been blogging as a way to get things off my chest, and that was how Gareth found me online, when he'd done a search for Olwen Nia Evans.

Dad stopped me. "Wait—wait. Gareth just happened to look up your name on the Internet? I don't understand."

"It's a little creepy, don't you think?" Mom added.

I smiled nervously. "That's the thing. Gareth was doing a school project on his family tree. A few months before that, he'd been here in Cwm Tawel with his family, visiting his great-granddad, and while they were hiking he found a grave marker from the 1940s that said Olwen Nia Evans."

Mom sat up straight. "Quite a coincidence," she acknowledged.

"Gareth also dropped his phone into a cromlech—in that churchyard we went to the other day, but it wasn't fenced off then—and when he went inside to get it, he..." I swallowed. "He saw a little girl in there. She told him her name was Olwen, and she was lonely. When he turned around to help her out, she was gone."

"What?" Dad was leaning forward now, his elbows resting on his knees. "So maybe he imagined it."

I sighed. "While he was researching his family, he got curious about Olwen. That's why he looked up her name online. But all he found was my blog."

"Don't tell me you've put your full name out there in public," Mom said, frowning.

"It's fine," I started, ready to rail against my mother's paranoia, but then finally there was a knock at the door, saving me from whatever I was going to say next.

"Just a minute now," my mom warned. I ignored her and jumped up to open the door. Gareth was standing there, and not just him, but his great-granddad too. I felt a million pounds lighter and couldn't stop the relieved smile that spread over my face. I lunged for Gareth and hugged him.

He turned pink, which made me grin even harder. I was even happy to see Edward Lewis. Something about him looked different, though I couldn't quite pinpoint what it was. He was standing a little taller, maybe? He leaned to one side, peering around me, and addressed my parents.

"Mr. Evans...Mrs. Evans." He nodded at them crisply. "I'm sorry if I've arrived unexpectedly, but I feel that an apology is overdue. I should have come earlier to express my condolences on the loss of your grandmother."

He addressed that last part to my dad, looking at him expectantly.

It took my dad a moment to recover his composure, but then he said, "Oh, well. We've all needed time to cope, anyway. But I don't see the need...we're in the middle of a bit of a..."

"Well, in light of my prior acquaintance with Rhiannon, I'm afraid my behavior has been a bit poor. But one does what one needs to, to get by, you see." Mr. Lewis's thick gray eyebrows beetled into one of his dour frowns. Somehow it didn't seem as forbidding as it had before.

Gareth caught my eye and gave me a small smile.

"Prior acquaintance? So you knew my gran?" Dad still looked perplexed.

"I did," Mr. Lewis said. "It's rather a long story, but I think you might be interested in hearing it. From what Gareth tells me, he and Wyn have been quite busy incurring your wrath."

Dad raised his eyebrows at the mention of the two of us. "Perhaps you'd better come in, Mr. Lewis. Can I get you some tea?"

Mom frowned, but she stood aside as Dad gestured for Gareth and his great-granddad to come in. I started to worry. What had they planned? With all five of us in the small sitting area, the cottage seemed cramped instead of cozy and I felt uncomfortably warm.

Gareth gave me an unreadable look as his great-granddad settled into the easy chair where I'd been sitting. I brought two kitchen chairs over and sat down in one of them. Gareth sat in the other, pulling it closer to me, and my parents took up their spots on the couch again. I picked up my teacup, now filled with milky dregs, and turned it around and around in my hands, very aware of Gareth sitting just inches away, but equally conscious of my parents and what felt like a sword hanging over my head.

"This may come as a bit of a surprise," Mr. Lewis began, "but Rhiannon and I had an … acquaintance … which I think you should be aware of, and I've been made to understand that you aren't." For once, my parents' attention was no longer focused on me. They were both staring at Mr. Lewis, and I could tell they were already full of questions. But they held off as he related his sorrowful tale: his evacuation to Cwm Tawel, his growing love for Rhiannon, the birth of their child, and the devastation he felt at having to leave her and the child to find work. By the time he'd finished, I'd refilled and drunk two more cups of tea.

"But how?" My dad said. He looked drained and pale. "How could this have stayed hidden for so long? And why wouldn't she have told me? Or at least, told my dad. We don't have secrets in our family."

Mom looked at me pointedly when he said that, but I ignored her because Gareth was pulling out a small pile of letters and putting them on the coffee table.

My heart stuttered, I was so anxious to see them. But first, I jumped up and got the metal box from my room and placed it next to Gareth's set of letters. I took out the two letters from Edward to Rhiannon, and also the birth and death certificates.

"Here's the proof," Gareth said, gesturing at the yellowing papers. My parents picked them up carefully and gazed at them in silence.

"I had no idea about this," Dad said after a moment. "And you knew?" He looked at me, then Gareth. "How in the world did you find out? I mean, I just don't understand why Gran wouldn't have told me any of this."

"It wasn't easy for Rhiannon," Mr. Lewis put in. "There can be a bit of a hostile climate in small towns sometimes, when something happens to disturb the status quo." He exchanged a glance with Gareth. "We experienced a bit of that this morning, in fact."

I looked at Gareth questioningly.

"Peter," he muttered under his breath, and I nodded, only a little surprised.

"What I don't understand is why this all came to light now," Dad said to Mr. Lewis.

"I'm sure that Olwen—Wyn—here can tell you more about it." Mr. Lewis gave me an encouraging look. It was so different from the glance full of fear he'd directed at me last night that I was taken aback.

I gathered my thoughts and said, "It's pretty much like I told you. Gareth found my blog, and the first thing we wondered was, were we related? When nobody knew of any connection, we did some research, and the more we found out, the stranger it got. I couldn't stop thinking about it. I kept having these dreams about Gee Gee, and weird things were happening to Gareth, too. The girl he saw at the gravesite…" I stopped, not sure how to explain his ghostly visitations without sounding insane.

Gareth cleared his throat. "I'm not the kind of person who believes in ghosts," he said bluntly. "So I assumed it was a prank. But it doesn't matter. When we found out our great-grandparents were from the same village, we thought it was far too much of a coincidence. It had to mean something. But nobody would tell us anything useful."

Mom had a weird sideways twist to her mouth, like she'd tasted something sour. "So you thought it was a good idea to dig up the past," she said. "Even though people obviously wanted you to mind your own business. You know, there are legal ramifications to that sort of behavior."

"It wasn't like *that*," I said. "Gee Gee kept talking about how hard life had been, but when I tried to find out more, she wouldn't answer my questions. I just wanted to know, Mom. Or it would all disappear forever." I tilted my head at her, willing her to understand. "And then Gee Gee was gone." For a moment I just sat there, tears sliding down my cheeks and stinging the wind-chapped skin there.

Gareth put a hand on my arm and I pulled myself back together. "All we could think to do was to go back to where Gareth had found Olwen's grave—where it all started for him. That's when we found the box. There's more in it, too." I removed the diary and locket and set them in front of my parents, along with my notes translating the diary.

Mr. Lewis watched closely as Mom and Dad pored over the pages. Dad's eyes grew wide, and even Mom raised her eyebrows, looking mildly shocked.

The more amazed they looked, the more I relaxed into my chair. Even if I couldn't tell them everything, they had the tangible evidence now.

"Oh, Gran," Dad said indistinctly, almost to himself. His face was anguished and I felt like going over to hug him.

Instead, I said, "It was no wonder Gee Gee wanted to come back. She'd finally be able to rejoin Olwen. And now she can, Dad."

"Olwen. I didn't realize . . . when she suggested the name Olwen Nia, I had no idea she'd once had a daughter." Dad thumbed gingerly through the diary and my notes. "I just didn't have a clue. How could I not have known?"

"She was good at keeping secrets, Rhiannon was," Mr. Lewis said with a sad grimace. "Both of us were, evidently."

"What made you open up, if you don't mind me asking?" Dad's voice was surprisingly gentle.

"There's no harm to anyone anymore," he said simply. "Ellen—my wife—is gone, and nobody else is left to remember or be hurt."

"Nobody who matters," Gareth murmured, probably thinking about Peter.

"Olwen remembers," I whispered. He looked at me with soft eyes, full of understanding, and I leaned over until I was resting my head on his shoulder.

"Well, now what?" Mom asked, glancing at me sidelong. "We're only here for a few more days. I don't see what else we can really do." She set down Olwen's birth and death certificates, her face sad. I felt momentarily like I was falling: only two more days until we'd take the train back to London, and then a few days later, we'd be on the plane to San Francisco. No more Wales, no more Gareth. I was about to drop from exhaustion, but it was time to speak up one more time.

"I think I know what we should do," I said.

It was a clear day, one of the few non-gray days we'd had. The sun shone warmly down on my hair though the air was still cold, and I shivered at the contrast in temperature, pulling up the zipper on my coat.

It had taken some time to convince everyone, but now it was afternoon and we were on our way to the cromlech, one final time. We'd packed a bag with the now-empty metal box and the two containers of Rhiannon's ashes, and then all five of us piled into the rental car and drove down to the beach. Even Mom was quiet as we made our way slowly along the grassy path. It felt like there was an expectant hush in the air. But there was also a feeling of rightness, like leaving Gee Gee's ashes as close to Olwen as possible was the right thing to do to bring them together again. We'd scatter some in the sea, like Gee Gee had always said she wanted—but I had other plans for the second container.

Finally, as we reached the clifftop just before the bend in the path, Dad stopped.

"I remember this place," he said, his voice incredulous. "I haven't been here since I was a toddler, but I've been here before. Gran and Gramps must have brought me."

He set down his bag and pulled out one of the containers of Gee Gee's ashes. With the crisp, salty breeze blowing out toward the sea, he upended it and set the ashes drifting down onto the choppy waves far beneath. He was quiet for a few minutes, looking out at the blue-gray water. Mom went over to him and put her arm around his waist, and they stood there silently, the wind tossing their hair into wild snaky shapes. Finally, they turned back toward us.

"Shall we continue?" Dad said, his voice hoarse. He walked back from the cliff edge and put his arm around me. "Come on, Wynnie. I think we've got a fence to climb."

In the end, we didn't have to do any climbing. If Gareth and I had been more patient, or less tired, we could have walked along the fenced-off area for another quarter mile and found the gate where the construction worker had entered. There was a large gap between the fence and the gate, which was secured in place by a padlock on a chain. With some difficulty, and a disapproving look from my mom in her fancy sweater, we all squeezed through the foot-wide opening. Gareth and I took the lead, walking along the path to where the ruined church lay. It looked just as it had a week earlier—deserted, mid-construction. My parents and Mr. Lewis followed us over to where the cromlech stood, stolid and unchanging, the humble cairns piled over to one side.

When I showed them the plaque marked *Olwen Nia Evans*, Gareth's great-grandfather slowly dropped to a crouch in the dirt and bowed his head.

I moved a short distance away. I couldn't help thinking about Mr. Lewis's story. He'd said it was awful during the war, leaving his home in London, where he had nothing left, for a place where he was a complete stranger. But because of how he'd acted, Rhiannon had had to leave her home too. She was forced to leave everything she knew. Had she felt, in the end, that it had all been worth it? Or had she regretted leaving some things behind?

When Mr. Lewis looked up, it seemed to unfreeze our quiet tableau. Dad opened the backpack again and took out the metal box, empty now, and Rhiannon's small memorial urn, which was a plain wooden cylinder with a lid. He knelt down next to Mr. Lewis. Gareth and I crouched on either side, and Mom stood behind Dad, watching.

My dad carefully, reverently, placed the urn of ashes inside the metal box and closed the lid, taking out the tiny key to lock it up again, forever this time.

"Wait," I said. I reached around behind my neck and unfastened Gee Gee's locket—the one with the baby picture. I placed it inside the box next to the urn. I would keep the other locket forever, the one with the photo of Gee Gee and Olwen, but this one felt like it had to be returned to Gee Gee.

Dad took out a trowel we'd borrowed from the gardener's shed and carefully dug a shallow hole just in front of Olwen's grave marker. He reburied the metal box and covered it with dirt. Gareth picked one of the lilies that grew semi-wild nearby and laid it on the freshly tamped-down earth.

Ar lan y môr mae lilis gwynion ... The old melody floated through my head, vivid and clear, but this time the words carried a sense of peace with them that hadn't been there before. Nothing was going to be quite the same, of course, but I'd known that for a while now.

I turned to Gareth as he got up, and we walked together, lagging behind a ways, as our group left the fenced-off area to hike back to the car.

"Did you hear—?" he whispered.

I smiled and reached for his hand, inordinately happy when he laced his fingers through mine. We walked like that for a while, not talking, his hand keeping mine warm in the cold, windy air.

"So what are you going to do now?" I asked, finally breaking the silence.

"I think I'm going to stay with my great-granddad for another week," he said. "We finally had a decent conversation about everything this morning. He could use the company right now."

I nodded. It hadn't been easy for any of us, especially Mr. Lewis. But things would be better now. I was still going back to the U.S. in a few days, with a packed sightseeing schedule between now and then, and I didn't know when I would see Gareth again. But I had no doubt we would stay in touch. After all, Gareth was my first and only faithful blog reader.

I squeezed his hand, and he squeezed back. I could sense him smiling even though he wasn't looking at me.

I would be back. I didn't know when, but I knew. And one day I would read Gee Gee's diaries for myself. I didn't know when that would happen, either, but despite everything else coming to an end, I felt like time was stretching out ahead of me like a promise. Like rolling green hills, like an ocean.

I felt a sudden prickle at the back of my neck, as though the wind was stirring the tiny hairs at the base of my skull.

Reflexively, I turned around. For just a moment, I thought I heard a snatch of melody, thought I could see a mother and child standing together on a grassy knoll overlooking the sea. And then, like a waking dream, it was gone.

Acknowledgments

This is the first novel I ever wrote to completion, and since I finished that long-ago initial version about ten years ago, I owe a lot of people a *lot* of gratitude.

This book would never have left the safety of my brain in the first place, or reached new heights, without my YA writing group. Thanks to those of you who were there during the early days: Katina Bishop, Tanita Davis, Jaime Lin-Yu, Erin Blomstrand, JoNelle Toriseva, Meeta Kaur, Jennifer March Soloway, Kim Yan, and Sarah Zacharias. And thanks, too, to those who read more recent versions: Tanita and Jennifer, Yat-Yee Chong, Kelly Herold, Sara Lewis Holmes, and Anne Levy. You are all amazing and extremely patient. Special thanks to Jennifer for a phone conversation that changed everything (and saved my sanity).

More people without whom this story never would have existed: Kathryn Reiss, Tom Strychacz, and the Mills College MFA Program in Creative Writing. Thanks also to Shin Yu Pai, Corey Sattler, Beth Tevebaugh Maday, and my mom, Bonnie Pavlis, for feedback and encouragement in those early days and beyond.

Major gratitude to a huge list of people for helping me with historical, cultural, and linguistic information, even though I'm sure they've long forgotten doing so by now (which makes it even more fun to thank them here): Harry Campbell, Carwyn Edwards, Roger Fenton, David Lewis, Louise Ostrowska, Andy Whittle, and especially my good friends Greg Cooper and Mark Stonelake, as well as numerous others from Cymdeithas Madog and the (sadly now defunct) Clwb Malu Cachu listserv. Thanks to my cousin-in-law Sam Horner for helping me not to butcher current British slang. (Any remaining butchering may be blamed on me.) I also owe a huge debt to Raynes Minns (*Bombers and Mash*) and Leigh Verrill-Rhys (*Parachutes & Petticoats* and *Iancs, Conshîs a Spam*) for their wonderful books about the lives of British and Welsh women in the Second World War; to the OpenLibrary.org copy of *The Proverbs of Wales*, compiled by T. R. Roberts, 1885; and to the extremely entertaining Effing-pot British Slang website.

I am forever and always thankful for my far-flung online network of writing and blogging friends, who are always there with words of encouragement and support. I am honored to be part of the Kidlitosphere with you.

Some people I'll never be able to thank enough: Brian Farrey-Latz and Sandy Sullivan at Flux, for sharing—and sharpening—my vision over the course of the past few years. Jennifer Laughran, who is as smart and hilarious an agent as I could ever hope to have. And my family, especially Rob.

About the Author

Sarah Jamila Stevenson is a writer, artist, graphic designer, introvert, closet geek, good eater, struggling blogger, lapsed piano player, ukulele noodler, household-chore-ignorer, and occasional world traveler. She is also the author of *The Latte Rebellion* and *Underneath*. She lives in Northern California with her husband and two cats. Visit her online at www.Sarah JamilaStevenson.com.